SINNERS REIGN

BOOK 8 IN THE WATCH ME BURN SERIES

R.E. BOND

Cover design by Samantha La Mar

TalkNerdy2me | www.tlknrdy2me.com

To everyone who's stood by my side while I figured this author thing out. This would not be possible without you.
Thank you for loving these characters as much as I do, and thank you for making this such an amazing debut series.
I love you bunches Xx

SPOTIFY PLAYLIST LINK

https://open.spotify.com/playlist/
72qo7KGTTUGnRC2UzRkeLS?si=24fdabdf9fc74dee

PROLOGUE

Rory

*B*eing drunk while rethinking my decisions in life wasn't a good idea. Every time I thought about the crash that had happened a few months earlier, it pushed me into an even darker mind space. Knowing death would take me that day wasn't something I thought I'd be facing so early in my life. I'd had a lot of close calls, but the moment I woke up with Charlie Hendricks in my face, my body burning with pain in my crushed Corvette, I knew my time was up.

Part of me figured I'd deserved such a dramatic exit after the way I'd been acting lately, my mind a mess and my attitude sour. My guys were slowly giving up on me, I could sense their defeat from a mile away.

I'd never gotten close with Charlie, but I was grateful she was there to hold my hand. I knew she wouldn't let me die alone, even though her innocent eyes had never seen something so traumatic before.

Everything about it was fuzzy, but I remembered waking

up in a hospital bed, managing to cheat death and live another day. I should have been relieved to have the chance to fix the things I'd broken, to assure the guys that I was fine and they wouldn't have to worry about me anymore.

I wasn't invincible, and my luck would eventually run out.

It was a shame I didn't keep that mindset for long, though, as my body healed and life went on as if I hadn't temporarily lost my life at the hands of Rage fucking Evans. I guess I never learned to stop bottling shit up, choosing to drown in it instead of facing it head on.

I really had to stop drinking.

"You okay, baby girl?" Skeeter asked as he sat beside me in the corner of our living room, watching the party rage around us while not really paying attention at the same time. I was too drunk to defend myself if someone tried to hurt me, but I knew my guys would keep me safe.

Skeeter nudged my knee with his, reminding me that he'd asked me a question. He'd been grumpy all evening, but that was my fault. I'd picked a fight with him earlier in the day, which had soured his mood.

I shrugged, taking a mouthful of my whisky before replying. "I'm fine."

"You've been saying that a lot lately. You know not to lie to me," he grunted, leaning back to get comfortable. "Talk to me."

I lifted my gaze and looked over at him through my drunken haze, his striking green eyes burning into mine intensely. He had no reason to be nice to me considering I'd thrown a knife at him in the middle of our argument earlier. I guess our fighting was getting worse, but he kept clinging to hope that we'd be okay. Everyone I came across knew we were toxic, but we'd never cope without each other. Not anymore.

Our love-hate relationship was a part of us now, and we got off on the anger and destruction we caused each other.

"I'm sorry about earlier. I didn't mean to lose my shit," I mumbled, his lips quirking up into a smirk.

"Yes, you did. That knife had a good aim. I know you don't like talking things through, but something's been eating at you for a long time. You need to talk to one of us, even if it's not me. Is this about the whole marriage thing? You know I don't give a fuck about it."

I drained my glass and scrunched up my nose, sick of hearing that word.

"You've all known from the start that I don't want a marriage. There's enough people in this relationship as it is, I'm not adding in the government, too."

"I know, and I respect that. I don't need a piece of paper to prove to the world how much I love you. I know Rivera and Diesel have been a little upset about it, but they understand your reasons," he said carefully, reminding me of the argument I'd had weeks ago with Hunter. He'd been pushing the idea of marriage for months, and he was lucky to still have his face intact.

I felt a little bad for lashing out over it, but there were only so many times I could say I didn't want to get married before I killed someone. Dad and Mom had a shitty marriage that obviously meant nothing, and every other person I knew that was married treated each other like shit. I didn't want that, and marriage wasn't for everyone. It didn't mean we weren't a family or lacking in love; it just meant we never signed a piece of paper to prove it to the rest of society.

We'd all kill and sacrifice ourselves for each other, so why the fuck did we need a piece of paper with signatures? Waste of fucking money.

"Donovan," Skeeter murmured, snapping me out of my thoughts.

"Hmm?"

"Talk to me," he repeated, my teeth grinding with annoyance. I understood their frustrations with me. I'd been difficult to live with lately and I'd closed myself off a lot, but my emotions were a mess that I wasn't ready to deal with yet.

"Just leave it, Skeet. Please," I asked, making him snort.

"You're going to put yourself in an early fucking grave if you keep bottling it up like this and thinking you can party it out of your mind."

"You drama queen, I don't drink *that* much. I'm not going to die from it," I scoffed. He leaned forwards to grasp my chin, almost painfully in his fingers, his eyes burning into me with frustration.

"The drinking won't kill you, but I fucking will. Stop shutting us out. We're supposed to be family, Aurora. If you're not leaning on us and you continue spending all day fighting us while we try and help you, then why the fuck are you still with us? I get it, you're not the type to vent about everything, but you're making the rest of us feel like shit. Do you still want us?" He growled, letting me go when I remained quiet. "Figure it out before we do it for you."

"Skeet?" I said gently as he stood to walk away, his eyes filling with hope for a moment before I squashed it like the petty bitch I was. "Mind your own fucking business."

"Sit here alone and be miserable, see if I care," he snapped, stalking off into the crowd, not giving a shit about knocking people over as he went.

Lukas spotted his abrupt exit from across the room and jogged after him, making me roll my eyes. They were an unlikely pair of friends, but over the years they'd grown closer, and Lukas was usually the person to make Skeeter see sense. I didn't understand why they spent so much time pretending to hate each other when we all knew they'd somehow formed a connection.

I managed to get to my feet, stumbling towards the bar where Harley and Caden were laughing at something on their phones. Probably another stupid cat video. Their bromance was ridiculous.

I reached for the bottle of whisky and almost dropped it as a hand snaked out and grasped my wrist firmly, anger burning through me as I met eyes with Slash. "Let me the fuck go, Russo."

He snorted, trying to yank the bottle from my hands, but I held firm. "For fuck's sake, Donovan. You've had enough. You can hardly stand straight."

"Bite me, asshole. I'll stop when I want to," I snapped, glaring at Caden who stepped closer. "Coming to his rescue?"

"No. I'll get you a glass and pour it before one of you breaks the bottle and fucking cuts yourself," he replied bluntly, holding his hand out for the bottle as if I were a child. I scowled but handed it over, knowing he'd do as he'd promised and get me a drink. He was the least likely to argue with me at the moment. He seemed to be letting me self-destruct while he waited on the sidelines to catch me, unlike the others who were acting like helicopter boyfriends who had to direct my every move.

"Thank you," I muttered as he slid the glass towards me, some of my anger subsiding as Slash took a step back and gave me space. They'd gotten into a terrible habit of over-crowding me, and it usually didn't end well for anyone.

"You're welcome. You want to sit here and keep me company? Harley needs to run out and pick up Jade from Devil's Dungeon," he stated, giving me a stern look when I rolled my eyes. "Babe, you know she won't go anywhere alone after Rage shot the house up."

"She's a little bitch," I hiccuped, narrowing my eyes as Slash slapped the back of my head firmly like a naughty child.

"Being drunk isn't an excuse to talk shit about your friends. Besides, she has every right to be fucking terrified after everything she's been through. I wish you'd take a page out of her book and take back-up everywhere too," he growled, shaking his head with disappointment as I pushed him back and almost landed on my own ass. *Definitely too drunk.*

"You're just pissy about your big brother. I say we talk shit about him instead."

"I'm not talking about Rage. Especially while you're drunk, which is all the fucking time lately. Do you even know what day it is?" he demanded, fisting my hair and yanking me closer. "You're a mess. Clean your act up, you're making a fool out of yourself."

"How about you go and fuck yourself?" I threw back, earning a snort in return as he let me go.

"Gladly. I'm not fucking you while you're like this, so I have no problem using my hand."

"Why is everyone fighting? I just saw Lukas and Skeeter in a heated discussion in the bedroom," Marco asked as he joined us, his eyes already on me for an explanation.

"Your boyfriend's a dick," I shrugged. "Not my problem he has anger issues."

"It might not be your problem to deal with, but it's definitely your fault that he's usually so grumpy," he scoffed, clapping Slash on the shoulder and turning his attention away from me. "I'm heading off with Harley to check in with Hunter. You got this?" *Which was code for, did he have me under control.*

I spun around, tripping over my own feet and watching as the floor rushed up towards my face. Arms wrapped around me and pulled me back against a solid chest, and I relaxed as I smelled Diesel's cologne.

"Time for bed," he murmured in my ear, and as much as I

wanted to fight him on it, I was struggling to keep my eyes open. I let him guide me away from the crowd and up to our room, where he stripped my clothes from my body and tucked me into bed, climbing in beside me to snuggle.

I didn't deserve any of them, and a small part of me knew it was only a matter of time before they realized it and walked away from everything we'd built.

I'd have no one to blame but myself, either.

CHAPTER ONE

RORY

*B*lood ran down my face as I breathed heavily, glaring at my opponent from across the cage as I flexed my tender knuckles. My ears were ringing, my sports bra and shorts were soaked with sweat, and the bottle of whisky I'd drank earlier in the evening was threatening to come back up after my recent kick to the stomach.

I blinked hard to try and focus, smirking through the pain. "You can't fight for shit."

"Take a look at yourself, Donovan. You're a disgrace," the woman in front of me chuckled, tilting her head. "I'm surprised they haven't thrown you out yet."

I snarled, lunging for her and ending up with a fist to my jaw, causing me to stumble sideways.

"Face it, you're done," the woman laughed, bringing her foot out to kick the side of my head. My vision dimmed as it connected, but I got to my feet and threw punch after punch into her face, the pair of us landing in a pile on the ground together as we fought.

Radioactive by Bullet for my Valentine blasted around the room as I used all my strength to beat the mouthy fucker's ass, but I was suddenly hauled backwards and a hand firmly smacked against my cheek, snapping me out of it.

Skeeter stared back at me, his fingers digging into my bicep. "The fuck are you doing?"

"Did you just fucking slap me?" I snapped, making him grin.

"Yep. You should see what I have planned for your fucking ass later. You won't be able to sit down for a month. Now, the fuck are you doing? We only said you could fight if you were sober. Getting in here drunk is a stupid decision, baby girl. You know better."

"I'm not even that drunk. I've only had a few!"

"Yeah, a few *bottles*. Get your shit, you're going home."

I yanked back from him, clenching my fists by my sides. "I'm not done."

He stepped closer, speaking in a low voice. "You're making us look bad. You're flailing around the cage, you've had the shit kicked out of you, and I'm not far off from bending you over right here to put you back in your place. Is that why you're in here getting your ass beat? To be punished for whatever the fuck you've been overthinking about for months? You should have told me, I would have happily obliged."

I eyed him with annoyance for a moment before taking a swing at him, apparently moving too slow in my drunken state, because he caught my fist with his hand easily and ducked down, forcing me over his shoulder and carrying me towards the door.

"Put me down you piece of shit!" I shouted, trying to thrash about to get free, but my limbs refused to work properly. I knew he was right, I shouldn't have been in the cage while this intoxicated, but I was angry and my brain wouldn't shut off to let me get some peace. Everyone expected too much from me, and it was becoming too much for me to handle.

I sensed people watching me as I was man-handled from the shed and into the cool night air, probably whispering about how I was going through a mental breakdown or something. I'd been fighting a lot lately, but I knew I was losing more than I was winning. I deserved those hits, anyway.

Skeeter dropped me into the passenger seat of his McLaren, slamming the door behind me as he made his way around to the driver's side and slid in, not looking at me as he started the engine.

"This has to stop, Aurora. We get it, you're a moody cunt and you need an outlet, but you're making yourself look stupid in front of everyone and you're losing the respect you've built over the years. You're making the Psychos look stupid, too."

"I can fight people in the street instead if you wish?" I offered, crossing my arms tightly and ignoring the sharp stab of pain in my ribs. I'd probably broken some again.

He growled, reaching around to grab my seatbelt and secured me. "Grow the fuck up. You can pout like a child all you want, but I won't let you make a scene for everyone else's entertainment."

I ignored him the entire drive home. Not that he continued with the conversation, and I bailed from the car the moment we arrived. He didn't let me get far, though.

His fingers wrapped around my ponytail, yanking me backwards so that my spine slammed against his car. "I've had enough of your fucking attitude. Don't you see how childish you look? You've been drunk for months, other than your little hospital visit which might I remind you, was because you fucking *died* in a car accident. We have too many enemies for you to be running around without a clear head all the time. You don't think you need babysitting? Prove it. Get your shit together."

I slapped at his chest but he spun me around, pinning me against the car with his muscular body, a snarl leaving him. "I'm not playing games with you, Aurora. You want to do dumb shit for attention? Well, you've got my fucking attention. What are you going to do with it?"

"Fuck you," I spat. "I'm not trying to get your attention."

"Too bad, you've got it," he snapped, shoving the back of my shorts down and forcing two fingers into my pussy. I gasped in surprise, not expecting him to try and put me in line outside, but he kicked my legs apart and unzipped his jeans as he finger fucked me, warming me up for what was to come.

"We're in the fucking driveway!" I said with annoyance, and he let out a bark of laughter.

"Like you give a fuck if anyone sees us. Shut up and take it until I decide I'm done."

I glared over my shoulder at him as he lined up his rock-hard dick with my pussy, his eyes meeting mine as he slammed inside. I let out a groan, loving the bite of pain as his hands went to my waist, harshly digging into my skin as he fucked me hard, his teeth sinking into my shoulder and making me cry out.

I noticed the curtains from the bedroom window upstairs move, telling me we had a spectator, but I didn't care if the others saw us. They'd either jerk off to it or join us, I didn't mind either way.

"You want the pain, baby girl? I'll paint your skin red with your blood if you think it will help," he grunted, the flash of his blade catching my attention in the moonlight, two seconds before a sharp sting hit my shoulder where he'd just bitten me.

My pussy clenched as the pain fed my demons, and the

moment Skeeter's tongue licked across the wound, his knife dropping to the ground with a clank as his other hand found my clit, I detonated. I was glad the neighbors weren't too close, but they probably still heard me.

"Oh, fuck!" I cried out, my legs giving out and leaving Skeeter to hold me up. He waited until I was done before pushing inside as deep as possible and finishing himself, his teeth biting into my skin near the burning cut he'd left on me.

His hand snaked up my chest, his fingers wrapping around my throat to tug me back against his chest. "Better?"

"Better," I confirmed softly, attempting to take a step away, but he fixed both our pants and lifted me into his arms, cradling me to his chest.

"I wish you'd talk to someone about whatever's bothering you. I hate that I can't fix it for you," he murmured as he carried me inside, heading up to our room where Lukas and Tyler were watching a movie. They both glanced up and Tyler smirked, telling me who'd been peeking out the window.

"Evening. Have a good night?"

"Yep," I replied as Skeeter put me on my feet, and Lukas frowned.

"What happened? Did someone kick the shit out of you? What condition did you leave them in?"

"I had a play in the cage. I'm fine," I snorted, stripping off and raising an eyebrow at Tyler who was shamelessly staring at me. "Like what you see, perve?"

"Very much. How about you come and blow me?"

"How about you ask Skeeter. He seems to be in a giving mood," I retorted as he stood from the bed and moved towards me, sliding his fingers between my legs and running them through Skeeter's come.

"You're just standing there letting his gift run down your

legs. Ungrateful," he chuckled, pushing it back inside me. "Don't waste it."

I snatched his wrist and lifted his hand, popping his fingers into my mouth to clean them with my tongue, his eyes darkening instantly. I pulled them out, giving him a small smile.

"I don't think it's a waste. Right, Skeet?" I asked without taking my eyes off Tyler.

"Definitely not," Skeeter agreed, dropping back onto the bed. "Feed her more. She looks hungry."

I liked how comfortable they all were about our relationship. Sure, it had been a little rocky while we'd been figuring it out at the start, but sex was one thing we'd all gotten used to regardless of who was involved. It was also the one time we didn't seem to fight.

Tyler did as he was told, pushing his fingers inside me to gather more come, before lifting them to my mouth. "Open."

I did as I was told, moaning softly as I swallowed.

"Good girl," Skeeter murmured, his eyes burning into me as I soaked in his praise. I might have been a strong independent woman, but I'd never say no to praise in the bedroom. There was something hot about it, no matter what kind of mood I was in.

Tyler wrapped his arms around me and pressed a kiss to my lips, chuckling as I groaned. They must have been extremely comfortable with their sexuality, because the moment they'd discovered I loved kissing them after one of the others had come in my mouth, they'd suddenly made a habit of it. I'd tried to push for all the guys to go further with each other because I thought it would be hot, but they drew the line early so I knew it would never happen.

It was a shame, because I'd pay good money to watch them go at it like rabbits.

"Go have your shower then come to bed. I want to snuggle," Tyler said as he stepped back, swatting my butt before jumping back into bed between Skeeter and Lukas.

"The image in front of me right now would be better if you were all naked," I grinned, earning the middle finger from Skeeter as I left the room.

"As if these two pansies could handle me!"

"I could handle you just fine," Lukas snorted, making me laugh as I shut myself in the bathroom. This was another common argument between them. One I wished they'd try and prove right.

I STUMBLED into the kitchen at lunch time the next day, beelining towards the fridge for a drink. I'd discovered the best way to deal with a hangover was to start drinking as soon as possible. I was not happy to find my beer was missing.

"Where the fuck's my beer?" I scowled, slamming the fridge door shut and cringing when the loud sound hurt my head. Hunter was the only one of the guys around, sitting at the kitchen table eating toast like he had nowhere else to be. He had a business to run, and it was rare he took time off. They didn't open until later, Devil's Dungeon was a nightclub with adult entertainment, but he spent a lot of time in his office outside of opening hours. I didn't remember the last time he'd been home for lunch.

"Gone. Sit down and I'll make you some coffee," he said firmly, making me snort.

"Excuse the fuck out of me? What do you mean it's *gone*?"

"Exactly as it sounds. You eat and have a coffee, and I might miraculously find you something with alcohol in it," he answered, pushing his chair back and walking towards the coffee machine. I glared at the back of his head, considering throwing a chair at him.

"I don't eat breakfast. Now, get me a fucking..."

"Sit the fuck down!" Hunter shouted, cutting me off. It was rare that he shouted at me.

"Who the fuck do you think you are?" I demanded, stalking towards him and giving him a shove. "You can't talk to me like that!"

"Oh, so you're the only person around here who's allowed to raise your voice? Sit down. I won't ask you again, hot shot," he stated, seeming to relax when I let out a huff and sat down heavily in one of the chairs. "Thank you."

"Why aren't you at work?" I asked, resting my elbows on the table. "Where are the others?"

"I'm taking the day off. Marco will open the club tonight so I can stay home. Slash and Skeet are at the shed, Caden's out with Hendricks and Harley at the bar, Lukas and Jensen are at the movies, and Diesel is helping Ty with gun training. Marco's at Red's and won't be home before going to the club. Alex had an appointment, so he offered to hang out with her so she could stay home." He walked towards me with a fresh cup of coffee in hand, sliding it towards me.

"Why are you staying home?" I frowned, eyeing the cup like it was filth.

"Because, we need to talk. I heard about what happened last night," he sighed, giving me the side eye as he sat beside me. "This shit has to stop, babe. You're going to get yourself killed. *Again*."

"The car accident wasn't my fault! Rage fucking paid that barista to drug me!" I exclaimed.

"I know. You need to realize how lucky you are to be alive right now. You need to hit something? Use the bag or spar with one of us. You don't need to drunkenly climb into the cage where someone could do some serious damage to you."

"You think I'm losing my touch?" I snorted, his eyes meeting mine calmly.

"You're losing your fucking control. I know you don't want to talk about it, but at least eat some breakfast and hold off on the booze for a little longer. If I have to send you to fucking rehab, I will."

"I don't want breakfast. You also can't force me into rehab. I have enough money to get myself back out," I scoffed. He smirked, having a bite of his cold toast.

"I can lock you in the garage, tied to a chair until you dry out."

"You wouldn't fucking dare."

"Push me and see what happens. Besides, you love breakfast. What do you want?"

I sipped my coffee, my stomach churning at the emptiness. I wasn't sure when I last ate, it wasn't something I remembered to do as often as I should.

"Can I have waffles?" I asked quietly, my mood simmering slightly as my stomach growled loudly, making Hunter chuckle.

"Of course. Want to go out and do something today?" he offered as he finished his toast and stood to make my waffles.

"Like what?"

"Whatever you want."

I tilted my head, trying to figure out what he was up to. "You mean like, a date?"

He glanced over his shoulder, his playboy grin taking over his handsome face. "Yeah. It's been a long time since we've had some alone time. I'll even be a gentleman and make you come." His face became serious after a second, a frown taking over. "I'm sorry I've been working so much lately. I'll make more time for us, I promise."

I stood and walked towards him, wrapping my arms

around his waist from behind as he mixed up the waffle batter. "I'd love to go on a date with you. I haven't been the best company anyway, I know you guys avoid coming home some nights because of it."

"We know you're struggling with something, and we hate that we can't fix it for you. I usually work late because I'm overloaded with paperwork. I'm not avoiding you."

"Slash is," I said softly. "He sneaks in early in the morning for breakfast, but I know he's been spending some nights at the shed."

He closed the waffle iron and turned in my arms, pressing a kiss to my forehead. "Slash is struggling with a lot. It's not just because of you."

Guilt ate at me for not realizing he was dealing with personal shit. I was so fucking self-centered sometimes.

"Is he okay? What's wrong?"

"He'll be fine. He's just angry and confused about Rage. He's spent his entire life hating him because of a lie. You know Rage actually invited him to dinner the other week?" he said, and I almost choked on my own saliva.

"He fucking what?"

Hunter chuckled, seeming amused by the entire situation. "Rage wasn't happy about it, so I'm assuming Charlie was forcing him. He seemed relieved when Slash declined."

"Charlie needs to mind her own business," I grumbled, but I smiled slightly at the image of the tiny woman forcing a brute like Rage to do anything. She had balls, I'd give her that.

"She's just trying to help. I won't lie, I'm enjoying not having to look over my shoulder for a pissed off Shadow King," he answered. "Sniper's called a meeting though, so please don't shoot anyone."

I rolled my eyes and sat back at the table, crossing my

arms as Hunter finished making my breakfast. "I don't trust him."

"He might be a King, but he's a damn fucking good one. He's on our side with wanting the wars to stay gone, so don't go proving to his men that we can't be trusted. A lot of them don't like you and your itchy trigger finger."

"I don't understand their problem. My itchy trigger finger likes them a lot," I grinned darkly. "I can't wait for Rage to lose his shit and give me a reason to aim at him again."

"Donovan, don't even think about it. Unless he shoots at you, do *not* shoot at him," Hunter scolded, placing a plate of steaming waffles in front of me. They smelled good, and I pulled a piece off before he'd even grabbed me the berries and cream.

"I'm sorry, I hold a grudge with people who have tried to kill me multiple times. Hey, can we go to the gun range or something? I want to burn through some bullets or break shit," I mumbled while shoving waffles into my mouth the moment Hunter handed me a fork. He smirked, sitting to watch me eat.

"Trust me, I have a better idea."

"You're going to fuck me?"

"When we get home. Finish your food, get dressed, and I'll take you on the best date of your life." It wouldn't be hard. Although I'd been dating the guys for years, we'd never really gone on dates. I didn't have much to compare this date to.

The moment I was showered and dressed, Hunter steered me towards my green Lamborghini that he'd been claiming as his and opened the passenger door, waiting for me to climb in before closing it behind me. He refused to tell me where we were going, but my eyes lit up as we arrived and I saw the sign.

"You brought me to *Break Stuff*?" It was somewhere I'd always wanted to go. It was literally a place that had multiple rooms that were filled with plates and other random things, and we got to let out our anger by breaking random items. I'd mentioned to Skeeter a long time ago that I'd wanted to go, but he rolled his eyes and told me I broke enough of our plates at home.

Hunter smiled proudly at himself, climbing from the car and running around to my side to open my door. "Yep. Figured you'd be able to let off some steam. C'mon, we have all afternoon."

I was excited to be able to destroy things without someone yelling at me.

The moment I stood beside the big pile of plates, I snatched one and threw it hard onto the ground, making Hunter snort.

"Wait a second, you need your eye protection."

"No I don't. I need to break more of these ugly ass plates and pretend they're people's heads," I threw back, but he snagged my wrist before I could grab another one.

"I'm serious. Put them on. Now."

I scowled, snatching the eye goggles from him and shoving them on. "Happy?"

"Very much. Proceed," he grinned, motioning for me to continue.

I lost count of how many I'd broken as I went crazy, the satisfying smashing sounds making me smile. I grabbed a bat and kept going until I was a sweaty mess, but I had to admit, I felt better.

"Jesus, I hope you're not picturing that as my head," he grunted, eyeing the pieces all over the room.

"Nope. I like you right now. Skeeter on the other hand..."

"Give him a break, he's worried about you."

I turned to face him, dropping the bat onto the floor. "How about he gives me a break instead? I'm tired of fighting with him, but he won't let shit go."

"Can you tell me why you won't tell us what's wrong? You're killing me, babe. I hate seeing you like this," he replied, leaning back against the wall. He hadn't even tried to take any plates away from me for his own fun, he was just letting me go crazy on my own.

"There's nothing…"

He grabbed my throat, shoving me back against the wall and wedged a leg between mine. "I've let you deal with this shit on your own because it's what you prefer, but don't fucking lie to me. That's what's pissing us off. It's the fact you won't even acknowledge something is wrong. Look me in the eyes and tell me you're fine," he growled, his thigh pushing against my pussy and making me groan.

"I'm handling it."

"No, you're avoiding it. You're going to combust at this rate. You could do anything to me, and I'd fucking stay. Do you not realize the power you hold over all of us? We're not going anywhere, no matter what. You're my ride or die, Donovan. When will you realize that?"

His eyes burned into mine as we stared at each other, my heart hammering in my chest. I tried to shove him back, but he leaned in closer, his voice gentle. "I promise. Nothing you can say would make me leave you."

"You'll change your mind. You all fucking will," I spat. "I'm no good for you."

He chuckled, a smirk stretching across his lips. "You want to have this talk now? None of us are good for each other. We're a goddamn mess, but you're my mess, and I'm yours. What the fuck is eating at you?"

"Rivera, I'm not fucking around. Back off. I want to go home," I snapped, his hand tightening around my throat.

"I'll back off when you talk to me. Then I'll take you home," he murmured, scowling at me as I tried to hit him in the ribs but missed. "The fuck is your issue?!"

"You guys have things you want out of life that I don't! I should have spoken about it sooner, but I was selfish, okay?!" I shouted, managing to yank the goggles from my face and tossing them aside. "You deserve the wedding you want, the kids you want, and that stupid white picket fence that's you're so goddamn obsessed with!"

He frowned, dropping his hand from my throat but not stepping back. "What are you talking about?"

"I don't want any of it, Hunter! I don't want things to change at all, this is all I'm willing to give you guys, don't you see that?!" I screamed, finally shoving him hard enough to get away from him for some distance.

I grabbed a plate and threw it as hard as I could, watching the pieces shatter on impact. "I don't want it," I said more quietly, exhaustion taking over. He was silent behind me, my heart hurting at knowing this was the end. I knew I couldn't keep them, I should have dealt with this years ago.

"You don't want kids?" he finally asked, his voice full of defeat. I shook my head, refusing to turn and look at him, knowing the pain I'd see in his eyes.

"No, I don't. I'd be a terrible parent. The only knowledge I have is how my own dad raised me. I don't want to fuck up some kid's life, which I will. I've already told you guys this when Jade announced her pregnancy."

"Fuck that, you'd be a good mom. All Max taught you was how *not* to be a parent. The cunt's been dead for five years, and you're still letting him in your head. We thought you'd warmed up to the idea since you've been excited for Jade. Look at me," he barked, getting louder when I didn't move. "Look at me!"

I glared at him over my shoulder, not appreciating his tone. "What? I can't be excited for my friend without wanting a baby too? Of course I'm happy for her. I'm not a complete asshole."

His eyes softened, and I realized I'd let him see into me too much in that second. He saw the pure terror I held, the uncertainty, and my pain. I never wanted anyone to see me as weak ever again.

"You're not your father. Don't let him control your life from the grave. You had a good mom, so focus on that. We don't have to have kids if you don't want any, so calm down and breathe. I'm not leaving," he said gently, frustration surging through me.

"But you should! You've always wanted kids, I hear you guys talk and…"

"I'd give up anything for you. Fucking anything," he answered, but I could see it was hard for him to say. I was breaking his heart, just like I knew I would.

"That's not fair. You shouldn't have to give everything up for me. That's not love. That's fucking torture. You'll resent me in twenty years, we'll fight, we'll break up, and…"

"What aren't you understanding? I'm not fucking leaving you. Let's go," he said firmly, cutting me off. I went to speak again, but he left the room, expecting me to follow behind him.

By the time I'd handed my goggles and bat back at the front desk, he was already sitting in the car with the engine running, not looking at me as I climbed in and we took off towards home.

CHAPTER TWO

RORY

"*I* wished you'd told us you were serious sooner," Hunter murmured as we arrived at home and parked in the garage, his face turned towards the window.

"You can still leave. I wouldn't blame you," I sighed, jumping as his gaze snapped to mine and he snarled.

"Get it through your head, I'm not going anywhere! It would have been nice to know so I hadn't spent so much time wondering about our kids. I've been so fucking excited thinking about seeing you pregnant, to know you'd be carrying our baby, so I'm sorry if me being upset is a problem for you. I love you, but I need a minute to process this. I didn't realize you meant you never wanted kids *ever*."

"I'm sorry," I snapped. "How about you carry a fucking baby around for nine months, ruin your body, and live in terror for the rest of your life that you'll fuck up their lives! I told you *no* months ago! It's not my fault none of you took me seriously!"

I shoved open the door and climbed out, slamming it behind me and heading inside, almost knocking Jade over in the process. "What are you doing here?"

She snorted, raising an eyebrow. "Good to see you too. What's up your ass?"

"Nothing," I gritted out, hating to be a bitch to her, but I felt trapped by all the damn baby stuff. She'd been spending a lot of time with Marco, updating him on her pregnancy progress and getting him excited for something he'd never have, and as much as it wasn't her fault, I couldn't take it anymore.

"It doesn't seem like nothing," she observed, flinching when I jerked towards her, my fists clenched.

"Why are you here all the time?!"

"Whoa! Time out, Donovan," Marco snapped as he got between us, gently nudging me back a step. "The hell's your problem?"

"Fuck off with her for all I care!" I yelled, smacking his chest with my fist. "Go!" Maybe Harley and Alex would let Marco into their little relationship. He'd been fucking obsessed with their baby since they announced it. Of course, I'd fucking kill her before I let that happen, friend or not.

"Ignore her. We've been talking and I've pissed her off," Hunter said bluntly as he joined us. "Probably best you head home, Red. C'mon, I'll take you."

"You can fuck off too," I hissed, spinning on my heels and heading into the kitchen, not expecting to find Caden's mother waiting for me.

Caden gave me a stern look, telling me they'd heard my melt down in the hallway. "I take it your afternoon with Hunter was pleasant?"

"Bite me," I growled, facing Josie and forcing my face to relax. "Hey. Sorry, I didn't realize you were here."

I wasn't a crier, but I came close as she hauled me into her arms and hugged me. "Don't be silly. You just need a mom hug." She always read me so well, being the mom I needed since my own mother was gone.

I hugged her back, some of my anger vanishing. "How are you?"

"Better now I get to see my favorite daughter," she replied, patting my back affectionately. "You haven't been visiting much lately, so I thought I'd come and see you while I was home."

Caden groaned, even though we knew he loved the relationship I had with his mom.

"Don't call her that. It makes me feel weird."

"Caden Holloway, I'll call her whatever I like. You had no issue sleeping with her when she was your step sister, so stop pretending," she scolded, making me laugh.

"Yeah, big bro, listen to Mom," I teased, my muscles relaxing and the tension leaving me. He faked a gag, looking at me like he was disgusted. He liked it when he was balls deep in me and I called him brother, I was pretty sure he'd turned it into a kink of his.

"Well, little sister, I'll leave you guys to it. I need a shower and it looks like you need some time with Mom," he smirked, walking over and dropping a kiss on my lips. "Love you."

"Love you too, asshole," I said sweetly, turning back to Josie with a smile. "So, how long are you home for?"

Caden left us in peace, and Josie filled me in on her previous trip away. She'd been overseeing some new changes in her company, so she'd been gone for weeks.

Marco wandered in and grabbed a drink, not looking at me as he left again, making Josie frown. "Are you guys okay? It's tense as Hell in here."

I sighed, leaning back against the kitchen counter. "Yeah. My problems are turning into everyone else's. I hate it. Can I ask you something?"

"Always."

"Did you want kids? Like, did you and Tristan plan

them?" I mumbled, staring at the floor. She chuckled, making me look back up at her.

"No. Caden was a surprise, one that I was terrified about. Kids are scary, and I was so young myself. Tristan wasn't happy when I told him, and he tried to push me into an abortion at first. I almost agreed, but part of me held back on the decision. The moment I heard his little heartbeat at that first scan, I knew I loved him something fierce. I can't explain the feelings I felt," she smiled softly. "Why do you ask?"

I shrugged. "I was just wondering. Would you be upset with me if I never gave you grandkids?"

"Is that what's been bothering you? You feel like everyone expects that from you?" she murmured, waiting for me to nod before speaking again. "It's a big decision to make, one that you need to think about clearly. You have plenty of time, so don't rush. If I never get grandkids, I won't hold it against you, sweetheart. Not everyone wants the commitment of children. It's a lot of work. Not that I think you'd struggle with all the extra hands you have."

"I haven't spoken to anyone about it yet, other than Hunter just now. I told them months ago I wasn't interested, but they didn't realize how serious I was. Every where I look, someone's having a baby or the guys are plotting fucking names for our own kids. It's obvious what they expect from me, and I can't handle the pressure of knowing I'll either wreck their dreams, or wreck a kid's life to keep them happy," I said softly. "I don't want them to sacrifice that kind of dream."

She hugged me, sensing me getting frustrated with the conversation. "Don't stress yourself out about it. Talk to them. Be honest and explain yourself to them. Those guys love you, Rory. They'll understand."

"Will they? Hunter's definitely upset with me, and..."

"He's upset because you just told him. Let him process it.

You need to speak to them all, okay? Putting it off is hurting you, which is hurting them anyway. Communication is the key to a successful relationship," she warned, patting my arm. "And please, next time call me instead of waiting for me to show up when you explode. You would have saved yourself a lot of stress."

I snorted. She didn't know the half of it.

Hunter

I WAS DEVASTATED. I couldn't have hidden it if I'd tried. I'd spent years imagining Rory pregnant, wondering what color eyes our child would have and what their little personality would become as they grew. I'd never push her into it, but I wished she'd burst my baby bubble earlier than this.

She wasn't wrong, she'd technically told us already, but I assumed it was something she'd want eventually. She wasn't going to change her mind, I could see that now.

I didn't remember driving Jade home, but I jerked out of my thoughts as a small hand touched my arm. "Rivera? You good?"

I turned to face Jade as she sat in my passenger seat with worry in her eyes. She'd become part of the family, and I was annoyed that Rory had taken her anger out on her.

"I'm okay. Just found some stuff out today that sucks a little. Sorry about Rory, she shouldn't have acted like that," I sighed, her lips quirking up into a sad smile.

"Don't worry about it. Maybe my pregnancy hormones are rubbing off on her. I know she didn't mean it. Is she okay?"

I ran a hand over my face, not wanting to talk about it yet. "I appreciate you wanting to talk about it, but I need to think about some stuff first. Sorry."

"No need to apologize. It's not my business. As long as you know I'm here for you guys. Maybe talk to Lex when you're ready," she smiled, running her hand across her swollen stomach. My chest ached at the sight, her voice breaking me from my thoughts. "He's kicking. Want to feel?"

I nodded, reaching out to place my large hand on her stomach, smiling as I felt the little kicks under my palm. "That's so cool. Is it getting uncomfortable now that he's getting bigger?"

"Sometimes when he gets my damn ribs. He's an asshole for that," she chuckled, tilting her head as I pulled back. "You'd be a good dad, you know? You like learning about this stuff. Rory's lucky."

I let a snort slip before I could stop myself, making her frown. "What?"

"Nothing. C'mon, I'll walk you to the door," I offered, avoiding the conversation. I knew I'd be a good dad, but there was no point wondering about it. Not now.

Jade didn't say anything else as we wandered inside, but her eyes burned into me the entire time.

"There's our girl," Harley smiled as we walked into the living room to find him on the couch beside Alex watching a movie. "Thanks for bringing her home, Rivera."

I shrugged, watching as he stood and hauled Jade into his arms, his hand instantly going to her stomach.

"Any time. Saved you guys coming out. I thought you were working tonight?" I asked, leaning against the wall and crossing my arms. Like me, Harley rarely took time off work himself.

"Luke and Jense have it handled. They basically kicked me out and told me to go home when Holloway and Hendricks left," Harley grinned, placing a kiss on Jade's head and letting her curl up with Alex. "Why aren't you working? You never have a fucking night off."

"Marco's running things tonight, and I'm up to date with paperwork so he doesn't have to go in early. I wanted to take Rory on a date and try to crack open her issues," I replied dryly, her words playing in my head on repeat. "It could have gone worse, but it could have been better."

"Where do you take a woman like her on a date? I doubt she'd sit across from you at a restaurant and bat her lashes at you," Alex asked, joining the conversation.

"You know that place in town where you get to smash plates and stuff?"

"I bet that got you laid. That girl's a wrecking ball when she wants to be," he chuckled, but I sighed.

"She had fun until we started talking about a few things. It ended with me taking her home, where she attacked Red and Marco."

Harley's eyes narrowed, but Jade spoke, defending her friend. "Rory's just stressed out. She didn't hurt me, she just shouted a little. I'm fine."

"That's not the point. You don't need to take on her stress," he grunted, still not convinced. They argued about it for a few minutes before I felt like I was intruding and made my escape, saying goodbye and heading out to my car, letting out a breath as I shut myself inside.

Harley was right, Rory's stress wasn't Jade's stress. I hated knowing my girl's issues were affecting everyone so much.

I didn't know where I was driving until I pulled up at Lexi and Archer's house, apparently needing my best friend. Lexi was easy to talk to, and despite her being best friends with Rory too, she never betrayed my confidence.

I knocked on the door, letting myself in as Lexi hollered out that it was unlocked. Archer would tell her off for that, especially since she didn't know it was me at the door. I didn't expect to see her crying when I walked in.

"Hey, what's wrong?" I asked, only just managing to catch

her as she threw herself at me, her arms going tight around my neck. Archer was sitting at the kitchen table, a stupid grin on his face which confused me more.

I somehow pried Lexi off me, meeting her eyes to find she was smiling through her tears. "You guys are freaking me out. Why are you crying and why is Hendricks grinning at me like a fucking crazy person?" I snorted, understanding dawning on me when I saw the pregnancy test on the table. They'd been trying for a baby for months, having no success with Lexi's fertility issues.

"We're having a baby!" she practically screeched. "It's actually fucking happened!"

I pulled her in for a hug, patting her back as Archer tried to scowl but failed, too excited to be mad at me for touching his wife.

"Get your hands off her or you'll lose them, Rivera."

"She threw herself at me, asshole," I chuckled, holding her tighter. "That's amazing, Lex. I'm so happy for you."

Tears pooled in her eyes as she beamed up at me, and I knew I couldn't bring up my issues with Rory and ruin her moment. She'd been waiting for this for so long, assuming she'd never get the opportunity. I'd never take away even a fraction of her joy.

Archer rolled his eyes at me but kept smiling, snatching Lexi's waist as she moved towards him and pulled her down onto his lap. "We need to go to the doctor to confirm before you go blurting it out to everyone, babe," he warned. I knew she wouldn't be able to keep it a secret for long, so a professional opinion was a good idea before they got too excited and started buying baby clothes and strollers. Especially after their miscarriage history.

Lexi's face dropped and pain filled her eyes. "What if something goes wrong again? What if..."

Archer fisted her hair gently to hold her attention,

calming the situation before she could put herself into hysterics. "Wait until tomorrow and book an appointment with the doctor, then we can go from there after you get the results. Let us enjoy this for one night, and don't stress yourself out," he murmured. "Rivera, what can we do for you, since you're interrupting us," he said with amusement, making me feel bad. I hadn't known they were in the middle of a private moment. I should have called ahead first.

Lexi slapped at his hand with a scowl. "Leave Hunter alone. Why *did* you stop by? Is something wrong?"

I scratched the back of my neck awkwardly, needing to vent but not wanting to change her mood.

"Uh, just some shit with Rory that can wait."

"No, you'll talk about it now. C'mon, I'll make you a coffee and we can sit outside. It's a nice night," she offered, not taking no for an answer. Archer followed me outside while Lexi made drinks, and I was surprised when he spoke.

"I know you guys have been struggling lately. Is Donovan alright?"

"She's just dealing with some shit. I found out what it was tonight, and I don't know what to think of it. I told her it's fine, but it hurts a little," I mumbled. "Would you sacrifice your happiness for Lex?"

He snorted, looking at me like I was stupid. "Of course I would. I do it often. Why? What do you have to sacrifice to keep the Queen of Hell happy?"

Lexi joined us, and I sipped my coffee before speaking, needing a second. "Rory doesn't want kids. Ever."

Lexi frowned, but Archer shrugged. "She'll come around. You guys have plenty of time. Don't feel pressured just because the rest of us want it now. She might change her mind in a few years."

"Nope. She had a complete melt down about it. I won't leave her, but kids are something I've been wanting for a long time. I know she told us months ago about not wanting kids, but I didn't think she was so serious about it."

"Why doesn't she want them? I honestly thought she'd change her mind and was just being defensive about it here that day. You know what she's like," Lexi asked slowly, not understanding her friend's choice. I didn't like talking about Rory behind her back, but Lexi would help me get my head around it, even if she didn't understand everything herself.

"Her father plays a big part. She's only known bad parenting, so she's afraid she'll ruin the kid's life. She doesn't want to ruin her body either, or carry it for nine months. I thought most women dreamed of this shit," I sighed. "I wish we'd had a serious talk about this earlier so we all knew it was non-negotiable."

Archer chuckled, annoying me slightly. "You think she was going to tell you when you first got together that she didn't want babies? Dude, she was basically a kid herself back then. You need to think of her for a second. I doubt she knew you'd all stick around this long. She's always been a bit of a lone wolf, so she's still adjusting to a family environment. You can't blame her, she did try and make it clear the last time you had this conversation with her."

"She's had years to get used to being part of a family."

"Doesn't mean she has yet. Let her process her own feelings without letting yours get in the way. I don't like her much, but kids are a big decision for someone who's had a bad upbringing," he stated, making me growl.

"We've *all* had bad fucking upbringings! It's what made us know what not to do as parents! Diesel had a terrible childhood, and he's going to be devastated by this. He's been planning names and everything!"

Lexi put her hand up to shut Archer up as he went to reply, her blue eyes meeting mine calmly. "The good news is she's opening up a little. Give her some time, talk to the others about it, and maybe she will change her mind later. If not, don't pressure her into it. She'll run and you know it. Especially since she's already told you her opinion on it in the past."

Dread pooled in my stomach at the thought of her running from us, terrified about our expectations from her. I never wanted her to feel like she couldn't lean on us when she was worried about things, but I also knew we wouldn't always understand. Like now, where she was making me decide between having her, or having kids. I'd always choose her, but at what cost?

"I don't want to lose her, Lex. She's the best thing to ever happen to me. Hell, all the guys are too. We're a family, and I don't want anything to get in the way of that."

"That's probably how she feels, and if I know her like I do, I bet that's why she didn't bring up the baby thing again. She doesn't enjoy fighting with you, you know?"

"You're right. That's her entire reason for not talking about this sooner. I get her concern, but it's something she really needed to talk to us about as a family, not something in a passing conversation. I know some of the guys won't really care, but some of us have been excited about the idea of starting a family together," I said tightly. "I don't think any of the guys will leave her, but I'm worried it might push some of them over the edge to know how serious she is about it. What if one of them *does* leave?"

She gave me a sympathetic look, telling me everything I needed to know. If someone left, it would tear us all apart.

"Don't think about it too much, okay? You'll end up running in circles and still not getting an answer. Don't stress yourself out more than necessary. Arch is right, she might change her mind. For now, just be there for her and prove that you're not going anywhere. Unless you really can't live without having kids in your future. If it's going to make you miserable, you need to think of yourself first. I don't want to see you guys break up, it would be a fucking mess and I love you both, but if she refuses to change her mind, you might have to let her go to make yourself happy."

"I won't fucking walk away from five years of shit with her. We've been through so much. I didn't do all that just to leave. She's it for me, Lex," I said desperately. "I'd give up anything for her."

"Then you need to stop wondering about the future and go home to your girl. Maybe she just needed to explode and get her feelings out in the open properly since none of you took her seriously last time. Either way, you definitely need to all talk about this," she explained gently. "Preferably while she's sober."

"She hasn't had a drink today which is good. She's probably had one by now though. She was really mad when I left to take Jade home. I thought she was going to punch her. She was screaming at Marco about how he could leave and play baby daddy with Jade and her guys," I said dryly, not surprised when Lexi cringed.

"She's surrounded by baby stuff right now. She's probably just overwhelmed, and Marco is super involved in everything to do with Jade's baby. She needs to talk to him about it in a calmer manner if she's bothered by it."

"She's usually fine with it, but she just snapped today," I frowned, earning a small smile.

"She's probably just been hiding her feelings on the subject. Marco is baby obsessed, so it's probably why she's freaking the fuck out. It's obvious he wants kids, so it's her panic response. Sounds like you all need a family meeting," she suggested, and I could already imagine the yelling it would bring. Everyone was arguing lately, so a proper discussion would be ten times worse.

I talked to them about how Wet Dreams was doing to

change the subject, and Lexi gave me a knowing look as she played along with my avoidance strategy, but when it was time for me to leave, she followed me out to the car with a serious look on her face.

"Talk to each other. You need to know how everyone feels about all of this. Don't let Rory's demons drown you all. Be open and honest and you'll be fine, alright? I love you, and I'm always here for you. No matter what," she promised, giving me a hug before waving goodbye, making her way back to the house.

"Hey, Lex?" I called, waiting for her to turn around before smiling. "I'm really happy for you."

She gave me a soft smile, her voice warm. "Thanks, Rivera. Goodnight."

I wished I could have stayed and talked about her baby more, but I knew I had to get home and see what kind of state Rory was in. My money was on her being completely wasted and fighting with someone.

Rory

"Leave me alone," I growled as the bathroom door opened and Lukas walked in. I'd been sitting in the shower letting the water run over me for half an hour after spending my evening drunk and arguing with everyone. Marco was still at Devil's Dungeon, and I hadn't realized Lukas and Jensen were home from Harley's bar until now.

"Move over," Lukas said instead of leaving, stripping down to his birthday suit to join me, ignoring my scowling as he climbed in and sat next to me. "Penny for your thoughts?"

"You don't have enough pennies," I mumbled, leaning on him as his arm wrapped around my shoulders. He chuckled, pressing a kiss to my head.

"Tell me about my money's worth then."

"If I took away your dreams, would you hate me for it?"

He was quiet for a moment before speaking. "It depends on the dream. I don't have many left anyway. My dream is to be with you, right here, with all those other assholes you insist on dating."

"You love those assholes," I snorted.

"Yeah, I do. I'm trying not to push you, but you seem like you really need to vent. What's wrong, baby? I heard you had a fight with Hunter and Marco," he sighed, his arm tightening a little more. "What was it about?"

"Can we just fuck instead?" I questioned hopefully, earning a disapproving look.

"Talk to me first, and I'll consider nailing you right here." I loved how confident he'd become in the bedroom. I wouldn't mind it if he and Skeeter had a competition on who could give me the most orgasms. In the end, I'd be the real winner.

I'd managed to tell Hunter about my issues, so I knew I couldn't keep it a secret for much longer. It wasn't fair to tell one and not the others.

"I think we all need a talk. It's something I've been avoiding, but we need to talk about it," I mumbled, making him snort.

"You think? You've been a mess lately. I get it, I've had my own shit go on over the years and I acted out too, so you know I have your back no matter what it is. Promise you'll talk to us?" he asked, tilting my face up to meet his gaze. "Promise me."

I swallowed, frustration burning in my stomach at being pushed, but knowing I needed to. I was going to lose them regardless if I didn't get my shit together and be honest.

"I promise."

"Good. Come here," he said with relief, hauling me onto

his lap, his dick rubbing against my pussy and making it clench. He wasn't afraid to take what he wanted anymore, the unsure boy turning into a confident man over the past few years since he'd cut his mother from his life. Knowing he wasn't afraid to express his feelings for Jensen anymore was one thing, but it had helped him feel more secure in our family unit. Meaning, he had no issue manhandling me and putting me in my place. It might have annoyed me at times, but it was a serious turn on to know I could make him lose control like that. Before, he always felt the need to be gentle and baby me.

He held my gaze as he pushed my drenched black hair out of my face, burning need in his eyes as he watched me. "Ride me. I have a feeling you won't feel like it later, and I've been thinking about being inside you all fucking day."

I lifted on my knees so he could line himself up with my entrance, a growl leaving him as I slowly lowered myself over him. "Fuck. You feel so good." He'd also become a lot more vocal, too.

I rode him slowly, my hands resting on his shoulders for balance, and I jerked as his hand connected with my ass cheek. "Faster."

I moaned at the demand, doing as he'd asked, pushing back as his finger brushed against my ass. He chuckled, easing it inside me slowly as his lips skimmed across my throat. "You want more?"

"Always," I panted, all sense of frustration leaving me as he replied.

"How about we climb out of here and Diesel can help me then? He's been waiting patiently."

I peered through the foggy glass to find Diesel leaning against the sink, completely naked with his fist wrapped around his hard dick. I hadn't heard him come in, let alone strip off as he watched us.

Lukas helped me to my feet, turning the water off and not even bothering to grab a towel as he tugged me into the cool air. He kissed my shoulder as he steered me towards Diesel, his voice quiet but firm. "Back up to him and let him fuck you from behind. I want to eat your clit while he stretches you."

My knees were going to give out at this rate. They all had a filthy mouth in the bedroom, but it always surprised me when it came from Lukas.

Diesel hauled me into his arms, giving me a kiss on the lips. "Hey, baby. I missed you today."

"So I can see," I teased, wrapping my fingers around his length. "You want to play, D?"

"Give me that pussy," he grinned, spinning me around and wrapping an arm around my middle to hold me up properly, bending his knees to line himself up. We'd gotten into some weird positions over the years, and as much as this one seemed simple, it wasn't good for anyone's leg muscles.

He pushed inside me, his teeth grazing across my back as he grunted. "You want Luke on his knees? I want you to watch him. See how much he fucking enjoys the taste of your pussy juices." I was going to come and they'd hardly started on me.

Lukas dropped to his knees, giving me a naughty smile in the process. "Hold on, babe. This won't take long."

"I could have told you that," I moaned, trying to thrust forward but Diesel's arm held me still. Lukas chuckled, not wasting any more time as he sucked my clit between his lips, his eyes on mine as he licked and sucked at my bundle of nerves, my breath hitching as my pussy clenched around Diesel.

My fingers threaded through Lukas' hair as my body tingled, and I groaned as Diesel's thrusts picked up the pace. Lukas' tongue traveled lower, causing Diesel to pause for a second with confusion. They might have all learned to play nice in bed, but that didn't mean everyone wanted their dicks licked on accident by the other person.

"Luke," Diesel warned as Lukas slipped his tongue into my pussy. "Pushing it a little, man."

"D, I'm close," I complained. "Can you stop standing there and fuck me?"

"Tell your boyfriend to get his tongue off my dick then," he growled as Lukas lifted one of my legs and rested it over his shoulder, getting deeper inside me. I wished I could see this from someone else's perspective. I bet it was hot.

"Just ignore him and fuck me. His tongue won't make you gay," I snapped, gasping as he thrust firmly into me.

"You like that? The thought of Lukas tonguing us both at the same time?" he snarled, pulling a low moan from me. "I'm going to fill your pussy with my come and let him eat it. Would you like that?"

"Oh, fuck!" I gasped as my body tightened and I came, fisting Lukas' hair as I dropped my head back on Diesel's chest. He slammed into me, somehow not knocking Lukas out with my groin in the process, not warning me before coming hard. I expected Lukas to pull away, but he kept licking at my pussy like a man starved, rolling his tongue around Diesel as he pulled out. He pulled my leg up further, letting Diesel take it to hold out of the way while he buried his tongue in my pussy again, having no issue with licking me clean.

He finally sat back on his heels and looked up at me, wiping his mouth with a grin. "Bend over the sink." *Oh, shit.*

Diesel was giving him a dirty look, still not happy about their latest bonding session, but he spun me around and positioned me how Lukas asked. "We're talking later, Lukas."

"Later's fine by me," he replied, not paying him any more attention as he grabbed my waist with both hands. "Come for me one more time. Then I'll fill you up until it's running down your thighs."

He pushed inside me, not giving me a second to get used to him before he was hammering into me, my breathy moans bouncing off the bathroom walls for everyone else to hear. I wasn't surprised when I came that the door opened and Jensen poked his head in, amusement on his face.

"It sounds like you're killing her in here. Hurry up, family meeting."

Lukas buried deep and came inside me, my body tensing at Jensen's words. "Now?"

"Yeah. Hunter's home and told everyone to meet in the office for a meeting." This wasn't good. I wasn't ready.

"I think I'll pass," I said lightly, but Diesel gave me a dark chuckle.

"Like fuck. You know exactly what this is about. We know you've told him about what's been on your mind, he texted Skeet earlier and said he'd gotten it out of you. It's not like you to run from shit, so get dressed and let's go."

I fumed silently as I went to walk away, but Lukas jerked me back by the arm and met my gaze. "Relax. It can't be that bad."

I guess we were going to find out soon enough just how bad it was to them all.

"Nice of you to fucking join us," Skeeter grunted from his seat at the table as I entered the underground office, anger pulsing through me at the knowledge that I was about to be backed into a corner.

"I was busy," I snarked, sitting in my seat at the head of the table and kicking my feet up to try and appear relaxed. "I don't have all night."

Hunter raised an eyebrow, not looking amused. "Would you like to start then?"

"Not particularly. You're the one who called a meeting," I threw back, making him shrug.

"Suit yourself," then he turned to the rest of the room and blurted out everything without even working up to it. "Rory decided to tell me today that she was serious about not wanting kids. I think that's something we all need to discuss."

You could have heard a pin drop. My stomach twisted uncomfortably as I stared at the table, anger burning inside me the longer the silence went on for. Eventually, I snapped.

"Well?! No one wants to fucking add anything?!"

I met eyes with Skeeter who looked pissed, surprising me slightly. He was the least likely to want kids. Sure, he didn't mind talking to Jade about pregnancy stuff, but he never showed interest outside of that like the others did.

"You're only deciding this now?" he asked in a low voice, and I did well not to cringe.

"I've never wanted kids," I said bluntly, his eyes narrowing.

"You didn't think this was something you should have discussed with us earlier?"

Everyone was staring at me, and I sat up, slamming my fist onto the table. "I did fucking tell you the day Red announced her pregnancy! You all just assumed I'd want to be a baby machine for you all? Fuck that. If you wanted babies, why didn't you talk to me about it? Why's it up to me to bring this shit to the table, just because my opinion is different than yours? Are you saying I'm the one with the issue?"

Guilt ate at me despite my anger as my eyes darted around the table to see everyone's expressions. Diesel looked broken, Skeeter was fuming, Slash didn't seem too upset, and

SINNERS REIGN | 43

the others all had equal looks of disappointment on their faces.

"Why are you adamant about this? Help us understand," Diesel finally asked, making me scowl.

"My dad was a terrible parent, what more do you need to know?"

Marco stood quietly, his sad eyes on me. "Don't throw away your chance to be a parent because of your asshole father. We can figure it out together, babe."

"You mean, *your* chance to be a parent?" I scoffed. "It's your dream, not mine."

"I get it, I really do, I just thought we were working towards making a family and you'd warmed up to the idea." *Well, that made me feel like a dick.*

"I'm sorry, but it's not something I want. I made it clear. If you don't like it, you can leave," I said defensively, but my heart was hurting at the thought of him walking away. Frustration, fear and anger was thrashing around inside my chest, knowing this could be the end of everything I'd worked hard for.

Marco eyed me for a moment before sighing in defeat. "I just need some time to think." Then he walked out, closing the door quietly behind him.

My heart dropped as Skeeter got to his feet too, but he pinned me with calm eyes. "I'm going to check on him. We'll talk more later, baby girl." At least he wasn't leaving me.

The rest of us talked for hours before going to bed, and I wasn't surprised when everyone headed into the spare bedrooms, needing a night for themselves. We'd all been emotionally ripped open, so I knew it would take some time to heal.

I stripped naked and climbed into bed, glancing up as the door opened and Slash walked in, Tyler not far behind him.

"What are you guys doing?" I mumbled as they stripped

down to their boxers and slid into bed on either side of me. They sandwiched me between them, and Slash pressed a kiss to my forehead as Tyler wrapped an arm around me from behind.

"Sleeping. You're allowed to feel like this. I know they're upset right now, but they'll be okay. I'll get a damn dog if that helps them," Slash murmured, making me snort.

"I don't want a dog."

"We're going to have a problem then," he chuckled, letting me bury my face in his chest. "But seriously, not everyone wants to be a parent, and that's okay."

"You don't want kids?"

"I'd like kids, but it's not the end of the world if I don't. I'm happy as long as I have you," he replied, and Tyler tightened his arm.

"Same. Everything will be fine, babe. Get some sleep, okay? It's been a long day."

Nothing was fine, but I managed to fall asleep in their arms, my worries following me into my dreams.

CHAPTER THREE

MARCO

I slept like shit. Knowing I'd never be a father was a kick in the guts. I'd spent so much time with Jade, learning all about pregnancy and the awful things women go through, hoping to make it a little easier for when we went through it with Rory. It had all been for nothing.

I shouldn't have expected her to change her mind, so I was mad at myself more than anything. I should have taken her seriously when Jade announced her pregnancy, but instead, I'd pushed it to the back of my mind and acted like it never happened.

I couldn't lie, I was excited for Jade to have her baby and see her as a mother. She was my best friend, and I was going to love watching that kid grow, but it still hurt to know all my questions weren't going to be necessary anymore.

I rolled onto my back, Skeeter's arm tightening around my waist as he stirred. "You awake?" he murmured sleepily, his eyes cracking open to look at me.

"Yeah. It's still early. Go back to sleep," I replied quietly. I wasn't going to be getting anymore sleep, despite the sun only just starting to crack through the curtains.

He shuffled closer, lifting his arm for me to curl up to him, wrapping both arms around me once my head was against his shoulder.

"I take it you haven't had much sleep?" he asked, fully aware that I hadn't. He'd woken up a few times to find me awake.

"Nope. I just keep thinking, you know? Why wouldn't she want to have kids with us? Why don't you seem mad about it?" I grumbled.

"You need to take your mind off it a little. She's making big choices out of fear and uncertainty. She'll come around one day. She's only twenty-three, Mark. Let her live a little first."

I glanced up at him with a frown. "You make it sound like we're old as fuck. We're only four years older than her."

"You know what she's like though. She's obviously not over the trauma her father caused. Maybe in a few years, she'll be at peace with it and she'll want her own kids," he stated, trailing his fingers up and down my spine.

"There's a lot of maybes in that. She won't let us marry her, she doesn't want kids. Is this it? Is this as far as it goes?" I questioned, wincing when I realized how bad it sounded. "I didn't mean it like that. I love her, nothing will change that, and there's no one I want to wake up next to other than you two. But, I pictured myself going further with her. Calling her my wife, seeing her have our kids, all that stuff. Again, why are you not upset about this? You didn't even seem that surprised last night."

He snorted, kissing my head in a surprisingly affectionate motion. "You and Rory are enough for me. I never really cared about getting married, and as much as I wouldn't say no to kids, they're not something I really saw in my future. I've thought about having them with her, but I haven't just assumed that was the plan, especially since she bluntly told us months ago that she wasn't interested. Starting a family is a big decision, but I am a little frustrated with her for not telling us about the severity of her choice. You guys have been talking about kids a lot lately, and since she didn't argue with you, I assumed she'd warmed up to the idea."

"I really want kids, Skeet," I said quietly, scowling when he rolled on top of me. "I'm not in the mood. You suck at reading body language."

"Maybe we could adopt one day? I know you've been wanting to help the homeless kids some more, so how about you focus on that for a while? Might be good for Rory to be around kids so she knows if she's made the right choice or not. I love you and I want you happy, but promise me you won't fight her on this right now. She's on the verge of running. She's fighting, she's drinking, she's on mental overload. Don't push her," he warned, but I was still focused on the whole adopting thing.

"You would be interested in adopting? Like, you and me?"

He raised an eyebrow, leaning his weight on me. "I meant all of us. If it's not something everyone else wants, then we can talk about adopting ourselves. I don't know how that would work since we all live together, but we'll figure something out. Besides, then I can teach our kids how to throw hands so they don't get bullied in the playground."

"I've changed my mind, I'm in the mood," I chuckled, wrapping my arms around him and pulling him down further for a kiss. I was probably pushing it, he wasn't the type to roll around in bed snuggling and kissing, but sometimes he let me. This was luckily one of those times.

He growled into my mouth as I palmed his erection through his boxers, and I'd just slipped my hand inside them when the door opened and Lukas wandered in without a care in the world.

"Oh, sex party. My invite get lost in the mail again?" he joked, and I couldn't help but snort.

"You don't get invited because you couldn't handle it, little boy."

"Bite me, Ortega. You just don't want to be put to shame when I pull my dick out. Anyway, I'm here to make sure you're awake. Slash just got a call from Sniper. He'll be here in an hour."

"The fuck for? Can't that cunt show up at a regular time?" Skeeter growled, rolling off me to my annoyance. We'd only been having angry sex lately, and as much as it was good, I missed being playful with him. My ass was starting to hurt, too.

Lukas sat on the edge of the bed, shrugging his shoulders. "Apparently, he's got a good tip about some kids being moved through the skin trade. He's made the trip down to sort it out with Rage, but he wants us to tag along too."

That made me frown. We didn't work alongside the Kings with anything, regardless of the situation. I didn't feel comfortable working with Rage, either.

"I don't think that's a good idea. Someone's going to end up dead, and it won't be the kid snatchers," I stated. "Besides, I doubt anyone's going to want to help them after last night's bullshit."

Lukas' face dropped a fraction, making me feel bad for bringing up our late night discussion about our futures. Lukas might have grown into his confidence a lot, but he still had a soft heart, one that I knew Rory broke with her speech.

He sighed, laying back beside us to get comfortable. "I don't know what to do about any of that. But I want to help those kids. A lot of them were sold by their parents, apparently. Who'd give up their kids like that? Knowing where they'd end up?"

My blood boiled at the thought, understanding his need to help. He knew what it was like to be thrown away like trash by his mother, even though he was better off without her. He wanted to prove to those kids that life could get better.

"Come here, you softie," I smiled, hugging him despite his protesting. Skeeter chuckled, throwing an arm over me to hug him too for support. I was glad they'd started building a friendship. They were good for each other.

"Alright, we're up. I guess we can help out for the kids' sake. Have you told the others?"

"Not all of them. Rory, Jense, Slash and Ty are awake, but I'm going to wake up Holloway and Diesel, then find Hunter so we can discuss it further. I have no idea where he slept. I don't think he's in any of the bedrooms."

"We'll find him. Let's go help those kids. Tell Slash to call BG to let him know what's happening. The last thing we need is the cops kicking down our doors when we have a bunch of kids in our possession," I muttered, knowing BG would keep them away from us until we needed them. He was one of the only cops who understood shit like this and wouldn't get involved. Sure, we had other cops in our pocket, but he'd do us a favor for free, unlike the rest.

We quickly got ready and went in search of Hunter, not at all surprised to find his phone signal pinging at the Devil's Warehouse. We told the others where we were going and headed off to get him, finding him sitting at his desk with a sour look on his face.

"What are you doing here?" he grunted, glancing behind us to make sure we were alone. The day wouldn't run smoothly if we weren't getting along.

Skeeter sat on the edge of the desk, noticing the empty whisky bottle beside him, not that he mentioned it. "We're helping the Kings today."

"Like fuck. I'm not doing shit for those assholes," he snapped, but his eyes softened when Skeeter continued.

"You know how they're trying to stop the skin market? A bunch of kids are being moved today. Sniper's asked for our help, so I think we should go. Lukas is pretty determined about going, so we have to go and make sure he doesn't get shot."

"Luke's coming? That's a first," he snorted. "Fine. When are we meeting Sniper?"

"He's due at the house in the next ten minutes. Let's head home and see what the plan is. Head's up, Rage is going to be there," I answered. "No shooting in the house, okay?"

"It's not me you should be worried about," he argued as he stood, following us outside to the cars. "Is Rory going to behave?"

"Doubt it," Skeeter and I both said at the same time, making Hunter snort.

"Yeah, I didn't think so. Let's go start this shit show."

Rory

I FELT BETTER AFTER A SLEEP, not that anyone else seemed to sleep well. Slash was cranky, but that was always expected when his brother was involved in any conversation. Skeeter and Marco had returned with Hunter, but he kept his distance from me. I couldn't believe he'd left the house to get away from me. I tried not to take offense, but I was mad about how everyone was acting. You'd have thought I had the plague by the way they were all staying away from me.

"Rory! Your friends are here!" Sarah, our housekeeper called as she wandered in with Rage, Sniper, and a bunch of Kings behind her.

"They're not friends, Sarah. They're the enemy, and the

big angry one has a death wish for looking at me like that first thing in the morning after asking for a favor," I replied, glaring at Rage who was glaring back at me. Sarah waved it off as if I'd made a joke, telling us she was going to the store for groceries as she left us in peace.

"Morning, Angry Man. You look cheerful as ever," I taunted, his jaw clenching as his knuckles cracked by his sides.

"Tempt me, Donovan. I fucking dare you," he spat, but Sniper stepped closer to shut down the argument fast.

"Morning. Sorry to bother you guys, but we really need a hand with this. We've found a building just outside of town that's been holding the kids, and it's got a lot of ground to cover. Most of the MC are a state over and we had to move fast."

"We don't mind helping you with this kind of thing. Anything else though? You're on your own. Why are your guys a state over? And why aren't you with them?" I asked, not giving a shit about playing twenty questions and digging into their personal business.

He grinned, finding my snooping amusing. "New chapter of our club opened. Had to build connections between our contacts and our new guys. It's like a family fun day, but without the fun."

"Sounds riveting. I'm so happy that you fuckers are multiplying," I deadpanned. "So, where are the kids?"

I might not have wanted my own kids, but I'd kill any mother fucker who sold kids or sexually assaulted them. No child deserved that.

"I love your enthusiasm, Donovan. I have a map of the building and…" I snatched the map from his hands before he could finish speaking, rolling it out on the table to get a good look. "And you're welcome to have a look since you asked so nicely," Sniper finished with a snort, standing back to let us get a good look. I had no idea how they got their hands on blueprints, but it helped us figure out how to navigate the entire building. Thank fuck, because the building had a lot of hidden doorways and passages.

"How many kids? Any idea?" Slash quizzed. "Ages? Genders? Anything?"

Rage grunted, surprising us by answering. "There's at least twenty. Mostly boys. Three of the girls and two of the boys are reported as missing. The rest seem to have been sold or orphaned. Either way, no one's looking for them."

"How do you know the identities?" he snorted, but Rage simply smiled, creeping me out. It was rare to see a genuine smile on his face, but he'd been doing it a lot more since Charlie had forced his stupid brick heart to crack open.

"Surveillance. Donnie can hack into almost anything. He managed to scan the surveillance through some fancy system he has, and compared it to a bunch of missing kid reports and personal documents. I love how everyone's personal information is stored on computers these days. Makes it so much easier to hack into."

"How's Charlie? I bet she can't wait to have that baby so I can punch her in the face for shooting at me," I smirked, causing him to take a looming step towards me.

"Don't think I won't kill you in your own house, cunt."

"For fuck's sake, do we have to do this now?" Skeeter snapped. "We get it, you're going to kill each other one day. Get over it, we have more important shit to deal with."

"Fuck off," Rage barked, and Sniper groaned.

"Guys, come on. You all want to help these kids, so put your shit aside and let's get this show on the road. I want to get there before they move them. Apparently, they're being moved in two hours, so I want to get there early and surprise them."

Rage grunted about him ruining all the fun, but I gave

him a sweet smile. "Alright. Let's go then. I'd love some spare time this afternoon to have it out with Angry Man."

"Donovan," Slash, Skeeter, and Hunter growled, making me shrug.

"What? He's asking for it."

No one seemed to find me amusing, so I rolled my eyes and motioned to the blueprints. "Who's going to be stationed where? We need a proper plan."

"Since when do you give a shit about planning?" Slash scoffed, narrowing his eyes. "You go in guns blazing."

"I can't do that or I'll shoot the kids, asshole," I growled, feeling proud of myself. I'd had a lot of personal growth, not that anyone seemed to appreciate it.

We all went over the plan, making sure all exits were covered by us to ensure no one could run off with any of the kids, then we headed out to the cars and drove towards our destination. The drive only took half an hour, and by the time we arrived, I was practically bouncing in my seat. Ever since the Kings called a ceasefire with the other crews, I hadn't had many opportunities to shoot at anyone.

"Follow the plan," Skeeter said firmly as he killed the engine and turned to me. "If you find any kids…"

"I know. I'll take them outside to the van where Luke and Jense will be with some of the Kings. I was listening, Skeet. Don't baby me with this shit," I gritted out, but he took my chin between his thumb and finger, peering into my eyes.

"I was just double checking. I doubt you got much sleep, so I want to make sure you're safe and have your head screwed on. I love you. No matter what. And for the record? That shit last night doesn't bother me. It's the fact you didn't have a proper discussion about it with us earlier that pissed me off. I've always got you."

"I love you too. I'm sorry. I really am. I just can't…"

"Don't worry about it. We're good, baby girl. Let's go save

these kids so we can get home," he said, cutting me off. Relief filled me, knowing I hadn't hurt him as much as I thought.

I nodded, climbing from the car and following him towards Slash who was talking with Sniper. We all moved into position and surrounded the building, all of us making a sudden entrance to throw them off guard.

Bullets flew, but luckily there were less than ten men on guard, so it didn't take us too long to get control of the situation. One of the Kings ended up with a bullet in the leg, but that was it.

We searched the building, thinking we'd been given the wrong information, but Caden's voice caught my attention from further inside. "Hey! I've found them!"

I jogged towards him, finding a roomful of kids cowering in the corner together, their eyes wide as they stared at us in the doorway. I couldn't see properly because Slash and Diesel were blocking my view, so I wriggled into the room, my heart breaking at the state of them.

Their clothes were torn and dirty, some had cuts on them that looked infected, but one boy stood out to me as he got to his feet and tried to stand in front of as many kids as possible, glaring at me through his fear. He looked to be around eight-years-old, but he'd obviously had to grow up fast.

"Hey, what's your name?" Slash asked him, making most of the kids jump. None of them would speak, and I was starting to think they didn't know how until one of the younger kids slowly approached me, causing the eight-year-old to speak.

"Mikey, don't!"

I turned to look at the others who were crowding in the doorway, knowing they were a scary looking bunch but not knowing how to make the kids feel safe. This was why I didn't want to be a parent, I wasn't good with kids in general.

The younger boy kept moving towards me despite his friend telling him not to, and when he got to me, he reached out to touch my leg. I didn't dare move, not wanting to scare him, but I was terrified. What was I going to do? Pick him up? He looked two, if that.

"Mommy?" Oh, fuck. What was I supposed to do with that?

I slowly crouched to his level, speaking softly and hoping my voice didn't shake. "I'm not your mommy, but I want to help you find her."

The kid touched my face hesitantly, and the older boy snorted. "She's dead."

I glanced up at him with a frown. "How do you know?"

"They killed most of our parents or found us in the foster system. Either way, no family," he shrugged, moving closer to try and protect his friend if needed. I sat on the floor, finding they relaxed more when I made myself look smaller.

"We want to get you out of here. There's people coming to take you away, so we need to move before they arrive. Can you help me get them outside?"

"You're bad too. You have guns," he stated, looking at me as if I were stupid. "I'm not going with you."

"Do you want to be sold for sex with old men then?" I snapped, making them jump.

"Donovan," Slash warned from the doorway, making me wince. I didn't know how to make them understand. Kids were hard to convince on a good day, let alone damaged kids who had trust issues. I should know, I'd been one of those kids who trusted nobody.

The toddler was scaring the shit out of me. He'd climbed into my lap to get a closer look at my face, leaving the other kids to stare at me in wonder. Before long, more of them crept away from the wall to inspect me.

"What's your name?" I asked the older boy since he never

answered Slash, and he finally stepped almost in front of me, his features guarded.

"Lloyd."

"I'm Rory. I promise we're here to help you, but we really need to move. We can sort you out some food when we get there," I said gently, some of the kids' eyes lighting up at the thought. They were all underweight and definitely hadn't been looked after. I hated to know they'd probably gone without food.

Lloyd stared at me a second longer before seeming to take charge of the kids, helping them towards the door. He headed back to the corner, and I wanted to throw up when he lifted a baby into his arms. He brought her closer, hesitating before speaking.

"She's been really quiet the last two days. I don't think she's doing good."

"When did she eat last?" I choked out, my hands shaking as I reached for her, but he pulled back, refusing to hand her over.

"I don't know. They don't usually have babies. They don't have milk."

"When did they take her?"

"Four days ago, I think," he informed me, tears filling his eyes as he dropped his guard a fraction. "She'll be okay, won't she? I've never had to look after a baby like her before. They can usually eat food, but she can't. I don't know how to feed her." Jesus, he'd been looking after them?

"Pass her to me. I'll carry her to the car and we can check her out at home. I'll get some food for her and a doctor."

He didn't look convinced, but he carefully handed her over. "I called her Angel because she looked like one when they got her."

"That's a pretty name. It suits her. What's this little guy's name?" I asked, motioning to the toddler who was still climbing all over me curiously. I knew he'd already told us by blurting it out earlier, but I was trying to keep the conversation going while he'd talk.

"Mikey. He doesn't say much."

The other kids were being ushered out by the guys, but Marco stepped inside the room and held his arms out. "I can take one so you can get up if you want?"

Lloyd stood in front of me, not letting Marco near us. "No."

He squatted, giving the kid a small smile. "I just want to help, man. I promise I won't hurt anyone except the bad guys."

Angel let out a squawking cry, and I almost dropped her in surprise. "What do I do?!"

Lloyd looked at me with confusion, but Marco chuckled. "Hand her here. She's probably just starving, the poor thing."

I wasn't going to say no, crying babies freaked me out.

He took her when Lloyd stepped out of the way, cradling her tiny body in his arms and peering down at her with the biggest smile on his face. "Aren't you a cutie? I'll get you some food and a warm blanket."

Angel kept crying, but Marco seemed at ease despite the demon in his arms, leaving me to walk out with Mikey and Lloyd. Mikey got tired after three damn steps and I had to carry him, but Lloyd wandered beside me without complaint, his eyes going wide when he saw the van.

"I don't want to go in the van!"

"I know it's scary, but it's the only way we can fit you all in. Can you hold Mikey on your lap if we take the car instead?" I asked, waiting for him to nod before motioning to Skeeter to join me. He jogged over with a frown, ignoring Lloyd's glare once he got close.

"You good?"

"Yeah. Can I drive the McLaren home? Lloyd doesn't

want to go in the van. He can ride with me, and Mikey can sit on his lap," I suggested, surprised when he handed his keys over without argument.

"Sure. Marco won't put the baby down anyway, so I'll drive his car home."

"Her name's Angel," Lloyd said loudly, stomping his foot and making Skeeter snort.

"I don't care. I'm here to save you, that's where our friendship ends, little dude."

"I don't like you," Lloyd replied bluntly, making me laugh.

"It's okay, we don't always like him either."

Skeeter scowled but let me take them towards the car, where Lloyd's face lit up. "This is his car?"

"Yep. We have lots of cars. I can show you when we get there if you want?" I smiled, relaxing slightly as we climbed into the car and I helped him strap Mikey in with him. It was easier to deal with older kids. They communicated better.

"More cars like this?" he beamed, seeming to relax around me too now that we were shut inside the car. I started the engine and chuckled as Mikey giggled with excitement.

I guess these two weren't too bad.

CHAPTER FOUR

RORY

"*A*urora! What is this?" Sarah exclaimed as we arrived at home and started bringing the kids inside through the internal garage entrance. We didn't want people seeing us moving a bunch of kids, it wouldn't look good.

I gave her a smile, motioning to Lloyd and Mikey. "Sarah, this is Lloyd and Mikey. We saved them, don't panic. We're not into the whole stealing kids business."

"You almost gave me a heart attack! Oh, look at them all! I'll cook up some lunch!" she suggested, shuffling off to the kitchen to make everyone some food, leaving us to settle the kids down. There were twenty-two, and BG was on his way to help sort out the missing children.

The rest on the other hand would have to find new homes which would be hard.

Lloyd stuck to me like glue, but he hovered closer to Marco when he found him, keeping his eyes on Angel. The kid had definitely grown up too fast, and I hated to see the weight of the world on his shoulders. Had these kids been sexually abused? How did you ask a child that?

I watched Marco who was rocking Angel, trying to soothe her without much luck, but he looked completely in awe of her. He looked so natural with a baby.

Jade shoved her way through the front door, Harley and Alex not far behind her. Jade cooed over Angel, and Lloyd gave me a look of confusion. The poor kid had dealt with enough strangers.

Mikey clung to my hand, so I picked him up and tried to balance him on my hip, joining Marco on the couch.

"Hey, Red. Thanks for grabbing the formula," I smiled and looked her over. I swore her stomach was bigger than it was the day before. She was popping out fast, and she looked a lot further along than five months.

She waved it off, all her attention on Angel. "She's adorable. What's her name?"

"Lloyd here named her Angel. The doc's coming to look at her. She hasn't eaten in days by the sound of it," I explained, and Mikey grabbed my face firmly with a smile.

"Mommy."

Jade basically melted, but I scoffed. "We talked about this, kid. I'm not your mommy."

His lip quivered, and Lloyd gave me a dirty look. "You suck at this."

"Thanks," I said dryly, internally panicking at his honesty. I knew I'd suck. Kids were complicated.

He rolled his eyes, patting my arm. "You'll get better. Maybe you can keep everyone? You'd get really good then."

I spluttered, not sure how to answer that, and I was horrified at the thought of raising all the kids that didn't have homes. *No thank you.*

Jade grinned at Lloyd, giving him a wink. "Be nice to Rory. Kids scare her. You're probably giving her a heart attack."

He turned to face me, tilting his head. "We scare you? I

didn't mean to be scary."

I laughed dryly, mentally flipping Jade the middle finger. "You don't scare me, I just don't know what to do with kids."

"Mikey likes to draw. I found some chalk once and let him draw on the concrete," he suggested, a smile hitting his face. "Oh! Do you have colored pencils? I haven't had any of those for ages!"

"How long were you with those assholes?" I asked, making him laugh.

"You said a bad word!"

"Assholes? How's that a bad word? A bad word would be fuck or…"

"Donovan!" Jade growled, shutting me up. "You're teaching them bad stuff!"

I put my hand over my mouth, but Lloyd was laughing hysterically. "You said fuck!"

The guys were looking over at us, giving me the stink eye, but Lloyd thought I was funny, so that was all I cared about. The kid liked me, even if it was for the wrong reason.

I grinned, leaning closer to speak more quietly. "Fuck's my favorite word."

"Aurora!" Jade scolded, but Lloyd cracked up, sitting beside me on the couch and getting comfortable.

"My dad used to say bad words. I said one once and he hit me."

I gave him a sympathetic look, knowing what it was like to cower to a parent. "My dad used to hurt me too."

"Is he still mean to you?" he asked curiously, and I shook my head.

"No. He died."

"My dad's dead too. He used to put needles in his arm. One day, he didn't wake up." He didn't seem upset about it which worried me. Most kids would be traumatized from that.

Jade was tearing up, but I gave him a small smile. "You'll get a new dad one day. He'll look after you and won't use those needles."

He looked bothered for a second before shuffling closer to me until he was pressed against my side. "I want to stay with you. I don't want a new dad." What the fuck was I supposed to do with that?

Marco gave him a warm smile, sensing my inner panic surfacing. "It's okay, you can stay here for a little bit."

Mikey was basically asleep on my lap, but he jerked awake when Lloyd threw himself at me. "I want to stay here all the time! I don't want to go!"

I was frozen, unsure what to tell him. I couldn't let him stay with us forever, but I didn't want to upset him more. He wedged himself under my arm curling against me tightly, and I tried to relax and hug him back. "I've got you, buddy. You're staying here, We'll talk about this later. Sarah will be finished with lunch soon, so we'll have something to eat and everyone can have a bath. I'll have to find you guys some new clothes."

Jade grinned, pointing towards Harley who was getting his ear talked off by one of the little girls across the room. "Those bags the guys have are full of clothes. We grabbed some on the way in case. Hopefully there's something to fit them all. If not, we can run out and get some more."

"You're the best," I smiled, turning to look down at Lloyd. "Does lunch and a bath sound good?"

"Can we watch TV too?" he said quietly. "I asked those people who took me, but they got mad and hurt me."

"You can watch as much TV as you like later, okay?" I promised, not wanting them to feel uncomfortable. "Make yourself at home."

Jade helped Marco mix up a bottle of formula for Angel, and the Doctor arrived to look her over. She was okay, but a little dehydrated. I didn't understand half the instructions we were given, but Marco seemed to, which was good.

All of the kids got checked over, and apart from a few small infected cuts that could be fixed easily, none of them had severe damage. They all ate lunch, and the sound of giggling filled the kitchen as everyone ate and relaxed, a smile forming on my face at the sight. I might not be good with kids, but I was enjoying seeing them so happy already considering everything they'd been through.

Lloyd refused to sit at the table with the other kids, so he stood beside me eating his sandwich, his eyes sharply glancing around the room for trouble. He never fully relaxed, especially when Rage wandered over with a scowl.

"We can't take them back to mine. BG's taking the kids that have homes, but there's still about ten left that definitely don't have families."

Lloyd stood beside me, trying to look tough but his eyes flashed with fear as Rage got closer. He was a scary looking man, I wasn't surprised that he was making the kids uncomfortable. He was fucking huge compared to them.

"It's fine. They can stay here tonight. Lloyd's going to help me look after them. Right, dude?" I asked, peering down at him. He jerked his head in a nod, taking a step forward.

"Yep. I'm helping."

Rage chuckled deeply, probably scaring the shit out of him. "That's nice of you. She'll need it. She's hopeless."

"Am not, fuck face," I muttered, and Lloyd crossed his arms and glared at Rage.

"Yeah. She's not!" God, I loved this kid.

Rage laughed, giving me an amused look. "Found a friend? You'll need it. Have fun with these snot nosed kids. I'm heading home, Charlie's throwing her guts up and she's miserable."

"I'd be miserable if I was stuck with you too. See you

later, Angry Man," I smirked, noticing Lloyd relax the moment Rage scowled and walked away.

"I don't like him," he said firmly. "He's mean to you."

"I don't like him either. We try to kill each other all the time. It's a fun game we play," I said dryly, his eyes flashing up to mine with worry.

"You hurt each other?"

"He's not very nice. Come on, let's get you all clean so we can put a movie on," I encouraged, not that it took much.

Bathing kids was the worst task I'd ever been given, but luckily some were old enough to bathe themselves. Marco was having the time of his life though, getting drenched from splash wars by all the kids he was helping. Luckily we had multiple bathrooms or we would have been doing this shit for hours.

"Feel better?" I asked Lloyd as he wandered into the living room after his shower, a cheeky grin on his face.

"Yep! Can we have TV time now?" he asked, his expression becoming unsure. Poor kid must have copped a lot of abuse for asking questions. He was strong, but he was nervous every time he asked for something, not knowing what the outcome would be.

I gave his shoulder a gentle squeeze, hating it when he jerked slightly. "You can watch as much TV as you like. C'mon, I'll put something on for you."

He relaxed, his eyes watching me as if I were God. I couldn't help it as warmth filled my chest as he followed with a big smile on his face. He was the least scary kid I'd had to deal with in my life.

"What do you want to watch?" I asked once we were seated on the couch, his eyes lighting up.

"I get to choose?"

"Of course, you do. Here," I offered as I handed the

remote over, his small hands snatching it to start flicking through the channels.

"Killer, I need help," Slash growled as he walked in with a screaming toddler in his arms, another clinging to his leg. I couldn't help but giggle, he looked completely out of his element.

"What am I supposed to do?" I asked, my eyes going wide in panic as he shuffled towards me and pried the kid from his arms, placing them on my lap.

"Take one, since you're sitting in here instead of helping," he grunted. I frowned, surprised when Lloyd growled. It sounded like a cute little puppy, but it was the thought that counted.

"She's helping lots! She was helping me with the TV!"

Slash eyed him with annoyance as the toddler on my lap screamed louder, but he kept his voice calm. "I'm glad you can relax, kid, but the rest of us need to get the other kids ready to relax too."

Lloyd turned to me, looking sorry for himself. "I'm distracting you."

"It's fine. I'll go and help, then I can come back. I'll go and check on Mikey and Angel for you," I suggested, waiting for him to nod and get comfortable with a cartoon, then I carried the screaming toddler into the kitchen to find Sarah rushing around trying to help. Most of the guys seemed to be having a blast, but Skeeter looked like he was getting impatient with the kid he was trying to dress, and Slash still had a scowl on his face.

Mikey wandered over and grinned up at me, holding his arms up to be held. I hesitated before hooking an arm around him and picking him up, not wanting to drop either kid I was now holding. They were fucking tiny, but so damn heavy.

"Where's Angel? I told Lloyd I'd check on her," I asked

Marco who was busy tickling one of the kids, the high pitched squeal almost bursting my ear drums.

"She's with Hunter upstairs. She was nodding off, so we wanted to try and get her to go to sleep now that she's been fed."

"Thanks, I'll go check on him. Do you need a hand?" I smirked as two of the little girls jumped on him, using him like a playground to climb on. They were cute, and they seemed to adore him. They didn't look older than five.

"We're good, aren't we, girls?" he grinned, making them giggle as he pretended to shake them off. At least he was having fun. Lukas and Caden were laughing at one of the other kids who got their head stuck in the shirt they were trying to put on, and Diesel was almost asleep on one of the kitchen chairs with a little boy on his lap, the kid's eyes drooping from exhaustion from the day.

They all seemed to be handling it well, and I sighed as guilt ate at me again for exploding about not wanting kids of our own. They'd all be good fathers.

Luckily, the screaming child I had on my hip had gone quiet, tiring themselves out with their melt down.

I made my way up the stairs, finding Hunter in our room on the bed, Angel asleep on his chest. It was the cutest thing I'd ever fucking seen, and he looked so pleased with himself as I entered the room.

"Hey," he said quietly, not wanting to wake her. "You okay?"

I sat on the edge of the bed, taking some of the weight off my arms from carrying the two toddlers. Both of them were half asleep, so I didn't want to disturb them by moving them too much.

"I'm okay. Lloyd's watching TV, and these two seem ready for a nap. You're making this shit look so easy."

"I got lucky, she was already half asleep when Marco gave

her to me," he grinned, peering down at the tiny baby on his chest, his face turning serious. "I'd hate to know what would have happened to her if we hadn't found them."

"Doc said she's only a month or two old. Who'd give up their baby?" I growled, cringing as Mikey jerked at the sound. He looked ready to cry, and Hunter gave me a small smile.

"Rock him a little. It soothes them."

I awkwardly tried to rock him, causing the other boy to stir. I was hopeless at this. I definitely preferred dealing with Lloyd.

"Don't panic. They can sense your emotions," he said gently, making me stare at him in disbelief.

"They have fucking mind reading abilities now?!" I whisper-yelled, making him smother a laugh.

"No. They can just sense when you're uptight and stressed, and it makes them upset too. Just rock them, take a deep breath, and relax."

"How do you know this shit?" I grumbled, trying to do as instructed, not wanting both boys to start screaming. I hated how out of control of the situation I was. Give me a gun fight any day over this shit.

"Marco told me earlier. He's like a Google search of information about babies," he replied with a small huff of amusement. "See? They're already relaxing."

He wasn't wrong. Mikey had snuggled into my chest more, his small fingers grabbing onto my shoulder for comfort, and the other little boy was growing quiet as he started drifting off to sleep again. I was too scared to talk in case one of them woke up, but Hunter chuckled.

"Just don't make sudden noises, they'll sleep through it."

"You're really good at this. You all are," I mumbled, staring at Mikey as his little eyes fluttered closed. Hunter sighed, looking sad.

"You're good at it too, babe. You just need to believe in

yourself. Kids are supposed to be hard, they're tiny people who need assistance all the time, but that doesn't stop people from having them. You're allowed to be scared, it's…"

"I'm not talking about this right now," I hissed quietly. "No stress, remember? They'll wake up again."

"I was just saying. Don't worry about it," he said with a smile that didn't reach his eyes. He was hurting, and having all these kids here wasn't helping. It gave him hope, a look into the future that he'd been chasing for so long, but it didn't change my mind. I had a headache from overthinking, and I knew I couldn't do this all the time.

I felt guilty for looking forward to the kids being gone, because Mikey, Angel and Lloyd were good kids, but I'd ruin them. Besides, there was no way in hell we were taking on any of them permanently. They needed stable homes, not one that had gunfire and shouting on a regular basis.

We stayed in silence for ages, stuck in our own thoughts, but I was just glad that the house had gone quiet and my head could have some peace for five minutes.

"Mommy!"

I jerked upright, my heart rate spiking from being woken up so abruptly. Mikey was crying softly in the dark, and I leaned over to switch the lamp on, finding that I'd climbed into bed at some point. I frowned when I realized none of the guys were there, Lloyd and Mikey being the only two in the room with me. I remembered Lukas offering to take the other kid, but that was it.

Lloyd stirred beside me, blinking against the light as I tucked Mikey against my other side, trying to figure out how to get him back to sleep.

"He likes back tickles," Lloyd mumbled. "It helps him sleep sometimes."

I carefully ran a hand up the back of Mikey's shirt, surprised when the kid basically passed the fuck out the moment my fingers started running circles on his skin. It was magic, there was no other explanation for it.

I left the dim lamp on, trying to get comfortable without waking Mikey again, and Lloyd shuffled closer slowly. "The man with the neck tattoos said I could sleep in here. Is that okay? I tried sleeping on the couch but..."

"Was his name Skeeter, Diesel, or Marco?" I asked quietly, making him shrug.

"I don't know. He had things in his lip." *Skeeter.*

"That's okay. I don't mind. Go back to sleep," I encouraged, feeling my own eyelids droop again, but they flew open when I felt a small body cuddle up to me. Lloyd might have acted tough, but he was still a little kid. He was in a stranger's house after dealing with fuck knows what trauma, and he was trying to feel safe.

I had no idea how to comfort a kid like this, and none of the guys were around to tell me what the fuck to do, so I tried to sound like I knew what I was doing. "Did you want a cuddle too?"

He hesitated before nodding, pressing closer to my side and throwing an arm over me, relaxing as I slid an arm under him. I had him on one side, and Mikey snoring softly on the other, and I laid like that for hours after they'd both gone to sleep, not knowing how I felt about everything.

I must have fallen asleep at some point, because the next thing I knew, I was gently being woken up by Jensen. "Babe? BG's back for the kids."

"He showed up last night?" I mumbled, trying to remember.

"Yeah. You were asleep. Twelve of the kids ended up

going home. Hunter helped BG track down some of their family on the web. He hacked into a heap of shit and BG pretended not to see it," he grinned, raising an eyebrow. "You have some new friends I see?"

I could feel the two kids still asleep against my sides, and I couldn't help smiling a little.

"Yeah. They like me, apparently."

"You're easy to like, don't act so surprised. We need to get them downstairs to get ready. You good with them?" he asked, and I jumped when Lloyd shouted.

"No! Don't take me away!"

Mikey startled, a loud wail leaving him and making me sigh. "It was nice while it lasted."

"I want to stay with you! You said I could!" Lloyd accused, betrayal filling his eyes as he sat up and moved away from me. "You said!"

I was freaking out. Lesson number one of being near kids was not to tell them anything, because they'd always remember.

Jensen took Mikey and tried to settle him, but Lloyd kept getting angrier. "I want to stay with you!"

"I..."

"You lied to me!" he snapped, climbing from the bed and storming from the room, slamming the door behind him. Jensen cringed, patting Mikey's back gently as his wailing died down.

"You told him he could stay?"

"Last night he was freaking out about it, so I said they were staying and we'd talk about it later. He kept getting upset over it and doesn't want to go," I groaned. "I thought I was doing the right thing!"

"Kids have the best damn memory banks in their heads. Marco's getting upset about saying goodbye to Angel, he's pretty attached. C'mon, let's go and say goodbye and try to calm things down. Lloyd will be fine," he promised, waiting for me to get out of bed before we walked down to the living room to find BG trying to herd the kids into one spot. It wasn't working very well.

Lloyd glared at me from across the room, and Marco looked torn in two as he handed Angel to another officer. He was devastated.

Jensen handed Mikey over to BG, and as soon as they got the kids out to the car, BG gave me a smile. "Thanks for looking after them for the night. We've found them all some wonderful foster homes until we can see if any more of them have family. It was hard to find enough places to put them on such short notice, but they're all organized now."

My heart was hurting. "They won't stay together?"

"No one wants to take on that many kids. Especially so many that young. The older one was hard to find a placement for, but…"

"He's going alone? No, he needs to stay with Mikey and Angel," I ordered, making him chuckle.

"I appreciate your concern, Donovan, but no one wants a nine-year-old, a newborn baby, and a two-year-old. It's too much to take on. Angel has a lovely couple waiting to meet her, and Mikey…"

"They stay together!" I snapped, sensing one of my guys stepping closer, ready to grab me in case I threw a punch at him. Assaulting a cop wasn't a good idea.

"I understand, but…"

I was ready to strangle him. Lloyd was clinging to Mikey's hand in the car, a defeated look on his face that broke me. I had no idea what I was thinking, but I couldn't stop myself. "Those three stay with me then."

He looked at me like I was crazy, his eyebrow lifting. "You want to foster them?"

"I don't care what you have to do, or how much it fucking

costs. They're not leaving or being separated. C'mon, Lloyd. You and Mikey get back out," I said firmly, Lloyd's eyes widening.

"Babe, do you think we should talk about this?" Slash muttered from nearby, but I shook my head.

"They're staying."

One of the cops snorted, giving me a dirty look. "You're the last person a child should be left with, let alone a fucking newborn."

BG groaned as I gritted my teeth, his hand going up to calm me down. "You're serious?"

"You're not considering this bullshit, are you?" the cop growled, but I nodded at BG.

"Dead serious. I'll sign all the forms, I'll take full guardianship, I'll pay whatever costs are needed. You're not taking those kids away and splitting them up. They've been through enough."

Lloyd bailed from the car, throwing himself at me and crying loudly with relief, and I somehow managed to hold him up while glaring at BG. "I won't lie, I have no idea what I'm doing, but these kids won't go without a thing. Between the ten of us, we'll make sure they're cared for. Please, don't split them up."

He looked thoughtful for a second before nodding slowly. "Alright. Foster kids get regular check-ins to make sure they're being looked after. There's a heap of paperwork since you're not a registered carer, and getting approval can..."

"I don't give a shit. Get me the paperwork," I snapped, hugging Lloyd tighter to try and soothe him. "Rush everything through so they can stay. We don't need to be paid to look after them either, so don't even worry about that. You want some funding for the foster agency? I'll give it to you."

What the fuck was I doing?

CHAPTER FIVE

SLASH

*R*ory had officially lost the fucking plot. She'd spent so much time the other night yelling at us about how she didn't want kids, and now she was offering our home up to three? I couldn't lie, I was glad the three kids wouldn't be split up. They seemed to have a strong bond, one that couldn't be broken. Angel was too young to understand anything, but Lloyd loved her so much.

It took hours of paperwork and dodgy deals for Rory to get what she wanted, and I was worried about how this would end up. It might have seemed like a good idea to help the kids, but this wasn't something that would get easier. She was taking on three damn kids.

Tyler wandered over to me on the back patio, watching Rory through the glass as she continued to sign paperwork, my chest tight with worry.

Would she regret this?

"What the fuck is she thinking?" Tyler murmured, making me grunt my agreement.

"I have no fucking idea. She couldn't wait to get rid of them yesterday."

Lloyd refused to leave her side, even when Lukas tried to convince him to watch some TV instead. The kid obviously had abandonment issues. Rory was too independent, she wasn't going to cope with him latching onto her for the rest of his fucking life.

Mikey was playing on the floor with a ball Caden had grabbed from his mothers, and I cringed at knowing how much shopping we would have to do. They needed everything from clothes to furniture, and Lloyd needed to go to school.

"How long do you think it will take for her to freak the fuck out and realize what she just commited to?" I quizzed, a light chuckle leaving Tyler.

"I give her a day. She'll go to bed tonight and realize she has to look after them full time."

"Fifty bucks says it takes her two days."

"You're on," Tyler grinned, bumping my fist.

Tyler and Caden wouldn't admit it, but they were basically unofficial Psychos. They'd been coming along to jobs with us over the last couple of years, needing to find their place in the family. Lukas and Jensen on the other hand preferred working the bar with Harley. They trained with us, learning to defend themselves against enemies if needed, but they didn't like moving drugs or guns.

"He won't put that kid down," Tyler observed as Marco wandered into view with Angel in his arms, and I couldn't argue with him. He was completely in love with the little girl.

He noticed us watching him and rolled his eyes, wandering outside and shutting the door behind him.

"What are you staring at?"

"You. You're like a proud parent," I smirked. "Not that I blame you. She's cute."

"She cried half the night but I think her stomach's upset

from her feed. It might take a little while for her to get used to it again after being so hungry," he mumbled, stroking her rosey cheek with his finger. "I'm relieved that Rory wants to keep them."

I snorted, giving him the side eye. "You know this will go to shit, right? She's going to freak eventually."

"She'll be fine. I've got Angel under control, Mikey's pretty easy going to care for, and Lloyd looks after himself. There's no reason for Rory to freak out," he said firmly. "Besides, I won't let her hand them back over. We're a family, we'll work around any difficulties we face."

"Has no one thought of the big picture? We all work, we're rarely home, and we forget to feed ourselves half the time. These kids need someone with them twenty-four-seven. Lloyd needs to be enrolled at school, too. I'm surprised BG is even allowing this."

Tyler laughed, but he was focused on Angel as he gave her his finger to grab hold of. "Have you tried telling our girl no? BG is smart to not argue with her."

"He shouldn't have said yes until he knew if he could push this shit through so fast. There was a chance it wasn't possible," I grunted. "Lloyd wouldn't have coped with hearing he had to go again."

"It's sorted now, stop worrying about shit," Marco scowled. "Charlie's coming around to help Lukas and Jensen with the kids tonight."

"Where's Rory going? She just took custody of three fucking kids," I growled, but he shrugged.

"She's fighting, apparently."

"Like fuck," I snapped, Rory's eyes darting up at me from inside, hearing my annoyance. "She can stay at home."

Her eyes narrowed, but she turned back to her paperwork, speaking to Lloyd who seemed to be deep in conversation about something.

"It's Friday night. You and Skeet decided to run that fucking fight and told everyone she was fighting. This is your fault," Marco replied. "I'll stay home and help with the kids. Hunter's needed at Devil's Dungeon with Red, you and Skeet need to be at the fight with Rory and Diesel. Caden and Ty can either go with Hunter or stay home. Everything's under control," he stated, lifting Angel against his chest to rub her back as she let out a small cry.

I raised my eyebrow, giving him a warm smile. "You're good with her. As much as I gave you shit about it, I can't deny you're coping really well with all this."

He grinned, rocking his body slightly to soothe her. "She's so fucking perfect. Hopefully she sleeps better tonight though, or tomorrow's going to suck."

"I doubt she'll sleep much. It's been a long twenty-four hours for her. At least Hunter's been helping," I offered, making him snort.

"I almost had to fight him to get her back. Skeet's not as helpful. Pretty sure it's freaking him out a little."

"He's not used to dealing with kids. He'll learn," I shrugged. "He's doing okay with Mikey."

"Mikey's easy. You make faces at him and he's happy," Marco said, rolling his eyes. "He's not getting along well with Lloyd. The kid keeps pushing his buttons."

"From what we've figured, Lloyd's been with those assholes for a long time. It's not like he was recently taken. He probably has a lot of anger and fear swirling around inside him, so if he only connects with Rory at the moment, who cares. As long as he's talking to someone," Tyler sighed. "Pretty sure we're going to lose our girlfriend to a nine-year-old."

He wasn't wrong. Lloyd stuck to her like glue, and he kept making her smile. He probably had a crush on her.

Rory

I WAS FUCKING EXHAUSTED. Lloyd talked my ear off all fucking day, Angel cried all afternoon, and Mikey refused to have a nap. I was going to fight like shit in the cage, I just knew it.

I managed to sneak away for five minutes of peace, sitting beside the pool and lighting a cigarette, savoring the silence.

"What are you doing?"

I bit back a groan, glancing over at Lloyd who was standing close by with a frown on his face. "Why are you out here?"

"I needed a minute. You shouldn't be out here while I'm smoking," I mumbled, making him roll his eyes as he sat beside me and dangled his feet in the pool.

"Don't smoke then."

"You know what happens when I don't smoke?" I quizzed. "People die. I can't exactly get drunk right now. I have you guys here, and I have a fight tonight."

His eyes went wide. "A fight?"

"Yeah. I fight for fun. People pay a lot of money to see me take down big fighters," I grinned, blowing the smoke away from him. I wish he'd go back inside, but he seemed uncomfortable around everyone else without me there. He kept glancing at the guys with uncertainty when he didn't think anyone would notice, but I saw it.

I didn't have the heart to tell him to leave me alone.

He frowned, tilting his head slightly to watch me. "Do those people get hurt?"

"Yeah, they do. They wanted to fight me though. They signed up for it."

He pondered my words for a moment before continuing. "Are you in a gang? I saw your jackets when you came and helped us."

I butted my cigarette out beside me and turned to give him my attention. It was hard to know how much I should tell him. He was a kid, but I didn't want to lie to him again.

"We're a street crew. Skeet, Slash and Diesel are part of the Bloody Psychos, and Hunter and Marco are with the Devil's Armada. We don't hurt people unless they deserve it."

"Are you their leader?"

"Why do you ask that?" I chuckled, leaning back on my hands, a smirk forming on his face.

"You tell them what to do a lot. Do you all live here?"

Fuck. How do I explain to a kid that I'm dating them all?

"I'm with the Psychos. Slash and Skeeter are in charge of the crew, but I help them a lot. And yes, we all live here. They're my boyfriends."

"All of them?!" he exclaimed in shock. "Like, they take you on dates and stuff?"

"Yeah, kid. I go on dates with all of them," I said tensely, waiting for him to tell me I couldn't do it. Kids always spoke what was on their minds, it was one thing I'd discovered.

"That's so cool!" he practically shouted, startling me. "Can I have lots of girlfriends too?!"

I laughed, ruffling his hair. "You can have as many girl-friends as you like. We'd better head back inside so I can get ready to go."

I stood, and he scrambled to his feet too. "When are we going?"

I shouldn't have said anything. *Shit.*

"You can't come with me. We don't allow kids at the crew events. It's not safe, and sometimes people try to hurt us," I explained, thinking I'd done the right thing. That was until his eyes widened and he grabbed my hand.

"No! You can't go! Someone will hurt you!"

I tried to walk, but he grabbed onto my arm tightly, planting his feet firmly onto the ground to anchor us. "I don't want someone to hurt you! What if you don't come back?!"

"Don't be silly, I'll be back," I scolded, his eyes welling up.

"What if you die and I don't see you again?!" *Jesus fucking Christ.*

"Lloyd, I'll be fine. You know I can handle the bad guys, remember? I came and saved you," I reminded him, but he became hysterical.

"No! You can't go! I need you to stay with me!"

"Everything okay?" Lukas asked as he joined us, his eyes on Lloyd. "What's wrong, dude?"

"She's going to fight with people and die! She has to stay home!" Lloyd yelled, clinging to me like fucking velcro. "Make her stay home!"

Lukas sighed, squatting down to Lloyd's level. "Rory doesn't listen to me when I tell her to stay home. You can stay with me and I'll make sure she calls us lots, alright?"

"I want to go with her! I don't want to stay with you!" He was crying angry tears, pure fear in his eyes. "I need to stay with her!"

"Maybe we can go too?" Lukas suggested slowly, making my eyes narrow.

"We can't take kids to the cage fights. They're kids, even I know that's a bad idea. They shouldn't be around that kind of stuff."

"We won't let him watch the fighting. He can hang in the office. Harley's going, right? He'd help watch him," he shrugged, Lloyd's grip loosening on me.

"I can go too?"

I groaned, peering down at the distraught kid softly. "Fine. But you heard him. You can't watch the fighting, you have to stay in the office, okay? I'll see if Lexi can come. She has one of the other girls helping her out at Wet Dreams, so I'll see if she can leave early."

"Who's Lexi?" Lloyd asked with worry. "Is she nice?"

"She's super nice, you'll love her. Her husband's a dick though," I said sweetly, making Lukas frown.

"Rory."

"What? He's nine, not three. I can say dick," I huffed, Lloyd cracking up with laughter.

"Can I call him a dick?!"

"Yes," I smirked as Lukas said no, earning me a disapproving scowl.

We headed into the house so I could get ready, and when I emerged, Skeeter was waiting outside the bedroom door, instantly backing me against the wall.

"You told the kid he could come?"

"Lukas did, actually. I agreed. He's going to stay in the office out of harm's way," I snapped, his hips pressing into me as he caged me in.

"What if the cops raid and find him there? He's not your kid, Aurora. They can take him away. What if the Kings turn on us and shoot the place up? He could get killed. The shed is no place for a kid," he spat. "Face it, you'll fight, get drunk like you always do, and end up fucking one of us in the bathroom. We can't take him."

I punched him in the ribs, satisfaction washing through me as he grunted. "I'm fighting, then I'll hang out with Lloyd. I'll even come home when I'm done if that makes you happy," I hissed. "Don't fucking..."

"If anything happens to him, it's on you. Remember that," he gritted out, cutting me off before stalking down the hallway.

"Fuck you too, asshole!" I shouted, clenching my fist. It was about time we threw hands. I was sick of his attitude, and apparently, he was sick of mine. I wished he'd get in the fucking cage with me, because I'd give him a few good rounds.

"Kick his ass!"

"Fuck yeah!"

"Knock him out!"

I grinned as the crowd screamed at me, eyeing my opponent and trying to figure out the best way to take him down. Diesel had tried to talk me out of it, but this guy had been running his mouth about me all night. I'd won all three of my fights, so I had no idea why he had so much to say about my apparent terrible fighting skills. I'd almost killed the second girl when I'd blacked out, not remembering anything from it other than Skeeter yanking me off her bleeding body.

The guy was bleeding from the nose, the cut on his eyebrow seeping too, and I was pretty sure he had a concussion.

"Got anything else to say, asshole?" I called, watching him stumble around the cage hopelessly. He'd only gotten two hits on me, and they did zero damage.

He lunged at me, managing to knock me off my feet, but I rolled so I was on top of him, pummeling my fists into his face.

"Rory!"

I kept hitting him, not stopping until someone ran into the cage and caught my eyes. Lloyd looked out of breath, his eyes wide as he took in the scene in front of him, fear punching me in the chest as I slowly stood and backed away from the man. Instead of running away from me like I expected, he threw himself at me, wrapping his legs around me tightly.

"Dammit, kid, you can't be in here," I growled, putting my arms around him to support him better. I was covered in sweat and blood, so it was hard for him to hold onto me.

"He hurt you!" he growled. "Can I hit him?"

I chuckled, trying to put him back on his feet but with no success. "No. I'm okay, I hurt him a lot more."

Skeeter was fuming at me from outside the cage, not happy to have the kid wandering around, let alone inside his cage. I helped Lloyd to his feet and convinced him to let go, taking his hand instead. "C'mon, we're going to get in trouble for having you in here."

He gave Skeeter a dirty look, kicking the man I'd been fighting on his way past.

"Don't touch my mom!"

My heart rate spiked and confusion washed through me. He was old enough to know I wasn't his mom.

"Aurora! Get him the fuck out of there!" Skeeter bellowed, slapping his hand against the cage wire. "Now!"

I flipped him off, leading Lloyd from the cage while ignoring the whispers and laughing as Lloyd tried to kick the man again.

Slash met me by the gate, a scowl on his face. "I thought he was staying in the office?"

"Back off, go yell at Lukas or something. He's the one that's supposed to be watching him," I snapped, heading to the office and gently tugging Lloyd inside. Lukas wasn't in there, so I sat at the desk and started unwrapping my hands. Slash had been forcing me to wear wraps lately, claiming it would protect my knuckles more. Looking at my busted knuckles now, told me that was bullshit.

"Does that hurt?" Lloyd asked, standing beside me to get a look.

"Yeah, a little. I'll give them a clean and they'll be fine," I shrugged, but he gently took one of my hands in his to get a closer look.

"They look bad," he mumbled, his eyes looking up into mine. My heart tugged at his concern, and I gave him a big smile.

SINNERS REIGN | 83

"They've been worse before. This isn't too bad, I promise. You ready to head home?"

He nodded, moving out of the way so I could stand. He stayed by my side as we walked towards the bar, and Lukas jogged over with relief on his face.

"He just took off!"

"He ran into the cage. How did he get past you?" I muttered, not wanting Lloyd to hear me.

Lukas sighed, running his fingers through his hair and causing it to stick up at all angles. "I had to pee."

"So you left him alone?" I demanded. "Luke, you can't do that."

"I'm sorry! Is he okay?" he asked with panic, running his eyes over him for injury. I let out a breath, knowing arguing wouldn't change what had happened.

"He's fine. I'm taking him home. Skeet's pissed about him going in the cage. He could have gotten seriously hurt."

"Drive safely?" he asked softly, waiting for me to nod. "Good. I'll see you when I get home. I love you."

"I love you too," I smiled, giving him a quick kiss before looking down at Lloyd who was eyeing us with worry. He probably expected us to beat him or something. "Let's get going."

He took my hand, and I had to fight the urge to pull away. It was freaking me the fuck out that he'd casually called me his mom. Especially since we didn't know each other. I assumed it was a coping mechanism, so I forced down the anxiety and led him outside, ignoring people who continued to glance at us and whisper to their friends. They probably thought he was a long lost love child or something.

Once in the car, Lloyd turned towards me, staring at me in silence until I sighed. "What?"

"I didn't mean to make you guys fight," he whispered,

toying with his hands on his lap. "I wanted to see you and make sure you were okay."

"I know, buddy. You can't do that though, alright? Kids aren't allowed at these events, and you promised to stay in the office. What if the other guy was winning and he hurt you? I mightn't have been able to help you," I said weakly, thoughts running through my mind of him getting hurt because of me. He stayed quiet for the rest of the drive home, and I was grateful for the silence. I rolled my eyes when my phone rang and Lexi's name popped up on the screen. She'd never answered the phone earlier when I'd needed her.

"Look what the cat dragged in," I drawled when I answered, holding the front door open for Lloyd. He looked at me with a frown, seeming confused.

"We don't have a cat?"

"It's a figure of speech, kid," I snorted, turning my attention to Lexi. "So, where were you? I've been trying to get hold of you."

"Sorry, I was dealing with something," she groaned. "Arch and I were busy, so I didn't hear my phone."

"I really could have used your help. We have a bunch of kids, and one had to come to the fights with me," I grunted.

"What the fuck do you mean, you have a bunch of kids? Like, you stole some, or borrowed them?" she teased. "Wait, you took one to the shed?"

I headed into the kitchen, jumping when I found Rage making coffee. "Jesus fucking Christ, you scared the shit out of me!"

He grinned darkly, enjoying my heart attack. "It's a shame I didn't scare the life out of you instead." *Asshole.*

"What's going on?" Lexi demanded. "Who's there? What the fuck were you saying about kids?"

"Ugh, it's just Angry Man. I'm not used to him being in my house. I knew Charlie was coming over to help with the other kids while I was fighting, but I didn't expect his ugly face to be in my kitchen when I got home," I scowled. "As I was saying though, we saved some kids and we kept three."

Lloyd stuck close to my side, eyeing Rage with suspicion. He probably sensed the burning need for us to kill each other.

"They're not stray dogs, Donovan! You can't just keep people!" she exclaimed. "You're going to get yourself arrested for kidnapping!"

"It's fine. The cops have already been here to help us sort everything out legally. We saved a heap of kids from the skin trade, and I didn't want three of them to be split up. So, I'm their legal guardian now," I replied dryly. "I didn't think about what to do after I got them though and it's freaking me out a little."

Lloyd took my hand, looking sad. "You don't want us now?" *Oh, fuck me.*

"That's not what I meant, shit. Of course I want you," I groaned. "I'm so bad at this!"

Lexi chuckled. "I'm coming over. I want to meet these kids."

"Alright. I'll see you soon," I muttered before hanging up. Rage grinned, tilting his head.

"You're going to fuck them up so bad."

"I know," I said quietly, looking at Lloyd with concern. "I don't know what I'm doing."

"That's obvious," he snorted, his face softening as Charlie wandered in with Mikey on her hip. He seemed completely smitten by her, and for a second I saw the pure love between them. I knew he loved her, but seeing him so infatuated by her was surprising.

"Hey, Rory. How was your fight?" Charlie smiled, placing Mikey on the floor who stumbled towards me, clinging to my leg.

"Up!" he squealed, raising his arms.

I bent down to lift him, frowning when I noticed he smelled. "Did he take a shit?"

Charlie rolled her eyes, tucking herself under Rage's arm. "Probably. He ate a lot after dinner."

"Can you change him?" I cringed, but she chuckled.

"Sorry, we need to get going. You'll be fine."

"Wait! I don't know how to change a diaper!" I snapped. "You need to help me!"

"You'll figure it out," Rage grunted. "It's not rocket science."

"If it's so easy, then you do it!" I growled, startling Mikey. He let out a loud cry, almost throwing himself backwards out of my arms.

"Have fun," Rage grinned, ushering Charlie from the room and leaving me with the screaming child, my heart rate hammering in my chest. Lloyd tapped me on the arm, speaking loudly over the noise.

"It's easy! I'll show you!"

"You know how to change a diaper?" I frowned, earning a flat look.

"Yes." *Alrighty then.*

I followed him into the bathroom, watching as he laid a towel on the floor. "Lay him down."

I went to place him on his stomach, and Lloyd snorted. "The other way around."

I felt so stupid.

I quickly did as he said, sitting on the floor by Mikey's flailing feet. "Now what?"

"I'll go get a diaper. You take his pants and dirty diaper off," he said with a nod, leaving the room.

"It's okay," I said tightly, trying to soothe Mikey who continued to scream, and satisfaction raced through me when I got his pants off without a problem, managing to get the diaper off too. I folded it into itself, scrunching up my nose at the smell. "You reek, you know that?"

Mikey rolled around, getting shit all over the towel, but the worst part was when he peed everywhere then ran his fingers through the smeared poop, not hesitating to rub it into his hair.

"No!" I scolded, causing his eyes to widen and his lip to tremble, his screaming starting all over again.

Lloyd sighed when he walked back in, seeming way too grown up for his age. "I'll do it."

"It's okay, I've got it," I insisted, despite my heart beating so damn hard in my chest that I was surprised I hadn't keeled over. He sat beside me, helping me change his diaper, and by the time we were done, there was piss and shit everywhere.

Jensen poked his head in and gave me a tired smile. "You good?"

"No," I mumbled, staring at the filthy child in front of me. "He needs a bath now. He got shit everywhere."

"It's okay. You go shower and I'll get him sorted. Angel's asleep so I have time," he offered, and I honestly wanted to fucking cry. I thanked him and bailed from the room, leaving Lloyd with him while I showered the sweat, blood, and baby shit from my skin, hating how much I sucked at this.

How was I supposed to help these kids when I relied on the oldest one all the time? I was hoping to make his life easier, not harder.

I got ready for bed and padded into the living room, finding Lexi sitting on the couch with Mikey asleep in her arms, her eyes darting up to mine with a smile.

"He's adorable. Are you okay? Jense said you had some trouble?"

I sat beside her, letting out a sigh. "I had to get Lloyd to help me change Mikey's diaper. I got baby shit and piss all through the bathroom, Lloyd had to come with me tonight to the fight but instead of staying in the office he ran out and into the cage to help me, and it's only day two. I'm exhausted."

"Lloyd seems like a good kid. I won't lie, I can't believe you took on three fucking kids," she chuckled. "You seem to be doing good though."

"No, I'm not. I keep upsetting Lloyd by saying dumb shit, I can't change a fucking diaper, and I'm going to fuck up these kids so bad. I haven't really had anything to do with Angel," I mumbled. "Maybe they would have been better off with a proper foster family."

"Don't say that. You're learning, so of course you'll make mistakes."

"Lex, Lloyd ran into the fucking *cage* tonight. He could have gotten seriously hurt. What if our enemies use them against us? What if…"

"You don't have enemies right now for starters. You're panicking over nothing. Lloyd loves you, he wouldn't shut the fuck up about how cool you are when I was talking to him earlier. He idolizes you, Donovan. Give yourself a chance, alright? You have nine guys to help you, so you're not alone. If you need a break, I can always take them for a while, or you can leave them with the guys and come see me. You did a good thing by taking them in. They've been through enough, so if they trust you, you're doing good. I promise," she said gently. "Where's Mikey's bed?"

"I'll show you," I sighed, leading her through the house and up to the room beside mine. "He can sleep in here. Where's Lloyd?"

She carefully placed Mikey's sleeping body in the bed, tucking him in before motioning for me to follow her into the hallway.

"Lloyd's in the garage with Jensen. He was freaking a little without you, so we took him down to the cars."

"He's alright?" I asked with worry, hating that I'd stressed him out. I knew I'd been too long in the shower.

"He's fine. He needs to get used to other people looking after him. It's not healthy for him to form too much of an attachment to you. He'll get separation anxiety otherwise, and he should be in school," she mumbled. "Have you thought of that?"

"Yeah. We're going to figure something out for him soon. I don't know whether to get him an at home tutor, or if we send him to school. Then we have to decide whether to put him into the public system, or that fancy private school on the edge of town."

"You'll figure it out. Maybe ask him what he wants?" she offered as we stepped into the garage to find Lloyd and Jensen sitting in Jensen's Camaro. Lloyd beamed at me, looking like a child for the first time since we'd met him.

"Jensen's going to let me drive his car!"

"Is he now," I chuckled, leaning back on my Ferrari. "That's nice of him."

I didn't get to drive my cars enough. I'd kept all the ones Dad had left behind when I'd killed him, but nothing felt the same as my Corvette. I missed that car so fucking much, but after crashing my second one, I knew it was a sign to move on.

"I want to race cars one day! Do you think I could?" he asked, climbing from the car and moving in front of me, his eyes wide at the thought. I ruffled his hair, smiling when he didn't flinch.

"You can do whatever you want. When you're a little older, we'll get you some driving lessons to teach you to race."

"Really?! Jensen! Mom said I can learn to race!" he squealed, and I felt Lexi's eyes burning into me at him calling me mom.

"Lloyd, I'm not your mom."

He frowned, pinning me with confused eyes. "But, you're like a mom. You help me, and feed me, and..."

"I'm not your mom," I gritted out. "Call me Rory."

His face fell, and he gave me a small nod. "Okay."

Jensen eased the situation by offering to let Lloyd rev the car, and the moment he was occupied, Lexi elbowed me in the ribs. "That was mean."

"What? I don't like him calling me that," I hissed. "I'm not his mom."

"To that kid, you are. He looks up to you. You saved him, and he's obviously very comfortable around you. Don't wreck that trust because you're scared," she warned.

I watched Lloyd as he revved the engine, but his face was still sad from my words. I hated that I'd hurt him, but I was right. I wasn't his mother, and he didn't need to call me that. It freaked me out.

"So, what's been happening with you lately?" I asked Lexi, her face lighting up as tears welled in her eyes.

"I went to the doctors today."

"And?" I snorted, my chest tightening as she beamed.

"I'm pregnant. I found out the other night when Hunter came over, but..."

"Wait, Hunter knew?" I asked bluntly, her smile dropping a fraction at my tone.

"Yeah. Archer and I did a home test just as Hunter arrived after you two had a fight. We didn't want to tell anyone until we got it confirmed."

"Of course he fucking knew. I bet he was over there blurting out all our problems, too," I spat, irritation filling her eyes.

"He was hurt and wanted help to understand your feelings. He wasn't bitching you out or anything, he..."

"He still fucking told you!" I snapped. "That was private!"

"He's hurt, Donovan. Let him vent. Besides, you were at my house having this argument months ago, it's old news," she growled. "It's selfish of you to take that opportunity away from him, you know?"

"Taking something away, means I've had something of his in the first place. He doesn't have rights to my fucking body. If he can't accept that, then you'd better set up your spare room since you're so fucking worried about him," I bit out, stalking from the garage and through the house, walking straight out the front door. I didn't care where I was going, as long as it was quiet.

I ended up walking for an hour, finding myself at the local Satan's Soldiers hang out. Most of them were still a town over, but since my uncle Axel had decided to stay here, they all seemed to stick around.

The Soldiers eyed me warily as I wandered towards the back office, one of them stepping in front of me to block my path.

"He's got a lady friend over."

"Like I give a fuck. Move," I demanded, shoving past him and throwing the door open, finding my uncle with his face in some bitch's pussy, her naked body laid out across his desk.

I smirked, leaning against the wall and crossing my arms. "Evening."

He glanced over at me, wiping his mouth with a scowl. "Why are you here? Who the fuck let you in?"

"Good to see you too," I grinned. "Aren't you happy to see me?"

The girl groaned, sitting up and grabbing her dress. "Nope. You didn't mention anything about a girlfriend."

"She's my niece," he grunted. "No need to leave, she'll only be a minute."

"Like fuck, I came here to have a drink with you. You

might as well go," I said sweetly to the girl, who wasted no time scurrying past me once she was dressed.

Axel got to his feet, giving me a dirty look. "Why'd you do that? It's been a while since I got laid."

"I'm having a bad night and sort of just ended up here," I shrugged, his eyes dropping to my bare feet.

"Did you drive?"

"No. I walked."

"Dammit, Aurora. Sit down," he sighed, pushing a chair out for me to use. "Put your feet up and let me look. They're probably cut to shit if you walked from your place."

I sat down, lifting one of my feet to look at it. "They're fine."

"You going to tell me what happened then? Since you ruined my plans," he muttered, cocking his head to watch me. I sat back in the chair and ran a hand over my face, frustration burning inside me.

"I want to fight, and fuck, and scream at people. I'm angry all the fucking time, and I hate that everyone expects things from me that I'm not willing to give. Oh, and I'm now the legal guardian of a newborn, a two-year-old, and a-nine-year-old," I deadpanned.

"Excuse me? You're a guardian to kids? Whose kids?" he asked, suddenly interested in the conversation. I explained everything that had happened, and by the end of it he chuckled. "No wonder you're freaking out. You're too young to be a parent, Rory. It was nice of you to take them in, but that's a lot."

"The guys all want our own kids, you know?" I mumbled, making him snort.

"I'm aware. Marco was here the other week, telling me all the names he liked for when you have kids. Usually the women are the baby obsessed ones, not the men."

I stood, pacing around his office with a scowl. "I've never

wanted kids. I told them months ago but they didn't take me seriously until now. They're devastated, Axel."

"But, you just took on three fucking kids. That doesn't really back up your dislike for children," he stated. "What's scaring you?"

"They're scary! I had to change Mikey's diaper tonight, and I ended up with baby shit and piss everywhere! I couldn't do it without the older kid's help! I'm dumb as fuck with babies and..."

"Jesus. Take a breath and relax. Kids are supposed to be difficult. They don't come with a manual, and you learn as you go. Where are the kids now?" he asked, guilt stabbing me in the chest.

"I took off from home. The oldest one, Lloyd, keeps calling me mom. I had a fight with Lexi about stuff, and I just had to get out of there. Jensen's home with them. I should probably call him," I mumbled. "See? I took off and didn't even think about the kids. Fuck!"

I kicked the chair over, cracking my tender knuckles and wishing I could break something.

"Is Lex alright?" he asked with worry, earning a disapproving look from me.

"Let her go. She's never leaving Hendricks." His love for Lexi was going to kill him one day. He'd been better lately, but occasionally he'd get lost in his thoughts about her. I always knew when she was on his mind, because he got this stupid smile on his face.

"I did let her go, didn't I? I let that stupid fucker marry her," he growled. "I still worry about her, though."

"I know. She's fine. We just had a disagreement, that's all. You need to find a good woman," I said firmly. "Someone who chooses you first."

He grunted, not impressed with me. "I'm trying, but you just scared her away."

"A crew whore isn't what I meant."

"She's not a crew whore. Besides, so what if she was? Lex works in the sex industry, and she's doing fine in her relationship," he snarked, making me roll my eyes.

"She's not in it anymore. Hendricks doesn't let her up on the pole."

"Well, he should. She loves dancing and he's a dick for taking it away from her," he seethed. "She'd always come home to him at the end of the day, so why try and control her?" He had a point, but Lexi seemed happy being a manager instead.

"She owns a strip club, Axel. She's more than happy about her job," I snorted. "Can I borrow your car? I'll drive myself home."

"Nope," he replied, holding up his phone. "I just texted Gilbert and told him where you are. He's on his way."

"I'm going to get my ass beat," I grumbled, making him laugh.

"Don't act like you hate it. Come on, let's go out to the bar and have a drink before he gets here."

I managed to have two drinks before I heard Lloyd's voice behind me, panic in his tone.

"Mom!" *Fuck's sake.*

I turned, bracing in time for Lloyd to launch himself at me, holding me tightly. "I'm sorry I made you mad!"

"You didn't make me mad, dude. We're cool," I sighed, hugging him tighter as he buried his face into the crook of my neck. He was practically shaking, and I knew I'd scared him by taking off.

"Sorry, I called you mom again," he cringed as he leaned back, his eyes red from crying. He'd probably cried the entire time I was gone.

"It's okay. It just freaks me out a little because I'm a terrible mom," I chuckled softly.

"You're the best mom ever," he insisted, my heart clenching at how serious he was.

I groaned when I realized Marco was with Jensen, Angel crying against his chest. Jensen had hold of a sleepy Mikey, and I couldn't help but frown.

"Why aren't they in bed?"

Marco was furious, but he kept his voice low. "Oh, I dunno. Probably because we had to come and get you? Lloyd refused to stay home, Mikey wouldn't let go of Jensen, and I couldn't leave Angel with Skeet and Lukas because they're killing each other in the living room. So, here we fucking are."

"Who's that?" Lloyd asked quietly, looking over my shoulder at Axel. I smiled, trying to calm down.

"This is my Uncle Axel. Axel, this is Lloyd."

Axel moved closer, his eyes running over all three kids with a smile. "Well, you definitely have your hands full."

Marco was rocking Angel, trying to get her to go back to sleep, and Axel approached with his arms out. "Can I hold her?"

Marco eyed him for a moment before handing her over, not liking her being taken away from him. Axel cradled her in his arms and gave me a grin. "She's adorable."

Her crying turned into hiccups as he talked nonsense to her, and I couldn't believe how quickly she calmed down.

"How did you do that?"

"She probably likes my voice. If she won't settle, I've heard soft music helps some kids sleep. Or sing to her," he chuckled. Marco was nodding, taking all the information in like a baby information hoarder, taking her back the moment Axel held her out to him. "I'm assuming this little guy is Mikey?"

Mikey was almost asleep, but he giggled when he heard his name, peering up at Axel with interest. No wonder the kid had been taken so easily. He loved people, and wouldn't have gotten upset by a stranger picking him up.

Lloyd finally let me put him down, but he took my hand and didn't let go, not wanting me to vanish again. By the time we left, all the kids were asleep and had to be carried out to the car.

"You're on Gilbert's lap," Marco grunted, motioning to the passenger seat.

"But I..."

"I don't give a shit, Donovan. Get in," he said sternly, cutting me off. I knew they'd be annoyed, but I guess I should count myself lucky. If it was Skeeter who'd picked me up, he probably would have put me in the trunk.

CHAPTER SIX

SKEETER

"I don't give a fucking shit!" I snapped as I shoved Lukas back against the wall. "You shouldn't have let him out of the office!"

"Yeah? Well you shouldn't do half the shit you do, but you do it anyway!" he growled, managing to bring his fist up and punch me in the jaw. I was surprised, not used to him being so damn aggressive, but he looked ready to strangle me.

"What the fuck was that for?" I demanded. "You want me to smack the shit out of you?"

"You can try, but I'll hit you back!" Sometimes, I missed the old Lukas. The one that was a little bitch and kept his mouth shut.

I sandwiched him between me and the wall, nose to nose with him. "You looking to fight me, Luke? You could just say so instead of all this fucking foreplay."

"You'd know if this was foreplay. You'd be on your knees," he chuckled dryly, his pupils dilating as I wrapped my fingers around his throat, leaning in to speak in his ear.

"You're wrong. If anyone's getting on their knees, it's you."

"Do you ever let Marco top you? Or are you too scared?" he smirked. He was lucky I didn't tighten my grip and choke him out.

"You know I've let him top me. I saw you watching. Does Jense know you've been fantasizing about me?" I murmured, running my hands down his chest and abs, stopping right above his groin. "Or is that your dirty little secret?"

"Does Mark know you've been trying to fuck me for years?" he threw back, wincing as I grabbed his semi-hard dick through his jeans and squeezed firmly.

"I've told you before, you couldn't handle me."

"I think it's the other way around. I don't think you could handle me."

I squeezed his dick more firmly, a gasp of pain leaving him, but I chuckled when he hardened more. "You like this, don't you? The banter, the threat of pain, the promise that I'd bring you to your knees. I know our girl likes a villain in her bed, but I didn't know you did too."

"Bite me, asshole," he sneered, hardly protesting as I spun him around, pressing myself against his back and biting his shoulder firmly until he yelped.

"Get it through your head, Luke. I'll never fuck you. You're weak, whiney, and everything I can't stand."

"I'm everything you want, and *that's* what you hate," he spat, my patience sizzling out fast. He wasn't completely wrong. I had no idea what the fuck had been going on between us lately, but I knew I didn't hate him anymore.

I reached around and grabbed his throat again, grinding myself against his ass as my dick swelled. "Keep pushing me, and you're likely to find out what it feels like for me to unleash my hate."

"What's going on in here?" Rory asked as she walked in. I hadn't heard the front door, so they must have used the internal garage access. Jensen and Marco were behind her, the kids most likely in bed already, and I stepped back from Lukas with a snort.

"I'm sick of his shit."

Marco eyed me silently, but Jensen snarled. "Leave him the fuck alone. Why do you insist on pushing him with your bullshit? Get it through your head, he doesn't want to fuck you."

"Grab his dick. I bet he's hard," I taunted, storming up the hallway and into our bedroom, forcing myself not to slam the door and risk waking the kids. How the fuck had we ended up with kids so soon after Rory's speech about never wanting any? The whole situation was fucked.

"What was that?" Marco asked bluntly when he walked in behind me, shutting the door quietly and making me scowl.

"What was what?"

"You two were dry humping against the fucking wall. What the Hell did we just walk in on?"

"Nothing. You think I want to fuck him?" I spat, glaring at him as he gave me a shove.

"Yes, I do. You could cut the sexual tension in the air with a knife. Be honest with me. Do you want to fuck him?" he growled, shoving me again. I landed on my back on the bed, his fists clenching by his sides. "Tell me!"

"Why would I want to fuck him? He's pathetic!"

"I see the way you look at him, Skeet. Don't fucking lie to me," he said more softly, defeat taking over his face. I scruffed the front of his shirt, hauling him on top of me and meeting his gaze.

"I don't look at him like anything. Don't feel threatened by him, alright? I love you, and I love Rory. That's it."

"Promise me," he replied, unconvinced.

"I promise." I didn't know why guilt kicked me in the stomach, because I didn't love Lukas. I never would. I didn't even want to fuck him. *Liar.*

I rolled so I was on top of Marco, not wasting time as I yanked on his shirt. "Get naked."

"No, I'm mad at you still," he huffed, making me snort.

"Good. You can scream your frustrations out into the pillow while I ride your ass as punishment for doubting me." The words tasted bitter in my mouth. I knew there was something going on between Lukas and I, but I'd never voice it. We didn't match in the bedroom, and I'd more than likely traumatize him. As much as he pissed me off, he was family, and I never wanted to fuck him up after he'd spent so many years finally becoming himself.

Marco sighed, pushing me off to get naked. "Can you take it easy? My ass hurts like hell."

"You can take more," I growled, crawling across the bed and reaching into the bedside drawer for lube. "Get on your knees."

He did as he was told, bracing when I kicked off my jeans and shirt. "Relax, babe," I murmured, running a hand down his spine. "You're tense."

"No shit? I just caught you trying to fuck Luke. I don't care if you want to fuck him, but don't lie to me about it," he muttered under his breath, groaning as I tipped some lube onto my fingers and pressed two into his ass roughly.

"I wasn't!" I snarled, leaning over his back and adding a third finger after a moment.

"Whatever, Skeet."

I thrusted my fingers a few times, making sure he was stretched a little, then I pulled my fingers out and coated my hand in lube, fisting my dick and making sure it was covered. I pressed the tip against his ass, kicking his knees apart more as I slowly sank into him. His back muscles bunched as he gritted his teeth, not being able to hold back a gasp of discomfort as I shoved the last of my dick inside him.

"Who owns you?" I demanded, grabbing his shoulders as I pulled out, yanking him back onto me. "Who?!"

"You do! Jesus fucking Christ, Skeet," he growled. "That fucking hurt."

"Good," I grunted, thrusting into him in long, fast strokes, loving the way his fingers curled into the bed sheets. I reached a hand under him and grasped his length, pumping it firmly in my fist.

The door opened and Hunter walked in, rolling his eyes as he noticed us. "Keep it down. The kids are asleep."

"Where's Rory? I need her to back her pussy up to his face and keep him quiet," I chuckled, making Marco hiss as I picked up the pace with both my dick and hand.

"Good luck with that. She's playing referee between Diesel and Luke. They're fighting in the living room," Hunter snorted. "Apparently, Lukas licked Diesel's dick or something when they were playing around with Rory the other day. The moment Jensen mentioned you and Lukas having a heated argument, he decided to pipe up and start a fight over the whole dick licking situation."

"Isn't he happy with Jensen? Why is he trying to fuck everyone else?" Marco snapped, wincing as I slammed into him.

"I wasn't trying to fuck him!" I bit out, grabbing his throat and jerking him back so he was flush with my chest. Hunter raised an eyebrow, dropping back onto the bed beside us.

"Oh, I walked in on an angry fuck again, didn't I?"

"What gave it away?!" I barked. "He thinks I was trying to fuck Lukas!"

"Well, you two do have some sexual tension," Hunter unhelpfully stated, pissing me off more. I tightened my hold on Marco's throat, cutting off his airways as I fucked him harder, making him wheeze out his response.

"See?" *Mother fucker.*

102 | R.E. BOND

I bit his shoulder firmly, drawing blood and tasting it on my tongue. My dick was painfully hard, and I knew I was leaving fingernail marks on his waist, but I didn't give a shit. I released his throat, letting him suck in a lungful of air. His choking drew me closer to my climax, and I shoved him forward again, grabbing his dick and jerking him roughly, the bite of pain sending him over the edge.

He let out a raspy groan, his body quivering as I kept hammering into him until I came.

"Feel better?" he snorted as I climbed from the bed and yanked my boxers on.

"No. Do you want a drink?" I snapped, looking him over and noticing a small trail of bloodied come sliding down his ass crack. "Or maybe a fucking tampon?"

"Go to Hell," he growled, gingerly standing from the bed and snatching his boxers off the floor, stomping off to the bathroom. Hunter winced, obviously seeing the blood too.

"Skeet…"

"Don't!" I barked, leaving the room and hearing Diesel still arguing with Lukas. I stormed past them, grabbing myself a bottle of water and downing it quickly, my heart rate thumping madly in my chest.

"You okay?" Jensen asked quietly from the doorway, making me scowl. I'd hoped everyone was too busy arguing to notice me sneak past.

"I'm fine. Fuck off, Gilbert."

He rubbed the back of his neck, walking further into the room. "Earlier…"

"I don't give a shit what you thought you saw. You didn't, okay?" I said, cutting him off. "Leave me alone. I'm not in the mood."

"This isn't about that. Well, it sort of is. Should I let Lukas experiment more? With other people?" His voice broke, telling me it was a stupid idea.

I turned, giving him a level stare. "He loves you. Don't offer things you'll regret. If you're not okay with him fucking someone else, then don't even bring it up with him. There's no point spicing things up if you're doing it for the wrong reasons."

"He's accepted his sexuality, and I feel maybe I'm holding him back a little, you know?" he mumbled, making me snort.

"How? You both didn't know what you wanted until you fucked each other. Do you want to try messing around with someone else?"

"No, but I'm getting the feeling it's what he wants to do. He ate D's come out of Rory and licked his dick," he grunted, sitting in one of the kitchen chairs, his shoulders drooping. "I don't know if I'm okay with it. I mean, sure, I don't mind if Rory likes a little bit of messing around, but I wasn't there. It feels weird."

I bit back a groan, knowing he was going to freak himself out forever about this shit. I sat in the chair beside him, clapping him on the shoulder. "Talk to him. It's not like any of the guys will mess around with him, so I don't think you have much to worry about."

"Not even you?" he murmured, meeting my gaze. "I'm not accusing you of anything, so don't explode at me, but I can sense the pull you two have on each other. It's been building for years, and I don't know if I should let it happen."

I chuckled, trying to keep my temper in check. "Trust me, I don't want your boyfriend."

"You might not, but I'm pretty sure he wants you."

I stared at him, unsure what to say. "Uh, I'll try to keep him under control?"

"I won't stop him if he wants to do anything, but if he chooses to do something? I guess that's up to him," he shrugged. "And if by chance you two do anything? Don't fucking hurt him."

"I'll try to restrain myself," I snorted, standing and patting his shoulder again. "You've got nothing to worry about."

Lukas

I KNEW PUSHING the boundaries with Diesel was a bad idea, but taunting Skeeter? Probably not my best choice. Diesel hadn't seemed too fazed by our encounter in the bathroom with Rory, but he'd obviously been thinking about it a little, because he was pissed.

"I'm not kink shaming you or whatever, but I'm not okay with you licking my cock," Diesel growled, giving me a shove. "You want to kiss me and get our girl all hot? Or lick her cunt full of my come? Go for it. But don't touch my fucking dick."

"Guys, keep your voices down, you'll wake the kids," Rory hissed, glancing towards the kitchen where Jensen had followed Skeeter. My chest ached at knowing I was bothering Jensen. I'd gotten lost in the heat of the moment with Diesel and Rory, and I couldn't explain the shit between me and Skeeter. I was drawn to him, wanting to piss him off so he'd put me back in my place. But only so I could throw his own shit back at him and put him in *his* place.

That asshole needed a reality check.

"You're looking into it too deep, D. It made Rory horny, I wasn't trying to convince you to face fuck me or anything," I replied, rolling my eyes and crossing my arms. I'd been working out more, the muscles in my arms bulging slightly. I wasn't as muscular as the others, but I was working on it.

Diesel scowled. "I'm not into dudes, you know that."

"I know. I didn't think it would be such an issue. I'm sorry, okay?"

He eyed me for a moment, before finally sighing. "Fine. Just, don't do it again."

"Noted."

"Are you two good now?" Rory huffed. "Can I go and check on Jense and Skeet to make sure they're not killing each other?"

As if on cue, Skeeter wandered out, giving us a filthy look. His eyes connected with mine, and I swore his eyes sparked with something I couldn't name. He didn't say anything, heading straight back up the stairs to our room, and I wondered if Marco was still angry at him. I'd heard them arguing, most likely fucking in the process, and I wanted to watch. I would have snuck off for a peek if Diesel hadn't started an argument with me.

Jensen joined me, taking my hand and giving it a small squeeze as we walked up the stairs. "I'm sorry."

"For what?" I mumbled, stopping at the top of the stairs and turning to face him.

"For holding you back. It's obvious you want to mess around with other people, but…"

Fuck that. I never wanted him to think he wasn't enough for me. Sure, I liked making Rory horny, she'd been wanting us to mess around more for her, but I'd never love another man like I did with Jensen.

I slammed my lips against his, kissing him firmly and grabbing his waist to keep him still, making him groan as I pushed my tongue between his lips. I slipped my hand down the front of his sweats, running my thumb over the tip of his dick, spreading the pre-come across it.

"Fuck, Luke," he groaned into my mouth, his head dropping back against the wall as his eyes closed. I wrapped my fingers around his length, my lips finding his throat in the dark hallway as I stroked him firmly. I knew his body like my own. I knew what he loved, what he hated, what he fantasized about. Every mark on his skin and every place to touch that made him fall apart, I knew it.

I dropped to my knees, yanking his sweats down and pushing him down my throat, loving the way his fingers threaded through my hair and pulled hard. I grunted, almost choking on him, but he pulled back enough for me to breathe. He always knew how far to push me and when to stop.

I shuffled closer, grabbing his waist and bobbing my head faster, not caring as I choked. I pushed him deeper, faster, harder, and by the time he came down my throat with my name on his lips, he was calmer.

I glanced up the hallway to find Skeeter's eyes burning into me, a blank look on his face as he turned and walked into the bedroom, shutting the door quietly behind him. I'd had no idea he was there or for how long, but it made me wonder what he'd like if I got on my knees for him. I wasn't attracted to him, but I'd seen how he fucked. It was intriguing.

I stood, shaking it from my thoughts and giving Jensen a kiss on the cheek. "Come on, let's go to bed, you look beat."

I didn't get much sleep, the guilt eating at me for thinking about Skeeter just after I'd blown my boyfriend. Hopefully, it was something that would pass soon, and no one would have to know. It wasn't love, it was simply curiosity.

Skeeter was right, my thoughts about him were becoming my dirty little secret, and I fucking hated it.

Rory

I woke up early the next morning to hear Lloyd crying. He sounded fucking terrified, and I leaped from the bed, not giving a shit about kneeing anyone in the ribs on my way past.

I found him in his room, Caden trying to speak gently to him. "It's okay, accidents happen."

He stepped closer to him and Lloyd screamed, his eyes full of terror, and I had no idea what the fuck was happening.

"What's going on?" I asked as I made my presence known, the kid diving at me and clinging to me like a monkey. Dampness soaked through my shirt, and I realized his pants were wet.

"He wet the bed. I can't get him to calm down," Caden murmured softly, cringing when Lloyd screamed at him to leave him alone. I tightened my arms around him, stroking his hair gently.

"C'mon, let's get you into some fresh clothes. Caden won't hurt you, I promise."

"He will! They always do!" he wailed, my heart breaking. He'd probably had a nightmare. If the people who'd had him before us hurt him for wetting the bed, no wonder he was hysterical.

I grabbed some clean clothes for him, carrying him into the bathroom and locking the door so he could relax. "Have a shower and get changed. It's okay, no one's going to punish you. It was an accident."

"You're not mad?" he asked quietly, his cheeks turning pink. "But, I ruined the bed."

"I'd never be mad at you for that. Get cleaned up and we'll go out today. We can get some new clothes and toys for you and the others," I offered, his hand wiping his tears as he nodded.

"Okay. Can we get ice cream too?" He flinched as he waited for my answer, making me angry at the people who'd hurt him.

"Of course we can. I'll go wait outside if you want?"

"No!" he exclaimed with panic. "Can you just face the door?"

I put him down and placed his clean clothes on the sink, sitting on the floor with my back to him so he had privacy. He turned the water on, and after five minutes he was humming to himself, seeming to calm down.

Once he was dressed, he took my hand and let me lead him down to the laundry, putting his dirty clothes in the wash basket. He waited outside my bedroom door while I changed my damp shirt, following me to the kitchen when I was done. I washed my hands and gave him a smile.

"So, where do you want to go? Maybe we can get the clothes first, then spend the rest of the day looking at toys?"

"Can I buy a bike?!" he beamed, seeming more sure of himself. "Or a motorbike?!"

I chuckled, grabbing him some cereal and juice. "We can probably do that. I'll have to get Hunter or Marco to help with the motorbike though. They ride bikes and know what they're doing."

"They do?!" he said with surprise. "I want to see them!"

"Maybe later, okay? Eat your breakfast," I grinned, leaving him to eat while I headed up to the bedroom to check on Caden. He looked devastated, but he forced a smile.

"How is he?"

"He's okay now, I think. I'm taking him shopping for a few things when he's finished breakfast," I stated, glancing at the bed to find only Marco and Slash still there. "Where are the others?"

"Harley's bar. Someone smashed the windows early this morning. Bunch of punk kids who think they're tough. Skeeter figured they'd go scare them," Marco mumbled, a small smile stretching across his face. "If I could move, I'd be right there with them."

"Ass hurts?" I snorted, making him grin.

"Babe, everything hurts. He was a little rough."

"So I heard. Need an ice pack?" I asked sweetly, laughing when he flipped me off. Slash sat up and stretched, my eyes darting to his abs with a groan. "Damn, Russo. I could eat you for breakfast."

He winked, patting the space beside him. "You can if you wish, my queen. I won't stop you."

"I promised to take Lloyd shopping," I muttered. "Rain check?"

"You bet. Take him around to Josie's. She needs to know about her new grandkids. Besides, she'll probably have a bunch of stuff in storage that used to be Holloway's," he suggested, climbing from the bed and giving me a kiss on the cheek. "And just so you know, I could eat you for breakfast every day."

"You and me have a date with a sixty-nine in the near future," I chuckled, swatting his firm butt. "Now, I'd better go. Let Sarah know that Lloyd's bed needs changing, and see if she can do pizza for dinner. I'm going to go and spoil Lloyd. Are you guys good with Mikey and Angel?"

Slash cringed. "Uh, you can't take them? I have a meeting with Hendricks this morning, and Marco's needed at the Soldier's hangout. Unless Holloway's free?" he asked, glancing at Caden who sighed.

"Not really. I told Skeet I'd go to the shed and start cleaning up from the fights last night. The place is a mess."

I rubbed my temples, feeling a headache forming. "I have to take all three of them? How am I supposed to do that?"

"Maybe see if Josie can watch the younger ones, and you can take Lloyd shopping alone. Buy one of those twin stroller things, too. We're going to need one," Slash said with a shrug. "If not, see if Red or Lex are free to help."

"Jade has enough to do as it is, and I need to avoid Lexi for a while," I grunted, his eyebrow lifting with amusement.

"And why is that?"

"We had a fight last night. She's pregnant."

He stared at me for a moment before narrowing his eyes. "You had a fight because she finally got pregnant?"

"No, we had a fight because... I don't know. Because Hunter knew and I didn't. Something like that. I was feeling overwhelmed last night, alright?" I snapped. "I'm going to get Mikey and Angel ready, then I'm going."

Marco leaped from the bed, wincing as he walked. "I'll get Angel ready."

"It's fine, you can rest. I'd hate you to shit yourself with that stretched asshole of yours," I teased, but he shook his head, poking me in the ribs.

"Minx. I want to help."

"You're going to have separation anxiety all day, aren't you?" I snorted, his eyes going wide.

"Wait, you're taking her all day?"

"You won't even be here," I deadpanned, walking towards the room she was sleeping in. "I've got it."

"Like fuck," he grumbled, darting past me, his face lighting up as he found Angel staring up at him in her make-shift cot. It was concerning me with how attached he was becoming. If by chance she did have family, they were in their rights to come and take her away. I didn't dare tell him that though.

"Can you get her a bed today? I'm worried she's going to hurt herself in this," he said quietly as he lifted her into his arms, scrunching up his nose instantly. "You smelly little girl!"

She stared at him, a satisfied look on her face. Luckily for me, Marco didn't have an issue changing diapers, because I sure as fuck wasn't doing it again.

"She won't hurt herself. It's a bunch of pool floaties under the sheet," I frowned, but he shook his head.

"I saw a youtube video about ways babies can get hurt. They…"

"Alright, new bed for the baby," I said firmly, cutting off his educational speech. If he said we needed it, I wouldn't argue.

"Can it be a princess one?" he added, making me scowl.

"If you're not coming, you don't get a say in the matter. I'm going to take Mikey downstairs for some breakfast."

"Yes, boss lady," he smirked, leaning over and kissing me on the cheek before gently placing Angel on the ground, changing her shitty bum. "Oh, and get more newborn diapers!"

"Don't we have heaps?" I frowned. "Jade bought some."

"Yeah, a small pack when we were supposed to only have them overnight. I have two left," he informed me. Fuck, kids could poop a lot.

Mikey was half asleep, a giggle leaving him when I moved over to his bed and lifted him into my arms. "Morning, little dude. You ready to go meet Grandma Josie?"

"Yosey!" he squealed, drooling all over himself and making me grin.

"Yeah, Josie."

"WHAT ON EARTH is going on here?" Josie asked with surprise as I carried Mikey and Angel into her house, Lloyd beside me with bags in his arms. I blew the hair from my face, putting Mikey on his feet.

"Meet your new sort of grandkids. I have guardianship of them. We saved them from the skin trade, and they were going to split them up. They're close, so I kept them. Yes, the cops know about it, and yes it's completely legal. This is Angel, Mikey, and Lloyd."

"Oh, my goodness!" she gasped, reaching down to pick up Mikey. "They're adorable!"

I motioned to Lloyd, the guarded expression back on his face after his meltdown that morning. "I'm taking Lloyd shopping, but I was hoping you could help with the other two. I can't carry them both, and I need to buy strollers and cots and stuff. I'm sorry, but all the guys are busy."

"Of course! They can stay here with me for as long as you need! Do they have diapers?"

"A couple, but I need to get more while I'm out. There's Angel's formula in the bag, some clothes, and they all just had breakfast, so they shouldn't be hungry any time soon. If Mikey needs a nap, he likes back tickles to help him sleep," I yawned. She gave me a smile, tilting her head slightly.

"You look tired."

"I was up late. Had a cage fight at the shed, then I had an argument with Lex and went for a long walk, then I got home and there was more fighting. I didn't sleep well, then we had an early start," I replied. "You ready, Lloyd?"

I turned to look at him when he didn't reply, finding him venturing further into the house. "Lloyd."

He jumped, spinning around to stare at me. "I was just looking!"

"It's okay, just don't touch anything," I warned, a big smile spreading across his face.

"Okay, Mom!" Then he ran down the hallway to explore. Josie chuckled, giving me a knowing look.

"That's freaking you out, isn't it?"

"You have no idea. He's an untrusting little kid, but he's attached himself to me. Maybe because I'm a woman?" I wondered out loud, Josie giving me a nod.

"Chances are high. Maybe the people who had him were all men. It's good that he trusts you. Is he coping okay? He seems a little guarded."

I explained everything since the kids had come into my care, and by the time I finished, Lloyd was coming back, happy with his inspection of the house. "This place is huge!"

"It is. This is where Caden lived when we met. I used to live here sometimes too."

"So, Josie is my grandma now?" he frowned with confusion, eyeing her suspiciously. "Is she nice?"

I ruffled his hair, giving him a smile. "She's the best. She's like my mom too."

"Because yours is gone?" he asked innocently, making me nod.

"Yeah, because my mom's gone. Let's go do some shopping. We'll come back later and pick up the others," I stated, worry filling his eyes.

"They can't come too?"

"Josie will be very nice to them, I promise. We can call her whenever we want to check in with them if you want," I promised, his features relaxing slightly. He looked up at Josie, taking a deep breath.

"If you hurt them, I'll be very mad."

She gave him a soft smile, not minding his attitude. "I promise, they'll have lots of fun. Maybe we can find some of Caden's things for you to take home."

Once she'd made him more comfortable about leaving the kids with her, Lloyd and I left, heading straight to the mall to stock up on clothes.

I had no idea what sizes the other two were, so I had to call Marco to ask him, but even then, I had no idea what I was looking at. There were so many styles and colors.

"How about this?" Lloyd asked, happy with his find as he held up a pair of small biker boots. "They'd look good on me!"

"They would! We'd better find you a jacket to go with it," I grinned, rifling through the stands until I found a small leather jacket. "Here!"

He beamed at me, holding his arms out to take it. He pulled it on, his smile wide. "Can I have it?!"

"Sure. Let's get one for Mikey, too."

"And Angel?"

"She's a little small for one of these. She needs a princess dress," I replied, his face turning to confusion.

"But, what if she wants to be a biker instead?" He had a point. He was smart for a nine-year-old.

"We can get her both. If she wants to be a biker, then that's what she'll be," I smiled, glancing at our cart that was piled high with an assortment of clothes. "Do you think we have enough?"

"Can we look at toys now?" he begged. "I want to look at them!"

We'd already filled the car with the bigger things like strollers and cots, so I hoped it would all fit. We'd taken the Hummer, something Marco had insisted on buying recently. Luckily, it had come in handy.

"Let's go pay for these, then go into the toy store," I chuckled, pushing the cart to the checkout and finding a familiar woman standing behind it. Her eyes widened when she saw me, slight fear taking over. She'd been one of Claire's minions when I'd first moved schools. I had no idea what her name was, but she'd been smart to back away from Claire when things got bad, not wanting to be caught in the cross-fire.

"Hey, Donovan," she stuttered, scanning items as I placed them on the counter.

"Hey. How are you?" I replied casually, and I swore the poor girl was going to pass out. I didn't have an issue with her, so she didn't have to worry about getting shot at. Besides, we were in public. I wasn't completely stupid.

"I'm good," she said quickly, trying to finish the job as fast as possible, not wanting to be stuck with me for longer than needed. Lloyd tugged on my arm, his eyes lighting up as he noticed the shop across from us.

"Mom! They have candy! Can we get some?!"

The girl's eyes nearly bugged out of her head. I could almost hear her calculating how long it had been since we'd left high school, trying to figure out how I had a kid that old. It was hilarious.

"Candy, or ice cream? You can't have both," I snorted, not wanting his teeth to rot out of his head.

"Can we come back for candy another time?" he asked quietly. "I'll be good."

"Next time, we'll get candy," I promised, taking my card out of my wallet, hoping the girl would hurry up with scanning everything. I was already tired, and we hadn't even done the toys which I knew would take the longest.

I startled as I heard a gunshot, immediately moving Lloyd behind me to keep him safe as my eyes scanned the area it had come from. The girl behind the counter let out a scream as someone wearing a mask walked through the door, a gun in his hand.

"Give me the kid, you cunt!" he boomed, my eyes narrowing as I took a step back. Lloyd was clinging to the back of my shirt, his body shaking in fear.

"Like fuck. Who are you? Too much of a pussy to show your face?" I snapped, discreetly moving my knife from my jacket pocket and passing it back to Lloyd. He took it, his shaking not as bad now that he felt safer. I had no idea if he'd held a knife before, but at least he could stab anyone who tried to grab him in case there were more guys.

"That's none of your business. You took him from us, so give him back!" he snarled, trying to step around me, but I stepped forward, kicking my foot out and slamming it into his knee cap, the sickening crunch sounding like music to my ears. He screamed in pain as he dropped, aiming his gun at me and firing, making me hiss as the bullet grazed my waist.

"That hurt, you bastard."

The girl behind the counter ran for it, making me roll my eyes. She wasn't going to be any help. She probably wouldn't even get the cops, she'd just keep running.

"Lloyd, get behind the counter," I said in a low voice, sensing his hesitation. "Now."

Once he was out of the way, I stalked closer to the man and kicked him in the ribs, dodging his gun as he tried to shoot at me again. I wrestled him, trying to get the weapon away, the next bullet hitting me in the shoulder. "Mother fucker!"

He smirked, but I kicked the gun from his hands, anger burning inside me as I started laying punches into him. "You think you can fuck with me, asshole?! You're not taking him, he's mine!"

Police swarmed the entrance, and I heard BG groan as he dropped his gun by his side. "Why am I not surprised to find you here?"

"Do your damn job and arrest him!" I spat. "He attacked me!"

"What for? Did you attack him first?" he grunted, his eyes widening slightly when Lloyd darted out from behind the desk and grabbed my leg, the knife still in his hand. "Whoa! Drop the weapon!"

I rolled my eyes, reaching down to take the knife and place it back in my pocket. "He's nine, BG. Do you really think he's a threat?"

"You gave him a knife?!"

"Only to defend himself if someone got him! The man's here to kidnap him!" I barked. "He's part of the skin trade operation!" That set BG into motion.

He started shouting orders, making sure the guy was cuffed and taken back to the police car, only turning to me when the rest left. "You can't be doing this shit with the kid in your care, Donovan. The state can still take him away."

"I'm sorry, I didn't realize I was the issue here. Someone tried to kidnap him, and you're blaming me?" I scoffed. "I just got shot twice defending him. I think you need to get your head checked, asshole."

"Mom? You're bleeding," Lloyd said softly, his eyes wide. "You're going to die!" *Jesus Christ, not this again.*

I squatted, looking up at him and keeping my voice quiet. "I'm okay. I can fix it. Are you hurt?"

He shook his head, throwing his arms around me and warming my heart. "I'm okay. You saved me again."

"I'll always save you, dude. You're my best friend, remember?" I grinned, leaning back to find him smiling at me.

"I am?"

"Of course, you are. We'll have to do toys another day though, alright? I need to go and get my shoulder and waist checked," I sighed. "I'm sorry."

"You need a hospital!" he exclaimed, but I laughed.

"Nah, I'll fix it up at home. I can stop at the shed on the way if I need to."

BG snorted, giving me a stern look. "We need to make a report, and…"

"You can come and bother me later. I need to get cleaned up, and I need to take Lloyd home. Stop by after dinner," I replied sharply, taking Lloyd's hand and giving it a squeeze. I frowned at my shopping, reaching around the counter and pressing the button to pay, scanning my card and waiting for it to be approved before grabbing the bags, snatching my receipt on the way. BG pretended not to see it, but he seemed amused that I'd paid. I was a criminal, but not a thief.

Lloyd fussed over me the entire drive, not convinced that

I wasn't going to die. We ended up at the Devil's warehouse, where I was bombarded by Hunter who looked furious. "What the fuck happened?! BG called and said you had a shoot-out in the mall?!"

I rolled my eyes, helping Lloyd from the car before turning to face him. "He called it a shoot-out?"

"Well? What else do you call it?! How could you do that?! You had Lloyd with you!" he shouted, my eyes narrowing. I shoved him back a step, my shoulder burning from the movement.

"The people who run the skin trade? They're not all gone. We got cornered by one in the mall and I got shot twice. Lloyd is fine, and I'm fine. I didn't shoot at anyone, but I defended myself. Move, I need to check my fucking injuries."

His eyes softened as he ran them over me, looking for the evidence. "You got shot?"

"Twice. The guy wanted Lloyd. I wasn't going to let him take him," I seethed, feeling Lloyd's hand squeeze mine. He didn't like us arguing, so I took a deep breath and tried to calm down. "Can we talk about this later?"

He nodded, turning to walk inside. "Come on, let me look at it."

This was the second time we'd spoken nicely in days it seemed. I was still mad at him about the whole baby thing, but I was trying to let it go. I understood that he was hurting, and I also knew I was hot headed when I felt backed into a corner. We needed to move on from it, so I'd try and be nice.

I sat in his office chair and pulled my jacket off, wincing when my shoulder burned. "How bad is it?"

Hunter poked at it, getting a good look before sighing. "It hasn't come out the other side." Fuck.

"Are any of the others here? I don't want Lloyd seeing this shit," I grunted, the kid scowling.

"I'm not leaving."

"No, but you could wait in the other room until I'm done," I offered. He didn't look impressed but he gave me a nod.

"Okay. Thank you for saving me."

"I've always got you, dude," I smiled, lifting my fist for him to bump with his. Hunter stood in front of me, eyeing my shoulder but speaking to Lloyd.

"Ty's in the back room. I'll take you to him and you guys can hang out until we're done."

Lloyd followed Hunter from the room, glancing at me over his shoulder on the way. I wanted to kill all the men who'd been part of hurting him. He looked his age for once. Scared and confused, his emotions working over time after the day's events. I couldn't wait to get him home where he could relax a little.

CHAPTER SEVEN

CADEN

"Hey, Mom," I smiled as I walked through the front door at her house, surprise shining in her eyes.

"This is a lovely surprise. Are you here for the kids? I haven't heard from Rory," she replied as I glanced around the room with a frown, the kids nowhere in sight.

"Yeah, she ran into some trouble today. I told her I'd pick the kids up. Where are they?"

I'd lost count of the times Rory had been shot. It was unnerving to know someone would try and take Lloyd in broad daylight. It wasn't something we'd expected, despite knowing the skin trade would have multiple people involved.

"They're both asleep in your old room. Worn themselves out I think. Angel slept most of the day, but Mikey wanted to have a play in the pool, so we did that until he got tired. Is Rory alright? What happened?" she asked with worry, knowing if Rory hadn't shown up, it wasn't good.

"I assume she told you how we ended up with the kids?" I questioned, waiting for her to nod before continuing. "One of the guys who run the skin trade tracked her down while she was shopping with Lloyd. Rory got shot, Lloyd's pretty upset, and they've been at the warehouse all afternoon patching her up. She's alright, just pissed as usual."

Her hand went to her mouth with horror, her eyes shining with tears. "She got shot again?"

"Yeah. Twice. Hunter had to dig the bullet out of her shoulder. The other was just a graze on her waist. She's mad because they didn't get to the toy store and she feels like she let Lloyd down," I sighed, running a hand through my hair. "We didn't expect retaliation, or she wouldn't have taken him out, especially not alone."

"Did they get the guy?"

"Yeah. Cops arrived and arrested him. Luckily for him, Rory didn't have her gun on her, and she'd given Lloyd her knife. It might have been a lot messier if she'd had a weapon," I chuckled dryly. "Why'd I choose a psychotic woman?"

Mom laughed, reaching out to give me a hug. I might be a grown-ass man, but I always needed her to hold me together with this shit. I'd gotten used to it, but it took an emotional toll on me.

"You wouldn't love her if she wasn't crazy. I feel better knowing she's there to protect you."

"Geez, thanks, Mom. In case you didn't know, I can protect myself. It's also supposed to be my job to protect *her*," I scoffed, hearing Mikey start to cry upstairs. "I guess it's home time."

"I can't believe you have kids," she smiled, looking ready to cry. I rolled my eyes but smiled as we walked towards the stairs.

"Me either. It was another one of Rory's impulsive moments. We didn't really get a say in it."

"Not bad for a woman who doesn't want children. She's

good with them," she replied, giving me a wink. "Maybe she'll change her mind."

"I doubt it. Angel's usually with Marco, Mikey's happy with anyone, and Lloyd's older. She seems to have connected with him which is good. I think they're helping each other. Can you imagine Rory pregnant? Fuck, she'd kill us," I groaned as I walked into the bedroom to find Mikey laying in bed screaming still, Angel happily blowing spit bubbles. I walked over and picked him up, kissing the top of his head. "Hey, little man. What's all that noise for?"

His screaming turned into soft crying, making me smile. "I know, life's hard."

He let out a giggle, reaching out to touch my face with his little hands, making my heart melt. He was the happiest kid I'd ever met, and I loved that he was always happy to see me. Lloyd was another story, but this kid liked me so I was rolling with it.

I sensed Mom staring at me, but I ignored her and focused on Mikey. "You ready to go home? Rory's got you a bunch of new stuff."

"Mommy!"

"Yeah, Mommy," I chuckled, sitting him on my hip and turning to Mom. "Thanks for watching them. Rory wouldn't have coped."

"You're so good with him," she said softly, wiping her eyes and making me snort.

"Don't cry. Please. He's not hard to look after. Did you meet Lloyd? He's a little more difficult. He doesn't like any of us, other than Rory."

"He's dealt with a lot, Caden. He probably trusts her because she's a woman. He'll learn to trust you eventually, just be patient with him. Don't sell yourself short, either. Mikey's still hard work, and he wasn't your problem. You still took him in and treat him like you would your own child. That shows I raised you right," she sniffed, making me sigh.

"Mom, of course you raised me right. You did a kick-ass job. I'm one of the only people I know who have good memories of my childhood where you spent time with me. The others never had that. I'm grateful to have you as my mom." That just made her cry harder.

"You're such a wonderful young man. How did I get so lucky?" she sobbed, hugging me and almost squishing Mikey between us.

"I love you, but please don't suffocate the kid," I chuckled, giving her a one armed hug, moving Mikey out of the way.

She helped me get them in the car, smiling when she saw the Hummer had car seats for the kids. "I see she bought them some new things."

"Yeah, it looks like the kids are a permanent part of our family now, so she's bought them literally everything. Pretty sure she's sent Sarah out to buy a heap of toys for them since they didn't get around to it today. Lloyd's requested a bike, so he'll be over the moon when Marco gets home with one for him."

"A push bike?"

"Motorbike," I corrected, her eyes flashing with worry.

"That's not safe. He's too young." That got my hackles up.

I strapped both kids in and shut the door before speaking. "We know what we're doing. Marco and Hunter were riding bikes before they could walk, so they'll teach Lloyd the safe way to ride, and they'll make sure his bike's safe. I promise. You don't think we can do this, do you?"

"I know you can. I just worry. I never let you have a bike because they're dangerous. I still wouldn't let you now and you're an adult," she scolded, making me grin.

"Hunter taught me to ride a bike. I have one at home."

"Get going, you're going to give me a heart attack," she growled, swatting my arm lightly.

"Love you, Mom."

"I love you too. Drive safely," she smiled, kissing my cheek before letting me climb into the driver's seat.

I had no idea what to expect when I got home. Rory was frustrated when I'd left, Lloyd was scared, and the guys were all equally pissy about what had happened. I'd been more than happy to escape the house for ten minutes.

I peered over my shoulder at Mikey and grinned. "You ready to see Mommy?"

"Mommy!" God, I loved this kid.

Rory

MY SHOULDER WAS ACHING, my mood was sour, and I wanted to get drunk. I was pissed that Lloyd wouldn't leave me alone for five minutes, too. I knew he was scared, but I needed some peace and quiet to think.

"Are you okay?" Tyler's voice rumbled from the doorway to our bedroom, stepping inside so he could sit on the edge of the bed. Lloyd was laying down beside me, refusing to let me out of his sight. I couldn't blame him, and I tried not to let my mood affect him, but it was hard.

I was feeling twitchy, unsure if it was from the day's events, or the fact I'd been sober for three damn days.

"Peachy. Is Marco home yet?" I wanted Lloyd to see his new bike. It might cheer him up a little, and it might mean he'd play with it for hours and leave me alone. I had no idea how parents did this twenty-four-seven. I'd had the kids for two days and I was starting to lose my patience.

"He's about five minutes away. Hey, Lloyd. How about

you come downstairs with me? Marco's bringing a present home for you," he smiled, but Lloyd shook his head.

"No."

"Rory can come too." *Ugh, not what I was hoping he'd say.*

I sat up, trying to keep the frustration off my face. "Yeah, let's go wait for Marco and see what he got you." That made him move.

He skidded from the room like his ass was on fire, making me let out a sigh. "I wish he'd nap like the other two."

Tyler chuckled, dropping an arm around my waist and kissing my temple. "You're doing really good with him. Hopefully, Marco will become his new favorite person and you'll get a break."

"I fucking hope so. I like the kid, but I'm tired and my body hurts," I grunted, glancing at my bandaged shoulder. "I could do with a nap myself."

"You can lock yourself in the bedroom if you want? I'll try and occupy him?" he offered. I winced, knowing that was a terrible idea.

"If he can't find me, he'll freak. I'll have to put up with him being clingy for now."

We walked downstairs to find Marco standing in the living room, a big grin on his face and Lloyd standing close by, but not too close.

"What did you get me?"

"It's a surprise. Come outside and I'll show you," Marco smirked, reaching out to take Lloyd's hand. He jerked back, his eyes immediately seeking me out.

"Mom? Are you coming?"

"I'm right behind you. Let Marco show you the big surprise," I smiled tiredly, letting Tyler lead me outside to find a little dirt bike parked in the driveway. Lloyd's jaw almost hit the damn ground, and he spun around to stare up at Marco.

"Is that for me?"

"Yeah, kiddo. I'll teach you how to ride it later. You want to go sit on it and get a closer look?" he asked, seeming surprised when Lloyd threw himself at his legs and hugged him tightly.

"Thank you! It looks so cool! Are those flames on it?!"

The kid was talking a mile a minute, and I couldn't help the chuckle that slipped past my lips. Tyler smiled, poking me gently in the ribs. "See? He'll warm up to everyone after a while."

Caden pulled in and stopped close by, managing to get both kids out of the car before joining us. "I see he likes his present?"

"I love it!" Lloyd exclaimed, waiting for him to place Mikey on the ground before taking his little hand. "Come look, Mikey! I'll let you ride it too!"

"Bike!" Mikey squealed, happily running after him to look at the new toy. Caden chuckled, placing Angel against his chest and patting her back as she started whining.

"How do you think he'll react when Sarah gets home with the other toys?"

"He's going to think it's Christmas," Tyler grinned. "I love this shit. Look how happy they are, considering what they've been through."

He wasn't wrong. Both kids were laughing and acting like regular kids. My heart tugged, warmth filling me at knowing we'd changed their lives so much.

The guys all seemed to relax at seeing the kids' joy, and Hunter moved beside me, nudging me gently.

"They're not that scary, right?"

"These three? No. Pushing one from my vagina? Yes," I snorted, knowing exactly where he was going with the conversation. He sighed, but he leaned down and gave me a kiss, not starting an argument.

The rest of the afternoon was filled with giggling children and a mountain of new toys. Sarah didn't disappoint. I'd told her to go crazy, and she had. She loved spoiling them.

"Mom! Look!" Lloyd shouted as he ran towards me in the living room with a dinosaur the size of him in his arms. "I got a dinosaur!"

"I can see that. Do you like all your new things?" I smiled, sitting on the couch and letting him scramble onto my lap, wincing as the dinosaur smacked into my tender shoulder.

"Careful, kid," Skeeter warned as he sat beside me, dropping an arm around my shoulders, making sure he didn't touch my injury. Lloyd apologized, babbling about his new toy before diving off my lap to find something else to play with, trashing the living room immediately. He was like a damn tornado.

Skeeter leaned closer, speaking quietly. "I want to drag you into my lap and fuck you so bad. My blade's itching to carve into your skin."

I shivered, tilting my face back to look at him. "Not in front of the kids, asshole."

"Obviously. Find a way to make it happen. Bring Rivera and Slash. I want to watch them fuck you into oblivion," he whispered, my thighs clenching together as I groaned.

"You don't play fair."

"I never claimed to, baby girl. Find an excuse to sneak away. Lloyd's fine. I'll meet you in the office. You have ten minutes." Then he bit my earlobe and stood, casually walking from the room as if he didn't just melt my panties.

I rumbled an excuse to Lloyd about needing a shower, but he was too busy with his new things to give a shit, so I grabbed Hunter's hand on the way past, finding Slash in the kitchen and dragging him with us.

"What's going on?" Slash chuckled, not putting up a fight in the slightest.

"Party in my pants, you're invited," I said quickly, tugging them into the office and locking the door behind us.

"Killer, you just got shot," he warned, but Hunter grinned.

"She'll be fine. If she's hurting, we're not distracting her enough."

Slash had softened a lot, but he was easy to convince when it came to my pussy.

"Fine. But if you start hurting…"

"Shut up," I snapped, yanking my pants down and almost tripping as they dropped to my ankles. Skeeter chuckled darkly, amusement in his green eyes.

"That was fast. I'm impressed, baby girl."

"Good girls get orgasms," I stated proudly. "Now, someone help me get my fucking shirt off."

Hunter wasted no time helping me get naked, stripping himself and glancing at Slash.

"You need a hand too, brother? I can help."

"I bet. No thanks. I've been able to undress myself for a long time now," Slash scowled, eyeing Skeeter with annoyance. "Are you just going to stand there and spectate?"

"For now," Skeeter smirked, sitting back in a chair and getting comfortable. "Sit your ass in a chair and make her face you. Rivera can fuck her ass."

"Oh, goodie. You're going to narrate the entire thing too," Slash deadpanned, doing as he was told despite not being happy about it. I practically jumped into his lap, being careful not to strain my shoulder too much. He fisted himself, lining up with my entrance and rubbing his length across my damp skin.

"You're fucking soaked."

"Do you blame me? I'm about to get railed by you three," I grinned, a soft moan leaving me as he slowly sank into me, pulling me down to sit on his lap. I rolled my hips, leaning forward to kiss him but Skeeter stopped me.

"Kiss Hunter." *Bossy prick.*

Slash growled, annoyed to have everything controlled, but Hunter had no problem with it. He moved in behind me, fisting my hair and jerking my head back to slam his lips onto mine, his tongue exploring my mouth as Slash gripped my hips and thrusted up. No matter what we did in bed, or who was involved, I'd never get tired of what these guys did to me.

Skeeter pulled a bottle of lube out of nowhere, tossing it to Slash who only just caught it before it could hit me in the head. "Watch it, asshole."

"Shut up, or you'll be lubing Rivera's dick up," he threw back, making Slash snort.

"Like fuck. You can if you want to play that sort of game."

"You think touching his dick bothers me? It's just a dick."

Hunter pulled back from me, giving Skeeter the stink eye. "None of you fuckers are touching my dick."

"Little bitch," Skeeter grinned. "You worried you'll enjoy it too much?"

"Go find Marco if you want dick that badly," Hunter chuckled, taking the lube from Slash and popping the lid. "I think you should let Rory rail you with a strap on."

I moaned low, moving my hips faster. The idea of dominating Skeeter like that was going to make me combust before we'd even started.

Skeeter pinned me with a glare. "Get that look off your face. That's never happening."

"You have no idea how hot it is when you're the bottom," I murmured, leaning forward to give Hunter some room to access my ass better. "My panties catch fire when you come with his dick in your…"

He stood abruptly, stalking towards us and grabbing my chin. "Stop talking."

"Make me."

I swore he was going to burst a blood vessel. His fingers tightened slightly, annoyance on his face. "Just you wait. I'm going to fuck your face so hard you'll be eating through a straw."

"Promise?" I purred, running my fingers up under his shirt to tease his abs. "You make it seem like it's a punishment to choke on your dick. Sounds pretty rewarding to me."

His eyes remained on me as he stepped back, but his voice spoke sharply to Hunter. "Fuck her. Hard."

"Yes, boss," Hunter snorted, lining his length up with my back entrance, taking his time to get it in. I gasped, pushing back on him as Slash watched my face in awe.

"Look at you. Such a good girl," he murmured, holding my waist firmly to stop me moving until Hunter was ready. I hissed as his fingers dug into the graze on my side, immediately making him move his hand lower on my hip. I tried to wriggle a little to hurry Hunter up, but he playfully scolded me.

"Give me a second, you'll hurt yourself."

"I've taken Skeeter's pierced python up the ass while he's been angry fucking me. I doubt me wriggling around will hurt me," I scoffed, a slow smirk spreading across his face before he started pushing in more firmly. I groaned, trying not to tense. It didn't matter how long you'd been taking it up the ass, your natural reaction was to tense.

Slash pulled me forward slightly, pressing my face against his chest, Hunter managing to push the rest of the way in with a grunt. "Happy now?"

"I will be when you actually move," I threw back, my fingers digging into Slash's arms as Hunter withdrew himself before slamming in harder.

"You got it, sweetheart." *Oh, shit.*

Slash patiently sat there with his dick resting in my pussy while Hunter went to town on my ass, showing no signs of slowing down as my legs started to quiver. "Fuck, fuck, fuck."

"Slash, move," Hunter demanded, earning him a sigh.

"Why's everyone telling me what to do? I know how she likes it and I'm quite capable of..."

"Fuck me!" I snapped, my orgasm close but not quite there yet. I needed him to move and hit that sweet spot that would send me over the edge.

He slipped his hand between us, rubbing tight circles on my clit as he lifted his hips slightly. "Such a greedy little thing," he grinned, starting to bounce me more as Hunter continued to rail me like a man starved. Just before I could come, Skeeter stopped them.

"Don't let her come." *What the fuck?!*

"Excuse me?!" I practically yelled, frustration burning inside me as the guys stopped moving, the tingles in my body starting to subside. "Let me come!"

"You can. When I say so," he growled, pulling me off them and slamming my chest down on the desk. I winced as my shoulder throbbed, but the pain faded when his fingers trailed down my spine, pushing inside my pussy when he got to the bottom.

"Good girls get orgasms, remember?" he mumbled in my ear as he leaned over my back, his teeth nipping at my neck.

"I've been good!" I argued, making him tsk.

"Good girls don't back talk," he chuckled, pushing his fingers deeper before sliding them out to spread my wetness over my clit slowly as he stripped his pants off one handed. "Watching you between Rivera and Slash made me almost come in my pants."

I shivered as he leaned back, licking the base of my spine and dragging it up to the back of my neck, his teeth biting into my flesh at the top and making me moan. My breath caught as he fisted his dick, rubbing the pierced head against my clit and slapping it against my pussy every so often.

"I want to see your cunt filled with their release before you get to come. Understood?" he growled, making me nod. As long as I got to come, I didn't give a fuck.

I whimpered as he pulled away, motioning to my raised ass. "Slash, fill her up."

Slash chuckled, moving in behind me and running his hands down my sides. "You want hard and fast, babe?" He didn't give me time to answer before he was sliding inside me, starting a rough erratic pace that almost shoved me through the fucking desk.

"You look so pretty at his mercy," Skeeter groaned, yanking his shirt over his head and leaving himself completely naked as he stroked himself, his eyes burning into me. My shoulder was burning, likely tearing my stitches, but the feeling of Slash slamming into me overpowered it. I'd let the pain consume me if it meant they'd keep railing me like this.

Familiar tingles crept up on me, my pussy clenching around him in anticipation.

"She's going to come," Hunter murmured, a cry of frustration leaving me as Slash slowed down, not letting me come before he filled me up and stepped back, swatting my butt in the process. Come dripped down my thighs, and I rubbed them together to try and give myself relief, but Hunter pushed my legs apart, not letting me.

"Naughty girl," he smirked, rubbing his dick against my opening and spreading Slash's release like lube.

"I swear to god, all three of you fuckers are getting stabbed!" I spat, gasping as he pushed inside with slow, long strokes.

Skeeter rolled his eyes, standing to my side so I could

watch him. "The only thing getting stabbed is your cunt. Take his load, and I'll make you come so hard you see stars."

My eyes flicked to his hand as it continued to stroke his dick, licking my lips. "This is cruel."

"You know it's worth it," he stated in a low voice, causing me to shiver. He'd been enjoying games like this lately. He wasn't lying either, the outcome of holding off my orgasms was explosive and intense.

Hunter never picked up the pace, choosing to fuck me slowly while placing kisses across my back, my name sounding like a caress as it left his lips. He let out a quiet groan as he came, my pussy dripping as he pulled out to admire his work.

"Damn, babe. You have no idea…"

"I've seen you watching porn before. I know all about your cream pie fetish," I said, cutting him off sharply. He frowned, tilting his head.

"You said you didn't mind. I was learning new shit to do to you."

"I don't mind. I'm a little on edge right now," I gritted out, my eyes darting to Skeeter. "Please. Fuck me and make me come. I'm going to die if I don't get to."

"That's a little dramatic," he chuckled. "Sit on the desk."

"I'll get come…"

"I don't give a fuck. Sit on the desk and lean back. I want to watch your face when you come apart," he demanded, grabbing me and dropping my ass on the desk. "You want to come? You got it, baby girl."

He shoved himself inside me, almost making me fall back, but he grabbed my throat and lifted one of my thighs, getting in as deep as possible. My body was on fire, and it had nothing to do with my injury.

His groin brushed against my oversensitive clit with

every thrust, my eyes squeezing shut at the pressure building inside me.

"Look at me!" he snapped, his fingers tightening around my throat. "Don't keep your pleasure from me."

I opened my eyes, staring into his and trying hard to focus on him. The moment his thumb touched my clit, I screamed. He hammered into me harder, holding me closer to him so I couldn't escape as my body pulsed around him. "Fuck!"

He didn't let up, stretching out my climax until burying deep and going still, allowing me time to recover. My legs were like jelly, and he chuckled as he stepped back and helped me to my feet. "Better?"

I nodded, leaning my forehead on his sweaty chest. "Can I go to bed now?"

"Shit, let me clean you up," Hunter murmured, drawing my attention to him and Slash. I'd forgotten they were there.

"Forget me, clean the desk," I mumbled, but Slash sighed.

"Your wound's bleeding. Let Hunter take care of you, then we'll…"

The lock on the door jiggled before swinging open, and Sarah walked in with Lloyd, gasping when she realized what she'd walked in on. "I'm so sorry!"

She spun Lloyd around, trying to usher him back out, but he wouldn't have it. "But we found her!"

Slash quickly dressed me, yanking his boxers on and trying to intervene. "Hey, kid. Rory's coming out in a second, okay?"

"I'll wait with her!" he argued, making me scowl. He had no understanding of personal space.

"Lloyd, go with Slash!" I barked, making him flinch.

"But…"

"Give me a minute alone, Lloyd!"

Sadness filled his eyes before turning into anger, his small fists clenching by his sides.

"I hate you!" That hurt me more than I thought it would.

I ran a hand over my face, cringing. "Lloyd…"

"I hate you!" he screamed again, storming from the room and leaving me standing there with regret. It was hard to bite my tongue with him. I wasn't used to worrying about hurting a kid's feelings.

"I've got him," Slash murmured, giving my cheek a quick kiss before taking off after Lloyd.

I sighed, glancing at Hunter. "I suck at this."

Sarah vanished, embarrassed about being in the room with us after finding us all naked, and Hunter dropped an arm around my shoulders, steering me towards the door.

"He'll be fine. It's a lot to get used to."

"Why aren't you guys stressed out over it then?" I growled. "I just bit his fucking head off."

"If you haven't noticed, there's nine of us to manage Mikey and Angel. Lloyd won't go near us half the time, so you have him glued to you. Slash will calm him down, and I'll clean you up while Skeeter cleans the office."

Skeeter grunted his annoyance but didn't argue, leaving us to head into the bathroom.

It didn't take long for Hunter to clean my wound, and after a quick rinse in the shower, I was nice and clean.

"I need to go and see Lloyd. I feel terrible," I mumbled as we walked into the living room, the kid nowhere in sight.

"All good. Go find him and I'll see you when you head to bed," Hunter smiled, giving me a kiss as I headed back through the house to Lloyd's room.

I opened the door, letting out a sigh. "Lloyd? I'm sorry, I…" The room was empty. I frowned, checking the closet before heading back down to the living room. "Hey, where's Lloyd?"

Diesel frowned, sitting forward on the couch. "Slash left him in his room. He was throwing a tantrum so he figured to let him do it in private."

"He's not in there, I just checked. He must have snuck down," I shrugged. He stood, looking concerned.

"I've been sitting here since he went to his room. He hasn't come down that I know of."

"He's probably outside," I muttered, walking towards the back door and almost running into Slash. "Where's Lloyd?"

"Probably putting holes in his bedroom wall. That kid has some serious anger issues," he chuckled, the amusement falling from his face after a second. "He's not there?"

"No. You haven't seen him?"

"Shit. Let's go look for him. He'll be around here somewhere," he promised, rounding up the others to help us search the property.

It was no use. We checked the security cameras to see if he was hiding around the property, but he'd ended up in a dead spot in the front garden that we couldn't see. He was gone, and it was all my fucking fault.

CHAPTER EIGHT

DIESEL

$\mathcal{I}$'d never seen Rory so upset before, and I'd been there when Slash had supposedly died. She was a fucking mess, frustration and fear seeping out of her in waves as she frantically called everyone she knew, seeing if they'd spotted him anywhere.

At first, she thought he might have been kidnapped, but then we mentioned he'd packed a bag, some of his clothes missing. The little shit had run away.

We stayed back while Rory tried to form a plan, her mood turning to anger towards us. We knew she didn't mean it, but it didn't mean it was pleasant.

The surprising part was when she called the cops for help. I never thought I'd see that day, but I also knew she trusted BG to a point. She'd called the Soldiers, the Kings MC up north, the Reapers, and even Rage fucking Evans. That's how terrified she was. She didn't care what price she had to pay the Devil for his help, but I was worried it would cost her something stupid. And probably a bit of pride.

"It's my fucking fault!"

I glanced over at Rory to find Caden holding her biceps, trying to calm her down.

"We'll find him, I promise. It's not your fault," he said gently as I approached. She tried to pull away, but he held firm as she kept yelling at him.

"It is! I shouted at him to leave me alone! He's gone because of me! Why did I take them in? I can't fucking parent them!"

My heart broke as her legs gave out and she broke down, Caden managing to catch her. I could count the times on one hand that I'd seen Rory cry. This wasn't a little teary moment, this was heart wrenching sobs, her voice breaking as she screamed nonsense about being the worst guardian ever.

She was borderline hysterical, which was worrying the guys. None of us were used to dealing with her like this. Usually, she'd get angry and start stabbing people for answers.

Caden sat on the ground, pulling her against his chest and whispering in her ear, but I could tell he was struggling.

"We've got to get her inside," Tyler murmured as he moved beside me. "She can't go out and look for him, not like this."

Lukas jogged towards her, speaking quietly before helping her to her feet. Surprisingly, she went with him into the house without argument. Caden joined us, his voice low. "Where the fuck could he have gone? We have to find him. What if those guys are still looking for him?"

"I'll call Hendricks and see where he's at. He was meeting up with Harley and Alex to start looking around the docks," I suggested, and Tyler frowned.

"You think he'd go that far? He's on foot."

"We need to cover as many areas as possible. He's probably not at the docks, but if he gets there, at least someone will be there waiting. There's heaps of shit he could hide in down there, and I don't want to risk him falling in and drowning. I doubt he knows how to swim," I muttered, grabbing my phone and calling Archer. The sooner we found him, the better.

Skeeter

I HOVERED in the doorway of our bedroom, watching as Lukas tried his hardest to soothe Rory. He stayed calm despite the situation, and I had to admit I was grateful to have him there. I'd be useless with her. I sucked at calming her down, I usually made it worse.

"What if someone takes him? We'll never get him back," she sobbed, her blurry eyes meeting mine as grief filled them. There was no way in hell I'd let anyone take that kid. He meant the world to Rory, and he'd grown on the rest of us too. He was family, and family stuck together.

"I'm going to go and find him, alright? You stay here in case he comes home. The others will spread out around town to look. He can't have gotten too far on foot. Hendricks is staying at the docks to make sure he doesn't show up there, Axel's in town keeping an eye out with the Soldiers, Milky's grabbing Lexi from Wet Dreams so they can keep an eye out near Harley's bar, and Rage and Charlie are driving around the park and the school. Hopefully he's just hiding and we'll find him soon," I said gently.

"Rage is looking?"

"Yeah. I spoke to Charlie. You know how Rage feels about abused kids. He's intending on driving around all night to find him." I'd never like Rage, he would always be the villain, but I had to respect him slightly for everything he'd been doing to keep kids safe. He wasn't driving around looking for Lloyd as a favor to us, he was doing it for the kid.

Rory nodded, her voice breaking. "Please, Skeet. Bring him home. If anything happens to him because of me…"

"Shut the fuck up," I growled, earning a filthy look from Lukas, making me clear my throat. "I mean, don't say that. He'll be fine."

"Promise?" she whispered, curling into Lukas like he was her lifeline. I didn't like seeing her like this. She was strong, fiery, a fucking warrior. This though? It made me realize just how human she was, and I didn't know how to make the fear go away. She was right, something could happen to him, but I wasn't going to admit that to her. Not when she was so devastated.

"I promise. BG's looking too, so hopefully it won't be long. Keep your phone on you. We'll call the moment we find him," I nodded, turning and heading from the room, meeting up with Slash and Marco outside.

"Let's go," I grunted, giving Marco a stern look. He was looking miserable, and I knew he was worried too. Josie had picked up Mikey and Angel, so luckily we didn't have to drag them around town too. "We'll find him, babe. He's fine."

I hoped I wasn't lying.

Rory

THEY'D BEEN GONE for hours. My heart was hurting, my throat was dry, and my eyes were stinging. Lukas placed a glass of whisky in front of me, sitting down and putting an arm around my waist. "Want me to call and check in with them?" *Yes.*

"They'd have called if they'd found him," I mumbled, reaching for the glass and downing it in one go, savoring the burn. No wonder I'd been grumpy lately, I was probably going through withdrawals for the past few days.

Headlights shone through the window, and I sprang to my feet, racing to the door. Slash and Diesel stepped out of the Mustang, and Slash shook his head slightly, telling me all I needed to know. They couldn't find him.

It was after midnight, Lloyd was probably freezing and scared in the dark somewhere.

I sagged against the doorframe, feeling helpless. "He can't be gone."

"He's not gone, he's hiding. It's late, he's probably sleeping somewhere," Slash sighed, pulling me under his arm and kissing my forehead.

One by one, I watched the guys pull in with no sign of Lloyd, genuine pain twisting inside my chest. Guilt ate away at me, knowing I was the reason he'd run off in the first place, and I swore to myself if he ever came back that I'd never get upset for him smothering me again.

Once all the guys were home, I went to close the door, but the sound of a car broke through the silent night, causing me to jerk it back open and step out onto the steps.

Rage stepped out of the driver's seat, fatigue on his face. He never let us see that sort of shit, I didn't even know the big bastard got tired. I assumed he fueled his body on all the souls he stole, so he should have been good for life.

"You lost something?" he asked with a small smile, my heart hammering in my chest as I practically leaped down the stairs. Charlie climbed out of the passenger seat, opening the back door to reveal a terrified looking Lloyd. The moment his eyes found mine, he raced from the car in tears, almost bowling me over with the force of his hug.

"Mom!"

Tears burned my eyes, and I dropped to my knees,

reaching for him and holding him tightly. "You scared the fucking shit out of me. Where were you?"

"Found him at the school. He was trying to sleep under the bleachers," Rage said gruffly, eyeing the kid with annoyance. "He gets his attitude from you. Little fucker bit me."

"I thought you were trying to kidnap me!" Lloyd exclaimed, making Rage snort.

"Even if I was, I'd have returned you, you little shit."

The guys wandered outside, but Lloyd didn't let go of me. "I'm sorry I ran away. I didn't mean to make you mad, I..."

I took his little face in my hands trying hard not to fucking cry again as I wiped his tears with my thumbs. "Don't apologize. You did nothing wrong. I didn't mean to snap at you, I'm not used to having someone relying on me all the time. I got overwhelmed, okay? Jesus, you gave me a heart attack, kid."

He threw his arms around my neck, squeezing tightly. "I don't hate you."

"I know. I love you, I'm sorry," I said, surprising myself. I knew I liked him, but love? That was a strong word. It was the truth though. Losing him for those few hours made me realize I'd do anything for him. Whether I'd birthed him or not, I was his mom.

He leaned back, his eyes wide. "You do?"

"You have no idea how much."

"I don't think anyone's said that to me before," he admitted, making those damn tears leak from my eyes. I needed to get a grip, especially while Rage was standing meters away from me.

I looked up at the big asshole, blowing out a breath. "Thanks, Angry Man."

"Keep a better eye on him," he grunted, but he didn't sound mad. He seemed curious about mine and Lloyd's relationship. I guess seeing me with a kid in general was probably amusing to most people.

Slash joined us, reaching out to offer Rage his hand to shake. "Thank you for finding him."

Rage was surprised, but he shook his hand and nodded. "All good. I'd hate to know what could have happened if we didn't find him. I'm glad he's okay."

The guys talked for a while, but I took Lloyd inside, not giving a shit about their conversation. I grabbed a blanket and curled up on the couch with Lloyd, putting the TV on and getting comfortable. Marco joined us, plonking down beside me and dropping an arm around my shoulders.

"I called BG and let him know we'd found him. Hendricks is on the phone to Holloway, and Rivera's calling Lex. How about you head up to bed? You look beat."

Lloyd was practically asleep in my lap, but I shook my head despite my eyes drooping. "Not yet. I don't want to sleep."

"We can sit here then, that's fine," he murmured, and that was the last thing I heard before drifting off to sleep.

LLOYD and I slept most of the next day, only waking when I was smacked in the face by a little hand. I jerked upright, making Mikey giggle. "Mommy!"

"Hey, buddy," I smiled, reaching down to pick him up, laying on my back and placing him on my stomach. He didn't want to climb on me for long, deciding Lloyd was a better option.

I remembered Jensen helping me into bed at some point through the night, but I had no idea when.

"Afternoon," Lukas smiled from the doorway. "Sorry, Mikey wanted to see you."

"He can wake me up anytime with a warm greeting like that hand to my face," I deadpanned, making Lukas grin.

"He did try to wake you gently. He called for you three times before bringing out the big guns."

"You *let* him hit me in the face?" I demanded.

"I told him to. It worked, didn't it?" he laughed, not fighting me on it as he walked into the room more and I tugged him onto the bed. He cuddled up to me, not minding when Mikey pushed his way between us for attention.

"Don't teach him to hit people, he'll get in trouble at school," I mumbled as he gave me a quick kiss.

"Sorry. You really were dead to the world, you know?"

"If you two are going to do that gross naked stuff, I'm leaving," Lloyd declared, making me groan as he bailed. I'd forgotten the poor kid had seen that.

Lukas raised an eyebrow, amusement in his tone. "What did he see?"

"Skeet, Hunter and Slash naked in the office with me," I cringed. "We locked the door, but Sarah was trying to help him find us. She let him in."

"I bet she'll never unlock a door again," he sniggered, grinning as Mikey laughed. "It's funny, isn't it, kiddo?"

"It's not funny. Luckily we'd finished and the guys weren't still fucking me," I muttered, cringing at the thought of what he could have seen only a few moments earlier.

"How about you come down to the kitchen and I'll make you something to eat?" he offered.

"I'm not hungry. I feel a little queasy, actually. I think last night fucked me up a little," I grumbled.

"You need to eat something. Even if it's just toast," he scolded, making me scoff.

"I rarely have breakfast."

"Yeah, but it's been around twenty-four hours since you

ate. You've slept through lunch and it's nearly dinner time. C'mon, I'll make coffee, too."

"I need some powder. I feel like shit," I grunted, his eyes narrowing as he sat up.

"You don't need it. You've been doing good the last few days, so keep going. Besides, you can't be around the kids when you're shoving shit up your nose." True. I'd never risk them seeing me like that.

I sighed, sitting up and pulling Mikey into my arms as I stood. "Alright. Breakfast it is."

We walked down to the kitchen and I couldn't help but notice the tension in the air. I glanced at Skeeter, finding him glaring at Lukas. The two of them needed a hate-fuck or a fist fight to deal with their bullshit. Their friendship was solid, but they had permanent tension between them that I didn't understand.

"Morning," I murmured, getting on tip-toe to kiss Skeeter's cheek. He pulled his gaze away from Lukas, his face softening as he looked at me.

"Morning, baby girl. Have a good sleep?"

"I feel like absolute shit, but I slept a lot. Lukas is making me eat," I grumbled, his eyes darkening.

"Good. You won't like what happens if you don't."

"Aw, are you and Lukey going to gang up on me? It's been a while since you competed against each other in the bedroom. I'm game," I chuckled, having no issue with the punishment.

"It won't be like that. You won't be able to sit for a month, and you'll get zero orgasms out of it," he warned, making me scowl.

"You wouldn't do that."

"Bet on it. See what happens."

Lukas snorted as he took Mikey, motioning for me to sit

at the table. "I'm not doing shit with Skeet. Keep me out of it."

"I want to test a theory," I hummed. "I need you two to fuck each other and see if you feel better. All this alpha-male testosterone is suffocating me. Have some hanky spanky so we can all live in blissful peace."

"I love you, but no," Skeeter growled, giving Lukas the stink eye before leaving the room, making me sigh.

"I really wish you'd do it for me."

Lukas rolled his eyes, turning to the toast that was ready. I hadn't even realized he'd started making me anything. "Never going to happen, babe. You want me and Jense to put on a show for you? That, I can get onboard with."

"I won't say no to watching you rail him," I smirked, my stomach rolling as he placed the buttered toast in front of me. He chuckled, sitting in one of the chairs beside me and bouncing Mikey on his lap.

"I bet. Maybe we should discuss this later when little ears aren't around."

Mikey giggled as he was bounced, not paying attention to us at all, but it probably wasn't worth the risk. He seemed behind in his speech, but he'd catch up fast.

"You're right."

I picked up the toast and took a bite, chewing slowly and hoping it helped me feel better. It didn't. By the time I'd finished the first slice, I was running to the bathroom to throw it back up.

Heaving up toast wasn't pleasant, and my throat burned as I sat back to take a breath.

"You alright, preggers?" Caden asked as he walked in and leaned against the sink, handing me a glass of water.

"You're not funny, Holloway. Yesterday knocked me around, it's probably from the fucking anxiety. I'm surprised I didn't throw up from the anxiety," I grunted, sipping the water slowly. I had to keep putting it down to throw up again, sweat beading on my brow by the fourth time. Caden frowned, kneeling beside me and taking my hair from my hands, holding it back for me.

"Lukas said it was only toast."

"It was. I haven't eaten since yesterday morning, and all the stress has probably twisted my stomach to pieces. I might go back to bed."

"You've slept all day."

"So? I feel like shit," I groaned. "I deserve to stay in bed."

"You never get sick," he stated. "Maybe it's withdrawals? You've basically been sober for days other than the whisky Lukas gave you last night. Maybe that's set you off?"

I heaved at the thought of whisky, making him sigh. "Alright, go back to bed and I'll bring you a bucket."

He helped me to my feet, escorting me to the bedroom and making sure I was comfortable before ducking out to find a bucket. He placed it beside the bed, climbing in behind me and wrapping his arms around my middle, his hand gently rubbing my stomach to try and soothe it.

"Go to sleep, I'll stay here in case you need me. I told Lukas to make sure everyone leaves you alone. Marco's teaching Lloyd to ride the bike, so they'll be busy for hours," he murmured, kissing my neck.

His warm hand on my stomach seemed to help with the uncomfortable twisting, so I tried to get comfortable and hoped I felt better after a nap. At least Lloyd seemed happy to spend time with Marco, because I wouldn't have coped with him demanding my attention while I felt like this.

CHAPTER NINE

RORY

*M*y nap helped. I woke up the next morning to find Caden still behind me, Tyler and Jensen asleep in the bed too. I slowly sat up, relieved when my stomach didn't twist or make me nauseous.

I let the guys sleep, wandering down to the kitchen and smelling something delicious. "I hope you're sharing that."

Hunter glanced up and smiled, giving me a nod. "Of course. It's just scrambled eggs and bacon though. No need to drool."

I moved in behind him, wrapping my arms around his waist as he flipped the bacon. "It smells so good. What are our plans today?"

He glanced over his shoulder, his voice firm. "My plans are to go to Devil's Dungeon. Your plans are to rest."

"I feel fine today. Where are the kids?"

"With Josie again. Lloyd wanted to go too, so they're at the park having ice cream."

"Lloyd wanted to go? That's good," I smiled, moving out of his way so he could dish up the food. My guys were all hot as fuck, but there was something about them cooking that always made my mouth water, and it had nothing to do with the smell of the food.

"Yeah. I think he enjoyed spending time with Marco yesterday. He's a fast learner with the bike, Marco's impressed. He listened really well to instructions. I think the hardest part for Marco was leaving Angel inside with Diesel," he grinned, handing me my plate and following me to the table.

We ate in silence for a while until Slash walked in, not looking happy. "I'm heading out. I'll be home later."

"Where are you going?" I asked, licking bacon grease from my fingers.

He watched my tongue for a second before he jerked his gaze to mine. "Shed. Harley needs help setting up for tonight. Skeet's already helping him, but the place is a bit messy so I offered to help too. Lukas and Diesel are helping Lex and Hendricks clean up Wet Dreams. It got rowdy early this morning and the place got trashed by drunk idiots who can't keep their hands off the girls."

"Should I go and help them?" I asked, knowing the answer before he even spoke.

"No. You stay here. Ty, Holloway and Jense are your slaves today, and I expect you to be laying around the house to make sure you're definitely better. No exceptions," he warned, giving me a knowing look.

I scrunched up my face, not enjoying that plan at all. "Can I go and visit Red at least? I'm bored. We can't get into trouble because of her pending crotch goblin."

"Don't call him that."

"Why not? She'll be calling him much worse when he rips her cunt in half," I smirked, making him crack a smile.

"You're a dick, Donovan. Fine, go see Jade if you want."

"I was going anyway. Since when do I do as I'm told, right?"

"You'd be correct," he grunted, leaning down and kissing my cheek. "I'll see you later. Call me if you need anything."

"I will. I love you," I replied sweetly.

"Love you too. Behave," he said firmly before heading towards the front door.

Once he was gone, Hunter sighed. "I suppose you won't let one of the others go with you to Jade's?"

"Nope. Alex is there, so there's some kind of adult supervision. I promise, Dad," I deadpanned, making him grin.

"If you're going to call me that, at least get naked and call me *daddy*."

"Sorry, I'm not following in Charlie's footsteps with that shit. I won't lie, I'm not even surprised Rage gets off on it. Always knew he had issues," I snorted, earning a dirty look.

"Did you just kink shame?"

"I just think it's hilarious that someone like Rage likes to be called daddy. I didn't mean it to be rude," I scowled. He dropped an arm across the back of my chair, motioning to my bandaged shoulder and changing the subject.

"When did you change that last?"

"Uh…"

"Aurora," he growled, shoving his empty plate back and getting to his feet. "Do you want a fucking infection? Get up."

"But I'm not finished with my bacon," I grumbled, fighting a laugh as he picked up the last piece and shoved it into my mouth.

"Chew while we walk."

"Yes, Sir," I mumbled around my food as I did as I was told, letting him lead me through the house and into one of the bathrooms. He pulled my shirt over my head, peeling back the bandage.

"It doesn't look too bad. I'll salt bathe it and rebandage it for you. Do I need to set up a sticker chart for you to make sure you do it regularly?" he grunted, giving me the side eye.

"I don't give a fuck about stickers, Rivera," I said dryly. "But if you want to tongue fuck my pussy each night before bed as an incentive, I might feel obliged to do as I'm told."

"You'll do as you're told anyway," he muttered, getting to work on my bandage.

"I might have a shower and head around to Jade's since Lloyd's occupied," I sighed, a groan leaving him.

"Couldn't you have said that before I started this? Don't get your bandage wet."

"I'll be careful," I said, rolling my eyes and waiting for him to finish before I headed up to the bedroom by myself to grab some fresh clothes.

Tyler and Caden were sitting in bed playing a shooting game on the Xbox, but Jensen gave me a big smile. "Hey, baby. You feel better?"

"I feel great today. I've had breakfast, so I'm going to shower then go have some girl time with Red while Lloyd's busy. You guys going to hang around here?" I asked as I walked into the walk-in-wardrobe and started rummaging for something to wear.

"I think you should stay home," Caden grunted. "But you won't listen so I won't even bother."

"You'd be right about that," I called back, making Tyler chuckle. I found some black skinny jeans and a white tank top, snatching my Psycho's jacket on the way back into the bedroom.

"Have you changed your bandage?" Jensen asked, smiling when I nodded. "Good. Can you tell Alex I'll stop by the bar tonight? I doubt Luke will be working, so I'll cover for him if he needs a hand."

"Will do. Luke's probably going to be a while."

"Yeah. He texted me earlier. Wet Dreams is a fucking mess. It looks like they had a riot," he sighed.

Once I'd convinced all three of them that I was fine to

shower alone, I headed into the adjoining bathroom and quickly got ready for the day. I winced when I lifted my arms to try and tie my hair up once my make-up was done and my teeth were brushed. "Hey, guys? Can one of you help me with my fucking hair?"

Tyler walked in, taking the band from my fingers and picking up the brush. "How do you want it?"

"Just in a ponytail."

"You got it," he smiled, brushing my hair into one hand and securing it high like I always did it. He gave me a scorching kiss when he was finished, taking my damn breath away.

"What was that for?"

"Just because I love you," he grinned, grabbing my waist and pulling me against him. "You know I love you in those jeans."

"You mean, you love it when they're around my ankles," I smirked, making him laugh.

"That too. You know you always look good, so stop acting surprised when I kiss the shit out of you. I've been doing it for years."

"You have, and I love you for it," I smiled, leaning forwards to kiss him. "I need to go. I texted Jade and she's waiting for me."

"Be safe. Take your gun," he said sternly. "And when you talk to Alex, let him know he can call me if he needs help with the bar, too. Jense can handle it, but if it gets busy he'll need someone else."

"Sounds good. I'll see you later?" I asked, waiting for him to kiss me again before letting me go, the other two getting the same treatment.

I said goodbye to Hunter as I headed through the house, shoving my feet into my black biker boots and grabbing the keys to Jensen's Camaro. I loved that fucking car, but it made me miss my Corvette.

It wasn't like I didn't have plenty of cars to choose from, but Jensen knew how much I loved driving his car.

It didn't take me long to get to Jade's, letting myself in as I arrived. "Honey! I'm home!"

"You're late," Jade said with annoyance, making me smirk.

"Oh, shit. You got those fun hormones going on. You sound cranky."

"You'd be cranky too if you'd been awake all night because the baby inside you was trying to kick his way out. I swear he's broken my ribs," she grumbled. Alex wandered in looking tired, telling me he was up half the night with her too.

"Hey, Donovan."

"Hey. Jense said he can fill in for Lukas tonight if needed, and Ty offered to help out too if you get busy," I said, knowing I'd forget if I didn't tell him straight away. Relief filled his face and he gave me a smile.

"No shit? Thanks. I'll definitely need them. I can't run the whole bar by myself without Harley, and Jade's busy at Devil's Dungeon tonight. Your guys are a lifesaver."

"You know they love working the bar. I think it's given Luke and Jense a purpose. I appreciate you guys letting them work there." It was true. Lukas was thriving, and Jensen always seemed happy to go to work and hang out behind the bar. Caden and Tyler helped if needed, but they preferred helping the crews with business.

"We appreciate them doing it. I need a nap," he muttered, Jade's eyes burning into him.

"Oh, you need a fucking nap? That's nice. How about you carry this fucking football star baby for a while and see how you feel?"

"Relax, the doc said to watch your blood pressure," he said gently, and I cringed, knowing she wasn't going to relax in the slightest.

"Relax? Fucking relax? You don't know what it's like to grow a person inside you! I can't relax! He's always kicking me, making me throw up, won't let me sleep properly, and I've had heartburn for three fucking days. Don't tell me to relax, Alex Crossin," she spat, impressing me slightly. Pregnancy had turned her into a raging monster at times, but this was a whole new level of anger.

"Men are stupid. Let's grab some ice cream and sit outside," I suggested, her features relaxing.

"They are stupid, aren't they? Ugh, that sounds so good. I'll grab the ice cream," she stated before wandering into the kitchen, leaving me with Alex.

"Thank you," Alex mumbled. "There's no stopping her once she starts and we can't calm her down. She's supposed to be resting."

"Is there something wrong with the baby for the doc to ask her to rest?" I asked with a frown, but he shook his head.

"No, but he's worried about her blood pressure. It was pretty high last time she went for a checkup, so he's trying to get her to relax more. A lot easier said than done when she likes to be busy all the time."

"I'll make sure she stays sitting down today. We weren't going to do much else other than hang out here," I promised.

"I appreciate it. Charlie came over yesterday to spend time with her, but Rage refused to leave and it made Jade tense the whole time. Hendricks' is being a helicopter husband at the moment with Lex, so he's always hanging around too," he sighed, running a hand over his face. "Did you know about Lex being pregnant?"

I nodded, cringing slightly. "Uh, yeah. We had a fight the night she told me. We haven't really spoken much since."

"You'll be fine. You two bounce back from arguments fast as fuck. Now, please go hang out with my girl before she comes back in here and kills me," he chuckled nervously, shooing me into the kitchen.

Jade was already eating ice cream out of the container with a spoon, guilt flickering across her face as she noticed me smirking at her. "Uh, I just wanted a taste, then I was coming to get you."

"Don't sweat it, Red. You can eat it all if you want. You're growing a baby," I pointed out. "But, I'd like to have a cigarette, so let's go outside and catch up. I feel like I never see you anymore."

She picked up the tub of ice cream and followed me outside, getting comfortable on a chair while I moved further away to smoke. I inhaled the heavenly smoke, blowing it out and glancing at Jade who was eating the ice cream like it was the last tub she'd ever see.

"Lloyd's finally relaxing a little, I think. He spent most of yesterday afternoon with Marco on the bike, and he's with Josie and the other two today."

"That's good. How do you feel? Marco said you were really sick yesterday. He thinks they finally knocked you up and he's freaking out a little," she said, surprising me.

"I'm not pregnant. Why is he freaking out? It's what he fucking wanted," I grumbled, earning myself a look of disapproval.

"Oh, I don't know. Maybe because if they knocked you up, you'd flip the fuck out. He told me how bad it was when you all talked about having kids. He doesn't want something like that to happen again," she said softly. "He was really hurt about it."

I took a long drag of my cigarette, looking away from her. "I know. I won't change my mind though. Having the three kids under my care is hard enough."

"So, what's your plan? Keep them for a few months and then find them new homes like lost puppies? You know you've got them forever now, right? You have nine years until Lloyd is eighteen. You have eighteen years until Angel is. I don't think you thought this through well, babe. I'm glad you have them, and it's obvious they love you, but…"

"I know!" I snapped, glaring at her. "I'm aware about how hard it's going to be, and how long for. I rarely have to help Mikey or Angel with anything, so I only really have Lloyd to think about. Losing him the other night fucked me up, Red. You have no idea how terrified I was."

"You're good with them from what I've heard. Every kid runs away from home at some point, don't be so hard on yourself. I bet you ran away plenty," she smirked, making me scowl.

"I ran away because Max kept beating me. It's different. I made Lloyd feel unwelcome, it's my fault he took off, and I'm worried it will happen again. I'll keep fucking up and…"

"Would you sit down and shut up?" she bit out, making me pause. "You took them in when you didn't have to. You've given them a home, discipline, and a family. You'll learn the right way to raise them, and you'll do a damn good job of it. Stop with the pity party, you're doing a good job."

"Wow, tell me how you really feel," I said slowly, butting my cigarette out and sitting near her. "I'm just scared of wrecking their lives."

She sighed, leaning back in her chair and putting her hand on her swollen stomach. "You can't ruin their lives, Donovan. You fucking saved them from a lifetime of pain and misery. Angel probably wouldn't have survived to see her first birthday, Mikey might not have been so lucky either. What if some creepy kiddy rapists bought them, huh? They don't care how old they are. They could have literally killed them by raping them. Lloyd was likely to have the same fate, but he would have been resold the older he got, beaten, and tortured. You might fuck up and say the wrong thing, but you'll never destroy those kids. Not when someone else has already done it. You're the best thing to have ever happened to them, so give yourself some credit. They call you mom, and no kid would do that unless they trusted the person. Especially not Lloyd."

Tears burned my eyes, and Jade looked at me in horror. "Shit, did I say something wrong?"

I scowled, wiping at my eyes angrily. "No, that was really nice of you to say. I don't know what's happening, I don't fucking cry over stupid shit. This is ridiculous."

"You sure you're not knocked up? All I did was cry over dropped spoons and dirty washing at the start," she snorted, but I shook my head.

"No way in fucking hell. I can't be."

"Why not? You fuck nine guys regularly without condoms," she pointed out.

"I have the implant in my arm."

"When did you get your period last?"

"I only get it once or twice a year with the implant."

"You know it's not completely foolproof, right? I got knocked up on contraceptives," she shrugged, panic filling me.

"No. No fucking way. I've just had an emotional week."

"I have tests in the bathroom if you want to double check. Ease your mind a little," she suggested. "Don't freak yourself out over nothing."

"I can't be, it's not possible," I said firmly, but she pinned me with a stern look.

"Go and check, Aurora. It will take five fucking minutes."

I didn't want to. If I was, I was going to freak the fuck out, so being in denial was a better plan. Jade wasn't going to take no for an answer though. She stood, grabbing my wrist and dragging me towards the house.

"You need to find out or you'll drive yourself crazy."

I tried to dig my heels in, but she kept pulling me through the house until we got to the bathroom, pushing me inside gently and pointing to the cupboard.

"They're in there. I'm not letting you out until you take the test."

"You can't fucking lock me in here!" I snapped. "I'll shoot my way out and you fucking know it!"

"Want me to call Marco and you can deal with him then?" she demanded. "I don't want to, but I will. You've been drinking like crazy for months, sniffing the entire town's cocaine supply, and getting your ass beat in the cage at the shed. You need to find out because if you are, you really should go to the doctor. I love you, which is why you need me to force your hand with this. Be an adult and do the right thing," she said bluntly, shutting the door and leaving me to freak out alone.

I stood there without moving for a while until finally walking towards the cupboard and opening it, the box of pregnancy tests staring back at me. I took one, building up the courage to sit on the toilet and pee on the stick.

Once I managed that task, I placed it on the sink and stepped away from it, my heart rate spiking with every passing second. It said to wait for a few minutes, so I took my eyes off it and looked at myself in the mirror. I looked like shit.

I frowned, turning myself sideways and lifting my shirt, running a hand over my stomach. It was a little rounded, but I wasn't surprised though, I'd been drinking a lot and slacking with my fitness. I moved my hand higher, poking at my breasts. They were tender, but that was expected when I lived with nine savage bed buddies. They always hurt.

"Stop being stupid," I scolded myself, picking up the stick, ready to tell Jade she was full of shit. My hands shook as the two pink lines stared back at me, and I threw it across the room and backed away from it like it was a snake.

"No! No! No!" I pleaded, stepping closer to look at it again. Still two lines.

"Donovan? You okay?" Jade called through the door, my lungs going tight. I couldn't have a fucking baby. My body was not a temple, it was a dodgy alleyway that kids should steer clear of. "Donovan?"

I yanked open the door, trying to dart past her. "I've gotta go. I'll see you..."

She grabbed my arm, forcing me back in front of her. "Hey, it's fine. What did it say?" she asked calmly, her eyes flicking between mine.

"Do you think I'd be freaking the fuck out if it was negative?!" I screamed. "I can't have a fucking baby!"

"You can. Breathe, before you give yourself a panic attack," she warned, steering me into the living room and pushing my shoulders down to make me sit on the couch.

"I don't want kids. I don't want to grow a baby. I don't want to..."

"Alex?! Can you get me some water?!" Jade called out, cutting me off as she gently pushed my head between my legs and rubbed my back. "You're okay. Deep breath in, and slowly let it out. You know the drill."

Alex joined us, his voice low. "What's wrong?"

"Just give me the water," Jade growled, taking it from him. "Rory, you need to breathe."

I shook my head, my chest burning as I tried to suck in air but couldn't.

"Call Marco," Jade barked at Alex. "They know how to pull her out of these things."

"I've got her," Alex replied, squatting in front of me and

taking my hand. "Donovan? Breathe with me, alright? Take a deep breath in, and squeeze my hand."

I tried multiple times, spots dancing across my vision from the lack of air.

"Breathe in when I squeeze your hand," he tried, giving it a squeeze and waiting for me to suck in a breath. I choked as some hit my lungs, his hand squeezing mine again. "And again. Let it out slowly."

I focused on his gentle squeezing, trying to breathe every time his hand tightened in mine.

"Have some water," he murmured as I sat up once my head stopped pounding so damn hard, offering me the glass. I took a small sip, glancing over at Jade who's eyes were filled with concern.

"I can't do it. What the fuck am I supposed to do?" I asked softly, my voice cracking.

She sat beside me, taking my hand as Alex stepped back a bit. "You can do anything. You're Aurora fucking Donovan."

"I don't want to though. I don't want to keep it," I choked out. "I don't want a baby, Jade."

Alex blew out a breath. "You're pregnant?"

I nodded, looking up at him. "I'm not supposed to be a mom. This wasn't something I wanted."

"You're already a mom to those three kids you saved. You might not have pictured kids in your life, but you already have it. Regardless of being pregnant, you're already a parent to Lloyd, Mikey and Angel. I know it's scary, Jade was terrified when she first found out she was pregnant, but you get a lot of help and support throughout the pregnancy, and you learn heaps of information from doctors and stuff. You don't go in completely blind."

"I need to think about it," I mumbled, getting to my feet.

"Of course. It's a lot to take in. Maybe get a doctor to run blood tests to make sure. Those tests aren't always correct, but it's highly possible it is."

"Can you guys not say anything about this to anyone?" I asked. "I don't want to talk about it and…"

Jade gave me a hug, not giving a shit when I tensed like an angry cat. "It's not our news to tell. Go home and wrap your head around it. Call me if you need anything, or have questions."

I couldn't have escaped faster if I'd tried.

Hunter

"INCOMING," Marco muttered as the Camaro drove up the driveway later that night as we stood on the front steps. Jade had messaged Marco two hours ago to see if Rory had gotten home. When we said she hadn't, she acted cagey about why she would have gone somewhere else, frustrating the fuck out of Marco. He knew something was wrong, and we were on the way out the door to find her when the headlights caught our attention. I'd hardly been at fucking work this past week, but luckily Violet knew how to handle the money and close.

Rory parked the car near the steps, climbing out with a cigarette hanging from her lips, not noticing us as she walked right past us, stuck in her own head.

"Princess?" Marco murmured, making her jump.

"Oh, hi. I, um… what are you doing out here?" she said, stumbling over her words and making me frown.

"We were coming to look for you. Are you okay?"

"I'm fine. Just need to pee," she said quickly, walking inside with us hot on her heels.

"Can you not smoke inside? It's not good for the kids," I

reminded her, her eyes widening as she threw it back out the door.

"Shit. Fuck."

"What's going on?" I murmured, reaching out to take her hand, but she jerked back from me like I'd burned her.

"Don't fucking touch me."

"Why not? Jesus, did something happen? Did someone fucking hurt you?" I demanded, hating the thought of anyone laying their hands on her.

"I'm fine."

"Obviously not," Marco argued, running his eyes over her for damage. "The fuck happened today?"

"Nothing! I said I'm fucking fine!" she shouted, drawing attention from the other room. Caden wandered in, Lloyd right behind him. He didn't need to see her having another melt down.

She surprised me though when she opened her arms and accepted his hug, forcing a smile. "Hey. You want me to sleep over in your room?" *What the fuck?*

Marco stiffened beside me, meeting my gaze with a frown.

"Yay! Can we watch movies?!" Lloyd beamed. "I want to tell you all about today! Josie is really nice!"

"She's the best. Let's go find a movie and get you to bed, it's late," she replied, not giving us a second glance as she let him lead her up the hallway.

The moment they were gone, Marco snorted. "What the fuck was that?"

"I have no idea. Maybe we leave her alone tonight. If she starts a fight, Lloyd will get upset. We'll get it out of her tomorrow," I sighed.

"She didn't say where she'd been?" Caden asked, crossing his arms and staring up the hallway.

"No, and she got really weird when I touched her. Some-

SINNERS REIGN | 163

thing's wrong, but I don't know what," I replied tightly, hating it when she shut us out. Marco growled, grabbing his phone.

"Jade fucking knows. I'll make her tell me because…"

"Leave her alone. She'd tell you if something bad had happened, and you know she's not supposed to be stressing. Don't corner her," I warned, his shoulders slumping.

"I just want to fix it."

"I know. I'm going to head back to Devil's Dungeon and help Violet. You guys staying here?"

"Yeah. We'll stick around in case Rory needs us, or if she takes off on the kids," Caden mumbled, making me scowl.

"She won't leave them home alone."

"She's not good with Angel and Mikey on her own anyway. She'd freak if we left her here with all three kids."

"Agreed. I'll be back in a few hours. Check in with Slash and see how everything's going at the shed, and let him know Rory's home," I nodded, snatching my keys from the bowl by the door and going back to work, hoping I wouldn't come home to mayhem.

CHAPTER TEN

RORY

I stumbled from bed at six in the morning, heaving my stomach contents into the toilet and trying to hold my hair back. I'd slept like shit, and I knew I wasn't going to have a good day when I woke up and almost threw up in bed. I managed not to wake Lloyd, but I didn't know how long I had until he realized I was gone.

I clung to the toilet bowl as I threw up again, tears burning my eyes as I heard the door creak open. I didn't want to face this shit, I wasn't ready, but it would be obvious to the guys what was going on.

Hands silently combed through my hair, pulling it back from my face to make sure I didn't vomit all over it.

When I was done, I leaned back, sitting on the floor and leaning into whoever was behind me, not giving a fuck about crying any more. "I'm pregnant." Might as well rip the Band-Aid off.

"I know. You've been showing signs. I didn't want to bring it up with you in case you flipped out," Slash murmured in my ear, holding me as I broke down for the millionth time that week. I cried until I threw up again, not having the energy to push Slash away. To be honest, I was grateful to have him there, holding me together so I couldn't shatter completely.

"You want to take a drive?" he murmured once I'd flushed the toilet and gotten to my feet.

"I can't. Lloyd…"

"I'll wake up Marco. He'll keep an ear out for him," he promised, grabbing my waist and hauling me into his arms.

"I can walk," I protested weakly, enjoying his comfort.

"I know you can, but I want to carry you," he replied, kissing my forehead as he carried me up to the bedroom. He opened the door, finding Diesel sitting up in bed checking his phone.

"Hey. Can you keep an ear out for Lloyd? I'm taking Rory for a drive."

"Yeah. You alright, babe?" Diesel said quietly, his eyes filled with worry. I nodded, not wanting to speak, knowing I'd start crying again. These hormones were fucked up, I'd never cried so much in my entire fucking life.

"She'll be okay. I have my phone so call me if you need me," Slash replied, closing the door and carrying me down to the garage. We didn't have shoes on. He was in his boxers and I was in my sleep shorts and tank top, but it didn't matter.

We climbed into the Mustang, driving around town for hours as the sun rose, ending up at the docks. Slash turned the ignition off, turning in his seat to face me. "Did you find out yesterday? Is that why you were upset? Hunter said you were acting really weird."

I fiddled with the hem of my shorts, nodding. "I was at Red's. She suggested I take a test. Well, forced me into the bathroom and refused to let me leave until I'd found out. I had a panic attack."

"She should have called me. It's been a long time since

you've had one of those. How bad was it?" he asked softly, taking my hand to stop me fidgeting.

"Alex was there. He helped. It was pretty bad, I almost blacked out," I mumbled. "I don't want a baby, Slash. I know everyone would be so excited, but I don't want it. It's selfish, I know, but…"

"No one's going to force you to have a baby. You haven't called the doctor yet?"

"No."

"Then we'll do that today. Make an appointment and get confirmation. They'll also tell you how far along you are, and let you know what your options are."

I frowned, holding his gaze. "How many options are there? Push, or be cut open?"

"I meant options about what you want to do. Like, have the baby, adopt the baby out, abortion," he shrugged. "They know everything that's available to you."

"As if you guys would let me hand over a baby to some-one," I snorted, turning my attention out the window and staring at the water. "My only option is to keep it."

"Killer, look at me."

I glanced back at him, his eyes soft. "You know I'd do anything for you and that baby. If you really don't want it, we can go to the clinic."

"Abortion?" I asked, discomfort swirling inside me. "I don't know if I could do that."

"Then that's probably telling you that you want the baby," he said gently, cupping my cheek. "I'll stand by you no matter what. It's your body."

"I'm scared," I whispered, hating that my lip quivered. "What if there's something wrong with it? I've been drinking, doing drugs and fighting. I've been smoking, and fucking hell I want a cigarette so bad."

"Then have a cigarette. Charlie's doctor got her to cut

back slowly when she first found out. It can be harmful to go completely off them suddenly. It will cause stress and anxiety. Don't chain smoke, just have one when you really need it. Eventually, you won't want them anymore," he smiled, making me frown.

"How do you know that? You don't really talk to Charlie."

He leaned back in his chair, running his hand over his face. "I've been talking to Rage."

"Like, Rage Evans?" I teased lightly, earning a scowl.

"There's only one Rage. Ever since we helped the Kings save those kids, we've been in touch. Only about the skin trade and shit, nothing personal. After he found Lloyd, we started talking more. I was with him and Charlie yesterday for a while, and Rage got pretty excited about the baby."

"That's good, right? That you're talking? I'm sorry, I didn't think to ask how you'd been doing with everything. I know the news about Rage protecting you was a shock after thinking he was a spiteful, murderous bastard all these years."

"I wouldn't have talked about it if you had asked me. He's a touchy subject, in case you hadn't noticed," he chuckled dryly. "I don't know if it's good. Having a truce with the Kings is one thing, but with my brother? I don't know if I can push it that far. Not yet. I need more time."

"I understand. How do I tell the guys about the baby?" I sighed, dreading it. Some would be excited, others would be worried about my pending explosion. Everyone would react differently.

"Just tell them. It doesn't have to be a speech," he smiled, grabbing me and pulling me into his lap, placing me sideways so my back was against the car door. "It's going to be okay, I promise."

I didn't reply. I curled against him, listening to his heartbeat as we sat in silence, only driving home when I said I was ready.

———————

WE WALKED into the kitchen when we arrived home to find everyone standing around with coffee, talking amongst themselves. Lloyd dived at me, a big grin on his face. "You're back!"

"Yeah, buddy. Can you go into the other room with Sarah? I need to talk about something with the guys that's private," I said gently, expecting him to explode, but he shrugged.

"Sure. Don't run away though when you guys fight."

"I'll try not to," I said dryly, waiting for him to run off to find Sarah before I faced the guys. Slash dropped a kiss on my temple, giving me the courage to just blurt it out.

"I'm pregnant."

"Wait, what?" Skeeter murmured, his eyes running over me. "How do you know?"

I sighed, feeling awkward. "I did a test at Jade's yesterday. I needed some time to think about it before telling you."

His jaw tightened, his voice low. "You're sure?"

My fists clenched as I glared at him, not expecting him to seem angry about it. "Yes, I'm fucking sure. I'm moody as fuck and I've been throwing up. The test said…"

"You're always fucking moody."

"You're a second away from getting stabbed," I bit out. "If you don't want it, then good. I don't want it either."

His face softened as he moved towards me, not fearing for his safety as he cupped my cheek. "I didn't mean it like that. I'm worried I hurt the baby the other day in the office. I slammed you down on the table." He wasn't wrong, we'd been pretty rough. "And you've been fighting in the cage a lot lately too."

"You don't want to keep it?" Marco snapped, hurt in his voice. "I know you don't want kids, but are you really going to get rid of it without asking us what we want?"

"I don't know what to do! I'm fucking terrified!" I threw back. "You don't have to grow it in your body for nine months, or worry about eating the wrong thing and…"

"No fighting!" Slash barked, dropping an arm around my shoulders to show his support. "It's Rory's body, and it's her fucking choice! She'll listen to your thoughts on it if you speak to her with respect!"

The room went quiet, and Marco managed to look ashamed of himself. "I'm sorry, babe. You know how badly I want to have kids with you. Maybe this is a sign that we're supposed to."

Hunter nodded, agreeing with him. "Yeah. I think it's a sign."

"I don't believe in signs. I believe in contraceptives failing," I deadpanned. "Anyone else have something to throw in?"

"Like Slash said, it's your body. I definitely want to keep her," Tyler grinned, making me scowl.

"Her?"

"Yeah. I bet it's a girl. We can call her Rory Two Point Zero," he chuckled, pleased with himself.

"You're a dick," I spat, annoyed that he was making a joke out of it. "This is serious."

"Fine. I say we call her something cool like…"

"Ty," Slash warned. "Not the time."

He grumbled to himself, shutting his mouth, knowing one of the guys or myself would smack him the fuck out.

Lukas, Jensen, and Diesel all agreed that they wanted to keep the baby, and by the time I looked at Caden, he eyed me sternly. "We're keeping it. I get that it's your body, but that's our kid in there. You going to tell Mom you aborted my kid?"

"Your mom has no need to know anything right now, no offense. This is private, and so is this choice," I growled. "And how do you know it's yours?"

He shoved his chair back, smacking his hands on the table as he leaned forwards. "It's all of our kid! I don't give a shit who's DNA it carries, it's still mine because you're their mom!"

I stared at him, not knowing how to react. They'd seemed happy to have a family, not knowing who actually created the baby, but I didn't think they were that serious.

"You really feel like that? You don't care who the bio-dad is?" I asked softly as he stalked towards me, gently tugging my hair back to make me look up at him.

"I don't give a fuck about that. That kid has nine fucking fathers, regardless of what DNA they have. I want to have this kid with you, Rory. When things get hard, you have so many people to lean on for help. You want a night off from the kids? Sure. Go out for the night and we'll watch them. You're sick of school drop offs in five years? Fine, we'll take turns. This doesn't have to be as scary as you think, and I know you'll be the best mom in the world."

"Okay," I squeaked out, his eyebrows jumping to his hairline.

"Okay, what?"

"We're having a baby," I choked out, only having two seconds to breathe before Marco pushed Caden out of the way to kiss the shit out of me. He lifted me, forcing me to wrap my legs around him.

"Thank you," he breathed, and I swore the fucker was tearing up. "This means everything to me."

"Put me down, you big softie," I snorted, but I leaned

forward and gave him a quick kiss, soaking in his excitement. All the guys started crowding me, wanting their share of kisses too, but Tyler couldn't fucking help himself as he smirked wide.

"I want to put bets on who the kid comes out looking like."

Caden gave him a shove, but Skeeter grinned. "We all know it's going to be mine."

"Like fuck. Most of your swimmers end up in Marco's ass," Slash snorted. "I bet it's Rivera's."

They discussed it for ages, making me roll my eyes. These fuckers would honestly bet on anything.

———

"Excuse me?" I scoffed, staring at the doctor like she was stupid. "That's not possible. I'd have known by now if that was the case."

The doctor sighed, taking her glasses off to look at me. She wasn't fazed by the nine baby daddies in the room, which was the one reason I wanted to keep her as my doctor.

"I can see the size quite clearly, Aurora. Can you see this?" she asked, pointing to an obvious baby on the screen as she moved the ultrasound wand across my stomach. "Your baby is measuring close to six inches in length. You're definitely four months along."

"Is it okay? Does it have any problems? Are..." I was panicking. I'd been getting the shit kicked out of me in the cage, I'd drank myself into oblivion, and I'd shoved thousands of dollars worth of cocaine up my nose. How the fuck was it even alive in there? I was surprised that even I was alive after that.

"Heartbeat is normal, the baby's growing well, and I don't

see any missing limbs if that's what you're worried about. Oh my," she chuckled, making me panic.

"What's wrong? I thought you said everything was fine?"

"Everything's perfectly fine. Can you see this flicker?" she asked with a smile, pointing to it. "That's a heartbeat."

"I thought the other one was the heartbeat?"

"It is. There's two." I was going to pass the fuck out.

Marco and Hunter almost tripped over each other as they tried to get a closer look, and something settled in my chest at seeing the love on their faces, despite my pending panic attack. They hadn't even met their kids yet and they were completely smitten.

"Can we tell what the genders are?" Caden asked, making me scowl.

"Don't ruin the surprise. There can't be two," I growled, squinting my eyes to see better. "It's probably just a little air bubble or something."

"We have to wait?!" Caden groaned. "I'll fucking die."

"Good thing you have back up daddies, right, Aurora?" the doctor teased, making me laugh. She was cool, I liked her. "But no, it's still a little too early. But everything looks really good, you have two healthy babies in there." I couldn't wrap my head around that.

"I thought I'd poisoned them or something. I was freaking out about one being in there, but two? Shouldn't I be showing more?"

"Babies are pretty resilient. Some women pop out fast, others are last minute. You're showing enough," she shrugged. "And since most first timers ask this question, yes, you can still have sex, you won't hurt them. They're very safe in there. Just don't cause too much body trauma if you're into anything harmful. I'm looking at you, grumpy."

Skeeter scowled. "No more knife play? Got it."

"Aw, really? We can't do that?" I pouted.

The doctor sat back, handing me a wipe for my stomach to remove the gel. "I don't recommend it. Apart from the risk of infection, you're also causing the body to go into a state of shock. The baby senses that, and it can be really upsetting for them."

"Fuck," I grunted, sitting up and swinging my legs off the table. "There goes all my fun. I can't fuck right, do any of my hobbies, or fight. What do I do with myself?"

"Rest," Slash muttered. "And drugs aren't a hobby, Donovan."

I rolled my eyes. "How about smoking? I smoke a lot."

I swore the doctor was sick of us already by the way she sighed. "If you can cut them right back, that's the best way to do it. If you need help quitting, we have many things to assist you like pamphlets and programs. Or, you can check in with me whenever you need while you slowly cut them out. If you don't smoke much, giving them up fast isn't that bad, but if you smoke a lot? It can cause the baby stress. The plan is to get rid of them though, right?"

"Yep. I feel sorry for these guys for having to deal with that," I grinned. "Can I have a print out, or do you just do them electronically?"

"I figured you'd want photos printed. Here," she smiled, handing over a stack. "One each. And here's a disk with the whole thing on it. You'll need to make another appointment for two week's time."

"Thank you," I nodded, leading the guys into the office, ignoring the judgemental glances other people sent our way. We were used to it. I understood, dating nine guys was a little ridiculous.

We sorted out another appointment and any paperwork, and by the time we got home, I needed a fucking nap. No rest for the wicked though, because Lexi and Archer were sitting in the kitchen when we got there.

"Make yourselves at home," I deadpanned, making Archer grin.

"Sarah let us in, don't panic. Lex wouldn't let me fart on your pillows or anything."

"I'm so grateful," I snorted. "What do you want? I'm tired and I don't really like it when you just show up. Well, Lex is fine to be here unannounced, but not you."

"You're a bitch," he grinned. "I wanted to let you know that Rage and I teamed up and saved two kids today. We found them locked in a storage container."

Anger burned inside me at the thought. "They're okay?"

"Yeah. Turned out to be some of the missing kids that were reported a week ago on the news. No sign of who took them though, which I don't like," he sighed. "I was ready to gun those fuckers down."

"So, you and Angry Man, huh? Budding bromance?" I teased, earning a snort.

"Doubt it. We can't be in the same room for long or we'll kill each other. I'm still pissed that he knocked my sister up."

"You mean that he kidnapped and raped her, right?" I said dryly.

"Yeah, that too," he growled.

Hunter moved into the kitchen and hugged the shit out of Lexi, and I knew he was going to blurt out our news. There was no point trying to stop him. "We're having a fucking baby, well, two! They're six inches long already, and their heartbeats are so good. Look!"

He waved the photo from the scan around, the biggest grin on his face. "I'm going to be a dad!"

Lexi's eyes whipped to mine, questions filling them as she hugged him. "That's great, Rivera. Who's the mom?"

I rolled my eyes, flipping her the middle finger. "You're hilarious. I found out yesterday with a home test. We've just been at the doctor's office finding out for sure. Four months along with twins, apparently."

"You're okay with it?" she asked, making half the guys snort. "Oh, I see. You weren't too happy then?"

I explained everything to her, and by the end, Archer was chuckling. "You're in for one wild ride with the three little devils you already have. Speaking of which, where's the little boy? He likes me."

"He's probably napping. Sarah was watching them," I shrugged. "I'll go let them know we're home."

I headed up to the bedrooms, leaning on the door frame and smiling as I found Mikey and Lloyd playing with their toy cars, Sarah sitting on the bed feeding Angel a bottle.

"Hey, guys."

Lloyd's head flew up and he grinned. "You're home!"

"I am. Where's my hug?" I teased, bracing myself as he launched himself at me. I caught him, chuckling as I tightened my hold on him. "I wasn't gone that long."

"It felt like ages!"

"Well, I was thinking we could spend the afternoon watching movies with popcorn."

"And pizza for dinner?!" he beamed, making Sarah smile as she stood.

"I'll make sure it's on the menu. How was your morning, Rory?"

I smirked, pulling the photo from my pocket and handing it to her. Sarah and I had grown close since we moved back into the place I'd called home for my early childhood. I wasn't going to keep it a secret from her. Not now I knew I was keeping them. I had no idea how I'd cope with two, but we'd deal with that later.

After seeing the little blobs moving on the screen, I knew I couldn't part with them. It melted away a lot of my anxiety, especially since I knew how hands-on the guys would be with everything.

"I'd say it went pretty well."

She frowned, taking the photo and holding it up to see, a gasp leaving her. "Is this what I think it is?!"

"I want to see!" Lloyd shouted, squirming until I put him down. Sarah handed it back to me, not wanting Lloyd to see it until I was ready, but I squatted on the floor to show him. He'd be so excited.

"See this?" I smiled, pointing at the blob. "That's a baby. And see the other little blob? That's a baby too."

He frowned, not understanding. "Whose babies?"

"Mine. They still have five months of growing to do though, so you can't meet them yet."

His face lit up as he took the photo in his little hands. "I get more brothers?"

"Or sisters. We don't know yet. You know what would make it better? I was talking to the guys last night and we want to ask you something." I'd been nervous about this. I knew being their guardian was already a commitment, so we'd been talking about making it more official. "Do you think it would be cool if we adopted you?"

"You'd be my real mom? Can I be called Lloyd Donovan?" he asked with excitement, turning to Mikey and waving the photo. "Look! We get two new brothers or sisters!"

I gently took the photo from him before Mikey could scrunch it up, placing it back in my pocket. "You can be a Donovan if you want."

"I do! I want to be a Donovan like you!" he squealed, running from the room and yelling it through the house. "I'm going to be a Donovan!"

Sarah chuckled, glancing down at Angel who was still drinking her formula. "You're going to have fun with all these kids. You know I'll help as much as I can."

I hesitated before reaching for Angel, waiting for Sarah to hand her over and offer me the bottle. I was awkward, unsure how to hold her properly, but Sarah helped get her in the right position so I could keep feeding her,

"Thanks. I'll probably need the help. Lloyd's one thing, but this little one is another. I need to learn though, I can't expect Marco to do everything," I sighed, feeling embarrassed. That wasn't something I was used to.

"Of course. You're lucky to have men who like to help. You'll get lots of practice with Angel before your little ones get here, too. Remember, it's okay to ask for help. All parent's need it," she promised, placing a small towel on my shoulder. "You'll need this when you burp her. Babies have a tendency to spew up their milk," she warned.

I cringed, laughing nervously. "Wonderful. I can't change diapers. I tried changing Mikey's and it was terrible."

"You'll get better at it. Try changing Angel next time. Mikey's a little wiggle worm, so he's harder to change. You'll get the hang of it."

I rocked Angel slightly as I watched her feed, tearing up when Sarah spoke again. "Marla would be so proud of you."

"You think?" I asked, hating that I sounded so fucking vulnerable.

"I know it. You've grown into a beautiful young woman, Rory. You've taken in three children who needed a family, and you're about to experience your own children. You're not perfect, but no one is. All she ever wanted was to see you happy," she smiled kindly, patting my arm on her way past, scooping up Mikey in the process. "I'm going to take Mikey downstairs. Let me know if you need help with Angel."

"I've got it," I said weakly, internally freaking a little about being left alone with her. So, I headed downstairs to where everyone else was, finding Archer holding Mikey, and Lloyd talking everyone's ears off about the baby.

Marco wandered over to me, reaching for Angel, but I stepped back. "Uh, I can do it."

"Of course you can," he smiled. "Sorry, I just missed her."

"Can you help me change her later?" I mumbled, feeling stupid, but his entire face lit up like I'd asked him to eat me for lunch.

"I'd love to. She'll go down for a nap in the next hour."

I frowned. "I should know that. Why don't I know that?"

"You've been a little preoccupied the last few days, babe. Don't stress. I'll help you figure out her routine, she's an easy baby."

"Promise me I'll be okay," I said suddenly. "That I'll learn all this stuff and be good at it."

He sighed, kissing my cheek affectionately. "You'll be the best at it, I promise. We're always here to help you figure things out, we're still learning too."

I hoped he was right.

CHAPTER ELEVEN

FOUR MONTHS LATER

Skeeter

"*I* swear to fucking God, Aurora!" I shouted as the frying pan narrowly missed my head. "I'm going to tan your ass! I said I was sorry!"

"I told you to be there at one! It's fucking four o'clock, asshole!" Rory screamed back. "It was important!"

"I didn't realize the time! Why aren't you yelling at Marco? He was late too!"

We were supposed to have been at a doctor's appointment, but we'd gotten caught up with the Kings. And by caught up, I meant we were burning down the skin trade hideouts and killing people in the name of the children we'd recently saved. I'd been having a little too much fun and hadn't noticed the time. It was hard to check the time when you were getting shot at.

"Marco messaged me to let me know he was going to be late home. You didn't tell me shit!" she threw back, pulling a plate out of the cupboard and getting ready to throw it at me.

"I was with him! We were sharing a fucking car!" I exclaimed, stalking towards her and yanking the plate out of her hand, walking her back towards the kitchen bench with a growl. "Stop throwing shit at me."

"She's right, you know. You're an asshole," Lukas hummed happily to himself as he walked in, being Rory's favorite for the week. He'd shown up the other day with fucking flowers and her latest craving of chocolate cake. Then he gave her a massage and ate her cunt until her juices were soaking into the bed sheets. *Bastard.*

"Don't you start. I can knock you out, unlike her," I warned, earning a grin.

"Try me. I bet I could put you on your ass."

I took a step towards him, but Rory got between us, shoving me back. "Leave him the fuck alone, you bully!"

"Me?! He just offered to fight me!" I roared, stumbling as someone shoved me from the side. I glared at them, finding Caden beside me.

"Watch it. You're going to knock Rory over, you dick head. Take this shit outside," he growled, his eyes darting over to Rory to check her for injury. I clenched my teeth, annoyed that he was right. Her stomach was huge, and she was unsteady on her feet these days. I thought she was the picture of perfection, not that she saw it.

I took a deep breath, closing my eyes to get control of myself. We'd clashed a lot through her pregnancy, her hormones out of control and my temper being short.

"I'm sorry," I finally forced out, meeting Rory's gaze. "I'm sorry I missed your appointment."

"Go fuck yourself," she hissed, making me sigh as she stomped off, slamming doors as she went.

"Well, that went well."

Lukas snorted. "She was fucking devastated that you guys missed it. She cried the whole way home, you dick." *Shit.*

"She did?"

"Yeah. You need to realize how bad this shit hurts her. You saw what happened when Ty said he'd bring her home a cheeseburger a few weeks ago and he forgot it," he grunted. That had been one scary day. I'd never seen her flip her shit so bad in all the time we'd known each other. She screamed, cursed him out, ended up crying, then got angry and went out herself to get it. She didn't talk to him for two days over it.

"We can't all be Mr. Perfect like you, Lukas," I said dryly. "It's like you can't even get in trouble."

"That's because I pay attention to her. Maybe you should try it sometime, you self centered cunt," he threw back. I grabbed the front of his shirt, shoving him back against the wall, hearing it crack.

"You don't think I put her first?" I snarled. "I always put her first. I'm aware I make mistakes with her, you don't need to rub it in my face."

I was surprised when he ducked out of my hold, spinning us around so he had me against the wall instead. "I'm not rubbing it in your face for the sake of it, Skeet. I'm hoping it snaps you out of your bullshit and you start acting right. She doesn't need the stress."

I went to move but his hand went to my throat, keeping me there. "Stop thinking you're the alpha in this entire relationship. Your attitude is half your issue."

"Wait, you think you can overthrow me?" I smirked. "You're weak as balls."

His eyes narrowed, and he pressed closer to me. "I'm not weak. You're just fucking arrogant. You don't think I could win against you? I'm stronger than you, because I don't let my emotions come into play. You think with anger, which causes room for error. You don't fucking think, you just act."

"Your emotions seem to be running this show, little boy.

Get your erection off my leg," I warned him, trying to shove him back, but the little prick had gotten a lot stronger over the years. He probably worked out more than I did, trying to prove that he was just as tough as the rest of us.

"You won't like it if my emotions get involved, because I'm a little pissed at you," he seethed.

"That's a funny word for horny. Now, get your dick off me before I rip it off your body and choke you with it," I spat, gripping his shirt in my fist.

"Make me," he said in a low voice, causing anger to rip through me like a hurricane. I shoved him, finding satisfaction when he stumbled, but he came at me again, punching me in the mouth.

"You'll fucking pay for that!" I barked, punching him in the nose, but he hardly flinched. He grabbed me, shoving my face against the wall and pinning me there. I heard his zipper, a laugh leaving me. "You want to top me, Luke? You think you have the fucking balls to dominate me?"

The bastard bit my back, definitely drawing blood as he yanked the back of my sweats down. I growled, my dick jerking to life as the pain washed through me, my hips jerking forward and squashing my growing bulge into the wall as his finger slid between my ass cheeks.

"You don't seem to be putting up much of a fight. I'm a little disappointed," he chuckled dryly, pulling away for a second, returning before I could turn on him, cool liquid smearing over my ass and dripping down my balls. I never should have told him to keep lube satchels in his wallet.

"I swear to god, you stupid fuck. I... fuck!" I shouted as he pressed his dick against my ass and slid all the way in, not giving me time to adjust. His arm pinned my shoulders against the wall, the other gripping the back of my neck as he slammed into me.

"What was that, fuck face? I can't dominate you? What do

you call this then?" he demanded. "I'd say this is me putting you back in your fucking place. You're not better than me, Skeeter. You'd do well to remember that."

I groaned, my fists clenching as I tried to turn around and punch his smug face, but he had one hell of a grip on me. He let out all his anger and frustration from years of build up, his fingers digging into my flesh.

"Fuck!" he shouted, going harder and harder until he came, a guttural groan leaving him as his balls emptied into my ass.

I swatted him away, pushing myself off the wall and spinning around angrily. "You're dead, Lukas."

"Am I? Don't lie to me. You've been wanting this so bad, I'm surprised you haven't exploded by now," he grinned darkly as blood ran from his nose, his eyes filling with defiance as I grabbed his throat.

"I always envisioned it being the other way around. Punishing you and making you realize you have no chance. You think you can take me? Then bend the fuck over and take it," I ordered. "Come on, show me you can back up those words."

He was breathing heavily, but he did as he was told, glancing over his shoulder at me as he laid over the table. "You think I'm scared of taking it up the ass? Show me what you've got, big boy."

I was going to break him in half.

I snatched some of the lube from his opened wallet, coating my dick and striding towards him, fisting his hair and yanking his head back painfully. "You've got it, you little bitch."

He tensed as I jammed myself inside him, not giving a fuck as he let out a sound of discomfort. He wanted to challenge me? He could deal with the consequences afterward.

His hands flattened on the table, trying to support his

weight as I kept his head back by the hair, curving his back as I slammed into him.

"I'm going to tear you to fucking pieces. There'll be nothing left for Jensen to fuck by the time I'm done, just a gaping, bloodied hole," I snarled, my free hand coming up to his throat and squeezing tightly. It was probably a little too tight, but he deserved it. He'd spent years pushing me to my limits, trying to get a reaction out of me. Well, he'd fucking gotten one.

"How does that feel?" I growled in his ear, biting his neck sharply.

"So fucking good," he said sarcastically. "I must say, I definitely fuck better than you."

I let him go, slamming his chest down on the table and holding him there, hammering into him relentlessly, a pained growl leaving his throat as his fingers dug into the table, scratching the surface. He wasn't going to admit defeat, and neither was I. This was a dangerous game, and I didn't think either of us were going to win.

I went as deep as possible, sweat dripping into my eyes as I focused on causing him pain, but he took it, just like he said he would.

"Jesus, fuck," he gasped, my balls tightening as I realized how much he was enjoying it. Who knew the quiet one had such a dark side?

"Don't bring Jesus into this," I gritted out through clenched teeth as I slammed deep one final time, my legs shaking as I came, resting my forehead on his sweaty back.

We stood like that for ages, catching our breaths as realization set in, and I discovered I felt better. Lukas would never make me feel like how Marco did, but there was something calm in the air now that we'd gotten our frustrations out.

"Feel better?" Rory said with amusement from close by,

making me jump. I moved away from Lukas, my eyes catching on Marco who seemed unsure of what he'd walked in on. I'd told him I'd never fuck Lukas, so his confusion didn't surprise me.

Slash was walking away, shaking his head, and Jensen was hovering close by with Diesel. I didn't know we'd had an audience.

"Yeah, a little," I panted, replying to Rory's question. I didn't miss the slight flinch from Marco. I knew he was worried that Lukas meant more to me, but that would never be the case. Sure, I had his back, he was family to me, but I didn't fucking love him. Not like I did Marco.

"That was so fucking hot," Rory grinned, fanning herself. "Do it again."

"Not happening, baby girl," I murmured, glancing at Lukas as he fixed his pants, throwing the lube away. "You good?"

He faced me, something similar to peace flickering across his eyes. "Yeah. You?"

I nodded, not saying anything else as Lukas left the room, heading up to the bedroom. I wasn't surprised. That had been intense, and he probably wanted to process what the fuck had just happened.

Jensen followed him, but Rory and Marco stayed in the kitchen with me.

"I thought you said nothing was going on between you two?" Marco said accusingly, but he didn't seem angry, just confused.

"There's not."

He snorted. "I found you with your dick in his ass. Don't bullshit me. If you wanted to change your relationship with him, why did you lie to me? I would have understood if you'd just..."

"I don't want to be with him, Mark. The only man I will

ever love is you. Nothing will change that," I replied as I fixed my clothes, wanting a shower to wash off the fucking lube and come from my ass. "This tension between me and him has been brewing for years. We were fighting, the frustration and anger eating at us until we snapped, but what just happened? It won't happen again."

He relaxed, stepping closer to me. "You really think so? Because that was pretty passionate. Be honest with me. Do you want to take things further with anyone in this house? Because I'm okay with it if it's in these walls. They're family, and I know we all cross lines sometimes, but it's okay. If you want to fuck other people outside this house though? We're going to have problems."

I shook my head, holding his gaze. "I swear, no one else. I can't explain the shit with Lukas easily. Of course I love him, but it's in a family kinda way. I don't even really know what the fuck just happened," I admitted. He cracked a smile, the worry leaving his eyes.

"I get it. You could have let us know though. We missed half of it." Thank fuck, because I wasn't a fan of having an audience while Lukas got one over me. "We walked in and you were already against the wall with his dick in your ass. I kinda wanna know how that happened." *Fuck.*

Lukas

MY ASS WAS on fucking fire. I stepped into the shower, letting the hot water run down my sweaty skin. I had no idea how the fuck I ended up with my dick in Skeeter's ass, but I didn't regret it. It seemed stupid, but all the tension between us vanished, and he seemed to see me as more of an equal. If I knew that was the trick, I would have fucked him ages ago.

Jensen stepped into the shower with me, his eyes running over my body before landing on my bloodied nose.

"Pretty sure your nose is broken," he murmured, reaching out to touch it. Now that the anger had worn off, I felt every little bit of pain, wincing as he poked and prodded at me.

"I'm not surprised. He punched me fucking hard."

"Why'd he hit you?"

"Because, I busted his lip," I chuckled, closing my eyes as he grabbed the soap and started rubbing it over my body. I hissed as he reached the bite mark on my neck, knowing the skin was broken. "Jesus, I'm going to feel this shit in the morning."

"Do you want to explore your sexuality more?" he asked randomly, making me open my eyes and look at him.

"What do you mean?"

"Do you want to mess around with other people?"

He looked unsure, but I knew he'd let me if it was what I wanted. I didn't though. Rory and Jensen were enough for me, Skeeter had just been something I'd needed to get out of my system.

"No. The shit with Skeet's been coming for a while now. And he's right, it's not something that will probably happen again. We're not into each other, but we lost control. Sure, I don't mind crossing the boundaries with the guys sometimes if it gets Rory off, but it's not something that gets me off, you know?"

"I saw you topping him," he continued, chuckling slightly. "That was some hot primal shit."

"You know I go hard on top," I smirked, grabbing his waist and tugging him closer. "Nothing compares to you and Rory. I'm sorry if I hurt you. I…"

He kissed me, backing me against the wall and nipping at my lip. "Don't be stupid. I don't care if you want to fuck any of them. I won't lie, I'm going to be thinking about you railing him like that next time my dick's in my hand."

"How about you think about it while I blow you?" I murmured, giving him a quick kiss before sinking to my knees, not giving a shit if I hurt my nose.

He was worth it, and I hoped he knew that.

Rory

I FELT LIKE SHIT. I couldn't get comfortable, everything gave me heartburn, and my feet and back were killing me. I was never doing this again.

"Mom?" Lloyd called as I walked past his bedroom door early in the morning, making me halt and poke my head inside.

"Yeah?"

"How much longer till the babies are here?" he questioned, moving over in bed so I could sit on the edge. He was full of questions, wanting to know everything that was happening and more.

"Four weeks. I hope they hurry up, they're running out of room and I'm ready to evict them," I grumbled, resting my hand on my stomach and wincing as I copped a foot to the ribs.

Footsteps thumped up the hall, and Marco tore into the room like his ass was on fire. I got to my feet as fast as I could, which wasn't fast at all, my heart rate spiking with worry.

"What's wrong?"

"Wrong? Nothing's wrong! Red had her baby!" he exclaimed, the biggest grin on his face. "I'm going to go and see her, you coming?"

"Wait, she had the baby? When?" I said with surprise.

"Three hours ago. She just called me and told me to go and meet him! So I told her I'd grab you and we'd go! Come on!"

He raced from the room again, and Lloyd giggled. "He's funny."

I chuckled. "He sure is. I'd better go or he'll leave without me. You have a good day at school, okay? I love you."

He scrambled to his feet, hugging me as best as he could with my stomach in the way. "I will. I love you too."

I waddled down to the kitchen, finding Marco impatiently waiting for me. "Are you ready?"

"Once I put shoes on," I snorted, glancing at Jensen who was leaning against the kitchen counter. "Are you good to drop Lloyd at school?"

"Sure thing. I'm going to grab Holloway and head to the bar. I told Harley we had it handled for a few days so he can stay at home with Jade," he stated, walking towards me and kissing me sweetly. "Have a good day, and tell Red I said congratulations."

"I'll see you tonight," I smiled, heading towards my flip flops by the door and staring at my boots miserably. I couldn't put my own fucking shoes on anymore, so I'd been living in shoes that I could slip on. I couldn't wait to be able to see my damn feet again. Or my coochie. At least the guys were happy to shave me, because I couldn't reach shit.

Once in the car, Marco started the engine and took off towards the hospital, almost bouncing out of his seat with excitement. "I can't believe he's here!"

"I know you're excited, but can you slow down a little? I'll throw up," I complained, his foot easing off the accelerator.

"Sorry. How are you feeling this morning? Skeet said you were awake most of the night," he asked.

"Yeah, I probably only got two hours, if that. I swear

there's more than two in there, I was getting kicked from all angles," I grunted, running my hand across my stomach.

"Not long now, babe."

"I have a whole month to go. If they grow anymore, I'm going to explode."

"The doctor mentioned bringing you on early if they keep growing. Maybe talk to her about it. They're big enough to come out," he shrugged.

We talked about names, making sure we had a mental list of everything else we needed, which wasn't much. When we'd told Josie about her grandbabies, she'd gone crazy with buying us things. Jensen's father had sent us money, not making the effort to visit, and Tyler's parents scoffed and refused to acknowledge them as their grandkids until they'd seen a DNA test. That wasn't happening, so it was their loss.

Once at the hospital, Marco managed to walk by my side the whole way, not wanting to leave me behind. I couldn't walk that fast, so it was probably a painful trip for him. He opened the door to Jade's room, forgetting about me the moment his eyes landed on the bundled up blanket in Jade's arms.

"Oh my God," he cooed, moving beside the bed to look down at his little face. "He's beautiful, Red."

Jade looked exhausted, but her face was lit up with the biggest smile. "He is. You want to hold him?"

Harley smirked from his chair in the corner. "You can't take him home though, alright?"

"That doesn't seem fair," Marco grumbled, taking the baby in his arms and staring down at him with awe. "What's his name?"

"Landon Alex Bates. The guys chose it," Jade beamed, looking over at me. "Do you want to hold him?"

I patted my stomach, giving her a grin. "I would, but I'd probably struggle. These babies are sitting so fucking high."

Alex stood from his chair, motioning to it for me. "Here. Sit and I'll pass him to you."

"Marco can have him a little longer. I doubt he'll let him go yet," I said dryly, moving towards the chair and sitting down. I winced as it felt like one of the babies kicked me in the damn coochie. It was their latest favorite game, apparently.

"You good?" Harley asked with worry, Marco's attention darting to me instantly.

"I'm fine. They're just kicking hard," I muttered. "They're assholes, like their daddies."

"You sure you're good?" Marco asked. "Want me to find a nurse?"

I waved him off. "I'm sure. You want to hand the baby over?"

He looked torn, but he brought him over and helped place him in my arms, giving me a good look at his tiny little face. "Oh, Red. He's perfect."

He squirmed in my arms, letting out a squawk before his rough crying filled the room. I was terrified of giving birth, especially to two, but I couldn't wait to hold my own in my arms.

"Uh, babe. You're leaking," Marco murmured, making me frown. I glanced down at my shirt, noticing wet spots across my breast.

"Shit," I cursed, handing Landon to him and standing. Harley handed me some round pads, confusing me. "What are these?"

"They're pads for your bra. Jade's milk came in weeks ago, so she's had to use them. Slide them in and they stop the milk seeping through your clothes," he smiled. "A lot of people said their milk came in when they heard babies crying. It's something to do with your hormones, I think."

"So, they're just going to keep leaking?" I groaned, but he shrugged.

"It's not always lots, but it's a good idea to keep the pads in there anyway."

I cringed, sliding the pads into my bra and hoping no one saw my tits.

Marco offered me his jacket to hide the wet patches, but it was hard to do up around me with the belly, so it didn't hide much.

"So, have you guys figured out your birthing plan?" Jade asked. "Who's going to be in there with you?"

I frowned, not understanding what she meant. "We'll come in here, the guys will all come with me, and then hopefully I'll push these fuckers out and go home."

"Babe, they won't let that many people into the room with you," she sighed. "There won't be enough space for nine of them, as well as the nurses and doctors."

"I'm not giving birth without them," I growled. "I don't care what it costs, none of them are missing out."

"There's not enough room," she murmured. "Even if you paid them millions, they physically won't fit in there."

I glanced at Marco with a scowl. "We're not coming here then."

His eyes nearly popped out of his head. "You can't *not* be here. What if something goes wrong? We don't know how to deliver a baby, let alone two. You know there can be complications with twins. What if one gets stuck? Or…"

"I'm having them at home, I'll find a doctor to help me there," I snapped, anxiety nipping at me. "I can't do it without you guys. I'm not having anyone miss out."

"We'll talk with the doctor and see what we can do. Home birth is an option, but we have to make sure we have professional…"

"*Fuck* professional. I need to get some fresh air. Congrats, guys. The others wanted to let you know they said congratulations too," I said calmly, turning and stalking from the room as fast as possible. I heard Marco muttered a goodbye before he chased after me, his arm going around my waist as he caught up.

"We'll figure it out, don't stress. It's not good for the babies, or for you."

I shrugged him off, needing some space. "It's sorted. It's happening at home no matter what."

"If the doctor says it's not safe, then you'll be coming in here," he said sharply as we headed outside. "I won't put you or the babies at risk. If I have to miss seeing them being born, I will."

"I don't want to talk about it right now," I said firmly, waiting for him to unlock the car before I shuffled inside. I turned the music up as we drove, not wanting him to use the time to talk, but by the time we got home, he was annoyed.

"You can't do it if it's dangerous," he insisted as we walked through the front door.

"I'll hire a full fucking medical team, don't panic," I gritted out, kicking off my shoes and stomping into the kitchen. Slash glanced up from his phone, sighing when he realized I was in a mood.

"What happened?"

"I'm hiring a medical team and I'm having the babies at home," I said confidently, sitting in one of the chairs and pulling Marco's jacket off. Slash's eyes dropped to my damp shirt, but he didn't mention it.

"I thought you wanted to have them in the hospital?"

"I did, until Jade said you all wouldn't be allowed in there. Fuck that," I seethed, wincing as I felt my stomach tighten. I rubbed my hand across it, trying to ease the discomfort, but Slash sat up straighter, placing his phone on the table.

"What hurts?"

"It's not really hurting, it's just uncomfortable," I mumbled, shifting in my seat.

"It's probably braxton hicks," Lukas offered as he joined us. "I'm surprised you haven't had them already."

"The fuck's that?" Slash demanded, getting to his feet. "Is it bad?"

Lukas rolled his eyes, standing behind me to massage my shoulders. "Don't you listen to anything? The doctor explained all of this, and it's in that book you said you were going to read."

"I haven't had time," he grunted. "So, what are they?"

"They're a form of contractions. It's the uterus contracting to prepare for labor. It's just her body getting ready, that's all. It's completely normal," Lukas informed him, making me smile. He'd been really attentive at appointments, and he loved learning about it all. Between him and Marco, I always had someone to give me answers about things I didn't even know.

"What does it feel like?" Slash asked, turning his attention to me.

"I guess a light period pain? It doesn't really hurt, but it feels like my muscles are tensing across here," I said, motioning to the front of my stomach. "It's weird."

"How about you go and lie down for a while? Ty and Diesel have taken Angel and Mikey out for a while, so you can have a nap in peace without one of them screaming," he offered, and I wasn't going to say no. The day had hardly started, but I was definitely ready to go back to sleep.

"Thanks. Maybe an hour or two couldn't hurt," I smiled, getting to my feet and waddling up to the bedroom, passing out the moment my head hit the pillow.

CHAPTER TWELVE

TYLER

I was definitely ready for bed. Mikey played for hours at the playground, and Angel fussed the entire time, apparently not liking the time out of the house. Diesel fed her, sitting back on a bench and watching Mikey who was still running around with some other little kids he'd become friends with.

"I never thought we'd be here like this," he chuckled, giving me a grin. "We're supposed to be shooting at shit and spending time in jail. How'd we end up sitting in a playground with kids?"

"Speak for yourself. I'm too pretty for jail," I laughed, sitting beside him and resting my elbows on my knees.

"Don't lie to me. You love that shit."

"It can be fun. I don't particularly like being shot at though," I smirked. He rolled his eyes, knowing I got a kick out of it. Caden and I had been spending a lot of time with the crews the past year or two. We'd learned to fight better, use weapons, and I had to admit it felt good to belong.

We'd always been seen as typical rich kids, getting what we wanted and throwing parties for no reason what-so-ever, but now people saw us and they thought of the crews, our family, and the girl we shared. It was pretty cool.

"You're so full of shit. You going to become a member yet? You know Skeet's ready to hand you over a jacket," he grinned, tugging on the collar of his Psycho's jacket. "You'd look good in one of these."

"Maybe I want to join the Devils?" I teased. "Their boss is nicer."

"You and Slash totally have a bromance going on. You'd sign up with us for sure," he laughed. "Besides, I haven't heard Rivera mention wanting to take on newbies."

"He'd let me join. He's my pussy pal."

"You tickle his balls when you cross swords, don't you?" he snorted. "Should have known."

"That's rich. I heard Luke licked your dick."

His eyes narrowed, his voice low. "You're lucky I'm holding Angel, or I'd punch you in the face."

"I also heard you liked it," I continued. "I guess it probably felt good."

"Asshole," he grunted, propping Angel over his shoulder to burp her.

I glanced over at Mikey, finding him sitting on the ground with one of the little girls, ripping grass out of the ground and throwing it at her, making her giggle.

"Look at this smooth talking bastard. He's already got a girlfriend."

"Only took you eighteen years," Diesel said with a straight face, making me snort.

"I didn't want a fucking girlfriend until then. I had plenty of girls that kept me entertained."

"Say that in front of Rory. She'll have your balls."

"She already has them in her fucking pocket," I grinned, not giving a shit. Rory could tell me to jump off a cliff and I'd ask her if she wanted me to do a fancy flip on the way down.

Mikey looked over at us and waved his hand. "Daddy! Come 'ere!"

I chuckled as I stood, walking towards him and plonking down on the grass beside him. "What is it, dude?"

"This Poppy!" he exclaimed, pointing at his little friend.

I gave her a smile, hoping her parents didn't mind me talking to her. I knew it was a kid's park, so all parents had a right to be there, but we'd noticed a lot of families didn't like it when one of us spoke to their kids. They always expected a mother to be hanging around, not a father. Marco had been accused of being a kid snatcher when he'd brought Lloyd and Mikey here a month ago and was talking to one of the other kids.

It was ridiculous, and the cops had been called. Luckily, BG had been the one to show up and smoothed it over quickly, letting the worried parents know that the boys were definitely in his care.

The little girl smiled shyly, reaching forward to poke my arm, but she didn't say anything. I hauled Mikey onto my lap, listening to them chatter to each other with amusement. He totally loved her, it was cute.

"Excuse me?"

I glanced up to find a woman standing behind me, uncertainty on her face. "Is this your little boy?"

"Yeah, this is Mikey. I'm not a kidnapper," I joked, luckily making her laugh.

"Good to know. I was wondering if I could give you my number? Poppy always plays with your boy when we're here, and I thought maybe we could set up a playdate with them?"

"Uh, I guess. I'll have to check with my girlfriend," I said slowly, wondering if she was more interested in me than the playdate.

Diesel walked over, his face wary. "Everything okay?"

The woman didn't even blink at his crew jacket or

tattoos. "Yes. My little girl seems to have taken quite a shine to Mikey. I was seeing if we could set up a playdate with them."

"No offense, but our girlfriend will murder us if we take your number," he chuckled.

"You both have the same girlfriend?" she asked, not seeming that bothered.

I nodded, placing Mikey on the ground so I could stand. "Yeah. She's got nine boyfriends." Might as well see if it scares her away.

Her jaw dropped and her eyes widened. "Wait, your girlfriend is Rory?"

"You know her?" I'd never seen her before, so I had no fucking idea who she was.

She shook her head, looking embarrassed. "Oh, no. I've heard about her though. She's the girl who runs that gang."

"She thinks she does," Diesel muttered, but I grinned.

"She helps run it, yeah."

"She's so cool! She's the reason I have three husbands," the woman beamed, and I instantly relaxed. It seemed Rory had a fan club.

"No shit? That's awesome. I'll have to let her know."

"Daddy? Me sleepy," Mikey said as he tugged on my jeans, making me grin as I picked him up.

"You wanna go home and see Mommy?"

"Mommy!" he squealed, throwing himself around in my arms like a wild animal.

The woman chuckled, picking up Poppy. "It's time for your nap too. So, do you think we could meet up with the kids soon?"

"Sure. I'll get Rory to call you," I nodded, pulling my phone out and typing her number into my notes. I had no idea how Rory would react, but she needed to get used to it.

The kids would start making friends, and they'd want to hang out with them sometimes.

Hopefully the woman being her number one fan would help.

Rory

"WHAT DO YOU WANT?" I said with surprise when I opened the door to find Charlie on my doorstep. Of course, Rage was with her.

"Rage is having a meeting with Slash, so I thought I'd come and see you too," she replied. "And by that I mean I had to tag along because I couldn't stay home alone."

"Ah, I see. Come in," I snorted, moving out of the way to let them pass. Charlie was still tiny, despite only being two weeks behind me with her pregnancy. She was only having one baby though, so that helped.

"How have you been?" she asked as she followed me into the kitchen, not hesitating to sit down. I couldn't blame her, my feet ached all the time.

"Ugh, like shit. I can't wait for them to get the fuck out of me," I snorted. "How's your little man?"

"The devil," she grunted, pressing her hands to her ribs. "He's beating me up from the inside, and I'm sick of it."

"Of course he's the devil, look at who his father is," I grinned, earning a scowl from Rage.

"Bitch."

"Asshole," I threw back sweetly. Rage was fun to play with. It was almost a shame we weren't still trying to kill each other.

He chuckled, sitting beside Charlie and putting his arm around her shoulders possessively. "Zane was kicking so hard last night that I swear the little shit almost bruised my face."

"Why was your face near him?" I grinned, my face softening as he smiled.

"I was talking to him. I guess he didn't like me resting my head on him."

"You're kinda nice when you want to be," I said honestly, relieved that he'd taken the idea of parenthood so well. I thought he was going to murder Charlie when she found out he'd knocked her up.

"My niceness only goes as far as Charlie and Zane," he shrugged. "That doesn't extend to anyone else."

I heard the front door close, just as little feet ran into the room. "Mommy! Home!"

"Yes, I can see you're home," I laughed, scooping him up and resting him on my knee. It was a tight fit, but he just liked being held.

Tyler and Diesel walked in, the pair of them looking wary. "What's wrong?"

Tyler shrugged. "Nothing's wrong. Don't cut me off while I explain this, alright?"

"Well, now I'm fucking worried," I scowled. "Just tell me."

Diesel sat down, cradling Angel against his chest as she stared at Rage and drooled.

"A woman at the park approached us and…"

"What did she look like? She thought she'd scope out the hot daddies? Hell no," I snapped, startling Mikey. Tyler rolled his eyes, giving me a flat look.

"I said, don't interrupt."

"You just said…"

"She's the mother of one of Mikey's little friends, Poppy. She wanted to know if we could set up a day for a playdate. Let me finish," he growled as I went to cut him off again. There was no way in hell I was going to let some woman prey on my guys like that. The kids were a pawn in her flirting game, I could see it from a mile away. "We explained we had a girlfriend and would need to organize it with you, and after some talking she realized who you were and fangirled so fucking hard, it was hilarious. She has three husbands because of you."

"Wait, she knows me?"

"She knows *of* you. She thinks you're awesome. So, I got her number, and you can call her to set up a playdate with Poppy and Mikey," he grinned, making me groan.

"I have to attend playdates? If you haven't noticed, I'm not the typical mother figure. I didn't even get invited to the school bake sale like the other moms did." I was pretty sure the school hated dealing with me entirely. One of the older kids punched Lloyd in the playground one day, so I'd had a meeting with his teacher. I guess they didn't like me threatening to beat up the other kid's mom.

"You'd tell them to go and fuck themselves if they asked you to bake a cake," Diesel snorted, making Rage grin.

"I could totally see you showing up with cupcakes and a big smile on your face. You'd probably put weed in it though."

"Bite me. I can bake!" I huffed, but Tyler scoffed.

"No, you can't. You get baked, that's about it." Asshole.

"I'm not good with other moms. They don't like me," I grumbled, glancing at Charlie. "I bet they'd all be too scared to go near you with that beast you insist on keeping."

"Moms love me at our pregnancy and birthing classes. They think it's cool that I have such a protective man in my life," Charlie smirked. "I'm not scary, but you are. You're blunt, opinionated, and you don't play nice."

"Thank you for that wonderful character reference. I'll add it to my resume," I deadpanned.

Slash and Rage vanished to have their meeting, so the rest

of us ended up laying around in the living room watching TV. When it was time for Lloyd to come home, Diesel offered to pick him up so I could rest. I was fucking tired.

The braxton hicks were driving me nuts. Every time I got comfortable, they'd start up and make me shift positions.

Charlie winced as she noticed me shuffling around. "They kicking?"

"Braxton hicks. Have you had them yet?" I sighed, sitting up as best as I could and letting Tyler drop an arm around my shoulders. The guys were all being super clingy, and I tried not to snap at them, but some days I didn't want to be touched at all.

"Yeah, not much though. Rage was sure it was contractions and had to get a good look to make sure I wasn't crowning or anything," she giggled. "He's acting like I won't know the baby's coming out."

"With the way he probably fucks you, I'm surprised you have any nerves left to feel it. Maybe his concerns are valid," I grinned, glancing up as Lexi wandered in. "Hey, didn't know you were coming over."

"Archer's pissing me off. I had to escape," she growled, sitting beside Charlie. "He won't let me do any housework. If I hear the word *rest* one more time, I'll kill him."

"He's only going to get worse the closer to labor you get," Charlie smiled. "He's always been like this with you though, you should have expected it."

"He's an overbearing asshole," she threw back, placing her hand on her small bump. She was five and a half months along, and she made pregnancy look sexy. She always looked good, her skin glowing and her outfits perfect. Then there was me, who was lucky to get dressed because nothing fit. I'd bet money on her never getting stretch marks too.

"Have you guys seen Jade yet?" I asked. "She messaged me earlier and said they're already sending her home."

"I have," Lexi grinned. "Isn't Landon the cutest?"

Charlie pouted. "I haven't. I can't go anywhere without Rage, and Harley politely asked me to wait until they got home. Jade's so tired, she doesn't need the added stress of Rage standing in the tiny ass hospital room with her."

"Tell Rage to go and fuck himself," I offered sweetly. "He can punish you later."

"Sounds good to me," she smirked, imagining all the filthy things he would do to her. I swore, all they did was fuck each other at every opportunity.

"Speaking of Rage, the guys are quiet. Should we make sure they haven't killed each other?" I grunted, noticing how peaceful the house was. Usually when they had meetings, someone was shouting.

"Probably. Can someone help me up?" Charlie chuckled awkwardly, making Tyler grin.

"Yeah, give me a second to help Rory up and I'll help you too."

He stood, taking my hand and pulling me to my feet, making sure I was steady before doing the same for Charlie. "You need a hand, Bryant?"

"I think I'm good," she said, rolling her eyes but smiling.

We all wandered down to the office, finding Slash and Rage leaning over one of their phones, talking quietly amongst themselves. It was fucking weird.

"No one's dead? This is a first," Charlie grinned as she made her way over to Rage, his arm banding around her instantly. His face looked slightly pale, making me grin.

"Something wrong?"

Slash peered over at me, worry filling his eyes. "Uh, we got distracted and decided to google some stuff."

"I wish we hadn't," Rage growled. "I can't unsee it."

"Show me," I demanded, eager to see what had the two big tough guys looking ill. It took a lot to make them uneasy.

Slash shook his head, Shoving his phone into his pocket. "Nope, you're not seeing it. We thought it would be a good idea to watch a birthing video. Please, don't look any up."

Lexi snorted, eyeing them with amusement. "It's not that bad. How do you think us women feel? We're the ones doing all the work while you sit back and complain we broke your hand."

Rage glared at her. "I don't want my girl going through that."

"Bit late now, don't you think?" she threw back, giving Charlie a wide grin. "He's going to be useless. Put me down as your emergency contact so when he faints mid-birth, they can call me to come and support you."

"Maybe you should," Rage grunted, peering down at Charlie and making me snigger. My money was on him passing the fuck out for sure, and it seemed he believed he would too.

"I want to see the video," I said to Slash, turning my attention to him and holding my hand out. "I know it's not pleasant, but how bad…"

"No!" Slash growled. "You've been freaking out since you found out you were pregnant. I'm not letting you see that shit. You'll put yourself into early labor."

"Good, I want these demon spawn out of me. Give me the phone," I ordered. He groaned, running a hand through his hair before digging the phone from his pocket and opening the web browser.

"Don't blame me when you're hyperventilating." *Shit.*

He held it up to me, and my eyes went wide as I saw a head coming out of some lady's poor coochie, the skin tearing slightly in the process. "Why's it taking so long to come out?"

"It's not a fast process," Lexi offered unhelpfully. "Archer and I watched heaps of birthing stuff when we found out we were having a baby. I think it's interesting to watch." There was something fucking wrong with her.

"Take it away!" I exclaimed as the baby's shoulders emerged, my pussy throbbing at the thought, making Slash roll his eyes.

"I fucking told you."

"I'm not doing that!" I choked out. "That looks awful!"

"Well, it's not supposed to be a family fucking picnic," Rage grunted, his eyes still on Charlie. He looked genuinely concerned, and I felt sorry for the nurses when she went into labor. Rage would strangle them over Charlie's pain.

"You can opt for a cesarean, but the healing process is longer. You're a badass bitch, Donovan. You'll be fine," Lexi smiled. "Besides, not all women tear or have long births. You might get lucky."

"I have to do it twice!" I snapped. "There's two in there, remember?!"

She frowned, nodding slowly. "True. Ignore what I just said, you're fucked." *Wonderful.*

Jensen

I'D WORKED the bar for days with Caden and Lukas, giving Harley and Alex some time with their new son. Jade seemed to be coping well, but we didn't want them to feel like they had to rush back to work.

I wanted to kill Slash for showing Rory that birthing video. It had been a week already, and she was still freaking herself out about it. My girl could take on the world, but pushing out a baby was a good reason for her to be afraid. I wouldn't want to do it either.

"Do you think she's going to be okay? With the birth?" Caden murmured as we walked through the front door after a long shift. It was two in the morning, and the house was completely silent.

Lukas nodded, not doubting Rory for a second. "She'll kick ass at it. Just try and keep her calm and focused."

"Have you tried to do that with her before? It doesn't work, so I doubt she'll listen while pushing a melon out of her pussy," Caden cringed. "I'm scared for our safety."

"Don't be a little bitch. If she breaks your hand, just thank her for the gift of life she's giving you and pretend you don't feel the pain. Whatever you do, don't mention it hurts. She'll be hurting a lot more than you ever will," he warned quietly. "Do *not* piss her off."

"I never plan on pissing her off. It just happens," Caden grumbled, placing his keys on the kitchen table and glancing at me. "We're dead, right?"

I grinned. "Yep. We're definitely not getting out of this alive. I love you, brother. I'll see you in the afterlife."

"Drama queens, both of you," Lukas replied dryly, rolling his eyes at us.

Rory wandered in, bags under her eyes and a forced smile. "Hey, how was work?"

"It was good. Why are you awake?" I asked softly, reaching for her and giving her a hug. She sank into me, her voice muffled by my shirt.

"Braxton hicks have kept me awake. I can't get comfortable, so I gave up."

"They're painful?" Lukas asked with a frown. "They're not supposed to be."

"No, they're just annoying. I kept tossing and turning, it was keeping everyone awake," she yawned, making me snort.

"So? Let them sleep like shit too. You want to climb into bed in one of the spare rooms? We'll sleep in there with you,"

I smiled, her pretty blue eyes peering up at me with exhaustion.

"Then I'll keep you awake."

"I don't care. We'll stay awake with you. It's our babies giving you hell," I replied, kissing her forehead and running my palm across her stomach. I didn't realize how active babies could be, it was like they never stopped doing somersaults in there.

Caden gave her a grin, moving in on her other side to kiss her. "Yeah. We'll lay down with you. We can put on a movie if you want?"

She shook her head, stepping into his arms. "I just want to sleep."

"I'll wear you out," he grinned, her eyes narrowing.

"I'm already worn out. I just can't sleep."

"How about a hot bath?" he suggested, but Lukas sighed.

"She can't have it too warm. Her body temperature will go up too much. It can cause her to pass out."

"Let's just go climb into bed and see what happens. You might be able to get some sleep with less people in the bed," I smiled, knowing she'd been feeling a little overcrowded lately. I wasn't surprised, it was hard for her to roll over before she got pregnant due to the amount of bodies in the same bed. So now she was baking two babies, she had zero chance of it being easy.

She followed us up to one of the bedrooms, sliding into bed and ogling us as we stripped down to our boxers. She'd had a pretty good sex drive the entire pregnancy, but she hated how gentle we'd been lately. She wanted a good hard fuck, but we didn't want to hurt her. She was already uncomfortable as it was.

Caden and Lukas laid down on either side of her, leaving me to curl up beside Lukas. We laid there for a few minutes in silence before she spoke.

"I lost my mucus plug the other day."

"The what?" Caden mumbled, making Lukas snort.

"You really haven't listened to anything, have you? Mucus forms in the cervical canal in early pregnancy to help keep bacteria out while the baby's growing. Her body's preparing for labor, so it's normal to lose the plug when you're getting closer to birth."

"Wait, she's in labor?" Caden blurted out, making me chuckle.

"Not yet, her body's preparing for it. He just said that."

"How long does it take after the plug comes out then?"

We'd left the lamp on, so I glared at him across the bed as I propped myself up on my elbow. "We've been told all this."

"It's a lot of information to take in! I can't remember it all!" he groaned.

Rory giggled, surprising me. She didn't like it when we forgot important pregnancy information, but that was probably her hormones talking.

"Any time in the next couple of weeks," she answered, rolling over to face him, her voice going soft. "I'm shitting my pants about it."

He gave her a small smile, tucking her hair behind her ear. "You'll do great. We'll all be there to help you."

"What if I can't do it?" she murmured. "What if…"

"Hush. You'll be amazing, I promise. If you need help, we'll get you into the hospital. Your safety is more important than us seeing the birth, alright? Lukas and Diesel can go in with you for support, and we'll wait outside," he nodded. "It will be okay."

"You'd be okay with not seeing it?" she asked with surprise, making me reach over Lukas and place my hand on her hip, her fingers instantly landing on top of mine to hold.

"Yeah. You can take whoever you want, we won't be upset if we're not picked. We thought maybe Luke and Diesel would be the calmest to go with you though," I explained. "They're the least likely to upset you by accident, too."

"Now we have the birthing plan sorted, can you guys fuck these babies out of me?" she chuckled dryly, "I'm really over my body being used as a boxing ring."

"You feeling needy?" Caden murmured, his eyes lighting up. "We can fix that."

"I'll grab some lube," I grinned, climbing from the bed and heading into the main bedroom, finding Marco and Skeeter awake, their voices low in discussion.

"Sorry, I need lube," I grinned. "Rory wants the kids out asap, so we're going to see if fucking her helps."

Skeeter groaned. "I knew I should have followed her when she left the room."

"Marco will blow you," I threw back, a devious smirk taking over his face.

"He already did."

"Wonderful. If you'll excuse me, I've got babies to evacuate."

"Lucky bastard," Marco grumbled as he tossed me a bottle of lube from the bedside drawer. "Don't give them brain damage."

"I'll try not to," I joked, heading back to the other bedroom to find Rory on her back with Lukas between her legs, his fingers slowly pumping in and out of her as he licked and sucked on her clit.

Caden's face was buried in her neck, his voice low as he whispered naughty things to her. We'd noticed how much she loved dirty talk, so everyone jumped on board with that pretty fast. She went off like a fucking rocket over it.

I climbed onto the bed, her hand instantly going to mine and giving it a squeeze. "Get your boxers off."

"How do you want me?" I grinned. "I don't want to push you with double penetration."

"I don't think it would be very comfortable," she murmured. "Then again, nothing's fucking comfortable."

Lately, we'd toned down the group activities. The positions were limited, and we wanted her to enjoy herself, not be uncomfortable.

I leaned down and gave her a soft kiss. "How about you get on your knees and one of us can fuck you, while another eats your clit? Or, we can all wait our turn if you're comfortable like this."

She closed her eyes, her teeth biting into her lip as Lukas brought her closer to release, my eyes darting between the bliss on her face and the way Lukas ate her. I didn't know which one to look at, I didn't want to miss any of it.

The moment she came, I kissed her, blocking out some of the noise so she didn't wake the kids. The last thing I wanted was them walking in to cock block us.

"Holy shit," she breathed, her eyes unfocused as Lukas sat back, her juices all over his lips and chin. He shuffled closer to me, his lips crashing down on mine to share her taste, making her moan. She loved this shit as much as we did.

I blindly reached for her pussy, not wanting to move away from Lukas' kiss, and I gathered her slickness onto my fingers before meeting Caden's eye and holding them out to him.

He was a team player. He opened his mouth and sucked on my fingers, a groan leaving him as her taste hit his tongue.

"I swear, I'm going to come again," Rory squeaked, watching us with interest. Caden didn't mind joining in with the *gayer* stuff. He didn't care if someone accidentally licked his dick or gave him a kiss. He was straight, and he was comfortable with his sexuality. He knew doing things to make Rory horny wasn't going to make him gay.

A few weeks prior, Rory had blown him and stuck a

finger up his ass to make him come. He didn't give a shit because it felt good.

Rory rolled onto her knees, keeping her weight off her stomach as she parted her legs. "Someone fuck me before I die."

Caden chuckled, pulling my fingers from his mouth and turning to her. "I'm on it."

He positioned himself behind her, not giving a fuck as I laid on my back behind him and scooted my head between his legs, his balls right in my face. We'd been here before, and he'd learned not to dunk them on me on purpose.

It was hard to avoid copping balls to the chin like this, but oh well. They were just balls.

We took it easy on her, taking it slow to avoid hurting her. She came once with my mouth on her clit while Caden slowly moved in and out of her pussy, then she decided she was uncomfortable and had to lay on her side.

Caden laid down behind her, continuing to fuck her slowly, and once he was finished, he moved out of the way for me to take his place.

I went a little harder, her pussy clamping around my dick with appreciation as she moaned. "Harder, Jense."

"You sure?"

"Please. I'm close," she murmured, her hand fisting the bed sheets as I went a bit faster and deeper. She tightened around me, my hand resting on her lower stomach as she tensed.

"That's right, baby. Come on my dick," I whispered, making her cry out as her pussy clamped down around me, probably waking the others. I slowed my strokes, giving her a moment to recover before picking up the pace again so I could finish too.

When I pulled out, Lukas groaned, watching mine and

Caden's come leaking from her swollen pussy. "Fuck, that's hot."

She let out a light laugh, fatigue filling her tone. "You'd better be quick, Luke. I'm going to fall asleep on you otherwise."

He sat in front of her, leaning down to kiss her forehead. "Then sleep. I can have you another time."

"You sure?" she mumbled, her eyelids drooping and making him smile, affection filling his eyes as he brushed her hair from her face.

"Positive. If my balls get blue, I'll make Jense choke on my dick."

She giggled sleepily, not arguing as she finally fell asleep, making Caden grin. "Well, that was easy. The guys should have fucked her sooner."

We got back into bed, making sure not to wake her, but she was out like a light.

Mission accomplished.

CHAPTER THIRTEEN

RORY

I slept like a log, not waking up until lunch time somehow. The kids had all gone to Josie's for the day, giving me some much needed sleep. That's what the text on my phone from Caden said, anyway.

"Morning, Princess," Marco smiled warmly as I made my way into the living room, finding the guys all lounging around watching TV. Skeeter and Hunter were missing, but everyone else was home for once.

"What's going on?" I asked, glancing around the room. "Why's everyone here?"

"Lazy day. Thought we'd stay home with you," he replied, shuffling over on the couch so I could sit between him and Tyler. Tyler instantly gave me a kiss, leaning down to kiss my stomach too.

"How'd you sleep?" he asked me, glancing at Caden with a grin. "I heard the guys knocked you the fuck out."

I chuckled, wincing as I copped a foot to my bladder. "I slept alright once I got to sleep. It was after four in the fucking morning."

"No wonder you slept late. Jade and the guys are coming over for a visit."

"I look like shit," I groaned. "Should I go and shower and..."

"Don't even bother. She knows what it's like to want to be lazy," Marco murmured, his eyes lighting up as we heard the front door open. "Landon's here!"

I couldn't wait to see him with his own kid in his arms.

Jade walked in with the guys behind her, all wearing matching exhausted expressions. Landon was asleep in Alex's arms, and he walked straight over to Marco and offered him the bundled up baby. "Here you go, baby daddy number three. Your shift starts now."

"You're funny," I snorted, but Marco eagerly took him into his arms and laid him on his chest.

Jade sat on the couch, wincing in the process. "I hope my pussy gets back to normal soon. This sucks," she grumbled, shifting to take the pressure off. Harley sat beside her, resting a hand on her thigh.

I cringed. "How bad was the damage?"

"Minimal. I didn't tear, luckily. It's really uncomfortable to sit down though," she sighed. "I'm bleeding a bit still, so I've been living in these sexy adult diapers."

"I can't wait for those," I mumbled sarcastically, hoping I healed fast. I doubted it. Two babies would ruin my pussy forever.

Jade filled me in on her fun labor, apparently threatening to murder Alex and Harley if they ever touched her again. They didn't find it funny, they'd been terrified at the time, much to the nurse's amusement.

I excused myself after an hour, needing to pee before one of the babies kicked me in the bladder again. I only got half way down the hallway before I felt liquid fill my panties and soaked into my sweats, making me groan. "Seriously? I'm at the stage where I piss myself now?"

I went to get changed, my braxton hicks feeling a little harsher and making me wince. "Can't something not hurt for five minutes?"

"You okay?" Diesel asked as he walked into the bedroom, frowning when he noticed my wet pants sitting on the floor. "What happened?"

"I pissed myself," I grunted with embarrassment. "Leave me alone to wallow in it."

"It happens. I've felt how hard those fuckers kick in there. I'd piss myself too," he said kindly, sitting on the edge of the bed to watch me put fresh pants on once I'd quickly wiped myself down in the bathroom with a damp cloth. I struggled, but he knew better than to help me until I'd asked. I wasn't an invalid.

My next braxton hick made my back ache slightly, and I reached around to rub my hand over it. "Fuck, these are starting to hurt a little."

"I didn't think braxton hicks hurt?" he asked with worry, running his eyes over me. "Shit, you didn't piss yourself, babe. Your water broke."

"I still have three weeks to go," I said with panic, and he was instantly on his feet, moving in front of me to take my face in his hands.

"It's okay. The doctor said they can come early, remember? They've probably run out of space in there, that's all."

"I can't have them right now! I'm not ready!" I exclaimed, his calm eyes holding my gaze.

"You're ready. You could have contractions all day before going into active labor. Don't panic, make yourself comfortable, and let me know if they start getting more frequent, alright?"

"Do I lie down? Or sit on the couch? I don't..." I couldn't

remember shit that the doctor told me. Not while I was freaking out.

"Whatever makes you most comfortable. Like I said, you could have contractions on and off through the day, so for now, try and relax. Would you like to stay in here?" he asked. "Or we can sit back in the living room with the others."

"Living room," I nodded. "Jade will be able to tell me when to start worrying."

"No worrying. You'll be fine," he smiled, giving me a kiss before leading me back downstairs, everyone's eyes going to me. *How long was I gone?*

"My water broke," I blurted out, looking straight at Jade. "What did you do? Did you sit down? Or lay down? When do I call someone for help?"

She looked so fucking excited for me. "I watched movies for hours and paced. Everyone's different though. Are you getting contractions?"

"A couple small ones, but nothing too bad. When does it get worse?" I asked, not liking the feeling of being out of control. I had no idea how long this could go on for, or what pain I was going to feel.

"It depends on the person. Again, everyone's different. When they start getting stronger and closer together, that's when you're closer to needing to push. When they're about 4 or 5 minutes apart, call your doctor and he'll come straight out. If you call them now, they'll tell you to wait anyway."

"I need to call Skeet and Hunter. Shit, what if they miss it?" I panicked, allowing Lukas to take my hand and gently tug me towards the couch to sit down.

"We'll call them, you have plenty of time. Relax," he soothed, glancing at Slash who instantly took his phone from his pocket and left the room to call them.

I tried to relax, I really did, but my mind was racing at all the things that could go wrong.

"Donovan, breathe," Jade said gently as she got to her feet and sat beside me carefully, not wanting to hurt herself. "You need to calm down or you'll put stress on the babies."

I nodded, trying to focus on my breathing, knowing she was right.

Slash wandered back in, sitting in his spot on the couch. "They're on their way."

Everyone was watching me nervously, making me realize I wasn't doing well at calming down.

The moment I heard the front door slam about ten minutes later, relief rolled through me. I needed them all there to help get me through it. Skeeter and Hunter skidded into the room, and Skeeter instantly knelt in front of me, taking my hand.

"How do you feel? Do you need anything?"

I shook my head, wincing as I felt another contraction. It felt like it was in my fucking back, and no amount of stretching would relieve it. "I just needed you guys here."

"We're not going anywhere, baby girl," he promised, giving my hand a gentle squeeze.

I had a feeling it was going to be a long day.

"WHAT DO YOU MEAN, he's not answering the fucking phone?!" I snapped, fear taking over as I stared at Skeeter. He was fighting to stay calm, trying not to yell back at me. I would have appreciated it if I wasn't so focused on the pain moving through my body.

"I've called him ten times. He won't answer."

"I can't deliver them without a fucking doctor!"

"We'll call around and see if someone else can come over. You focus on yourself, and we'll…"

"Fuck you! Call him again!" I demanded, leaning against

the kitchen counter as a strong contraction washed through me, causing me to grit my teeth. They were close together, so I knew we were running out of time.

"I'm trying, Aurora," he growled. "I can't make him answer in any other way than what I'm already doing."

"Try fucking harder!"

His jaw clenched, but I could see he wasn't angry with me, he was scared. No one had medical knowledge about assisting with childbirth here, so I couldn't blame him. His fear seeped into me, fuelling my panic even more.

"I know basic delivery stuff," Jade offered, making me glance over at her as she walked into the room with rubber gloves in her hands. "Skeet can keep trying the doctor, and I'll help you in the meantime."

"You've never delivered a fucking baby before," I snorted, but she shrugged.

"I know enough. What to look out for with trauma signs and small stuff like that. I've watched a lot of videos and…"

"Alright, Dr. Google. What the fuck do we do?" I barked, wincing as another contraction hit me. Someone's hands started rubbing my back, making me tense. "Don't fucking touch me!"

Caden took a step back, an unsure look on his face. "Sorry, I thought it would help."

"You know what would help? If one of you fuckers hadn't knocked me up in the first place!" I spat, considering punching them all in the face. Repetitively.

Most of the guys were smart enough to stay in the living room, not wanting to piss me off further, but wanting to be close in case I needed them. I wished Skeeter and Caden would do the same.

"Donovan? Come and lie down. I need to see what's going on up there," Jade said gently, making me scowl.

"Armageddon. That's what's going on up there."

She was struggling not to laugh at me. I could fucking sense it.

"I need to see if you're dilated."

"I don't want your hand up my fucking cunt," I hissed, but she kept calm and gave me a small smile.

"I know, but if you start pushing when you're not ready, you can cause harm to yourself and the babies."

I didn't like the pressure I felt down below, and I shook my head. "Nope, I've got to shit. I can't…"

"Chances are high it's the baby. I thought I had to take a shit too," Jade chuckled. "Let me look, please?"

"Okay, but you're responsible for your own trauma down there," I grunted, gingerly moving into the living room to lay back on the couch while she went to wash her hands. I didn't give a fuck if I wrecked the fancy couch, I'd buy a new one. If I laid down on the floor, I wouldn't be able to get back up, and I wasn't game enough to tackle the stairs to the bedrooms.

Harley and Alex took Landon into the kitchen, thankfully giving me privacy. Josie had said she'd keep the kids overnight, so we didn't have to worry about them coming home to this mess.

Jade hooked her fingers under the elastic of my pants, carefully pulling them down and leaving me exposed. "Part your legs for me."

Another contraction hit, and I grunted at the intensity of it. "I think I need to push. How do I know when to do that? I want to push."

"Give me a second and I'll tell you," Jade murmured and put the gloves on as Lukas bravely squatted beside me, giving me his hand.

"I've got you," he said firmly, some of my fear fading.

"Promise?"

"I promise. I'll be right here," he nodded, not flinching

when I gripped his hand so tight I heard his knuckles pop. I definitely broke something.

"Uh, babe?" Jade said from between my legs, just as I felt her fingers violate me. "You were right. It's time to push."

"How do you know?" I panted, trying to breathe through contractions as the pressure down below got worse.

"You're fully dilated, you're starting to crown."

"I don't want to do this. Luke, I can't…," I said weakly, but he cut me off.

"You can do anything you set your mind to. You're stubborn, remember?" he chuckled. "Do you want a drink?"

"No! I want this fucking devil child and their evil twin to get the fuck out of my body!" I snapped, but he wasn't fazed.

"I know, not long now, baby."

I went to push, but Jade stopped me. "Wait a second. Use the contractions, babe."

"I need to move. I can't lay down," I groaned, my back aching. "Can I move around?"

"You can give birth standing up if it's more comfortable," she nodded, moving away to help me to my feet.

Lukas stood beside me, letting me lean on him as another contraction started to sweep through me. "Breathe through it."

"You won't be breathing at all in a minute!" I practically screamed. "You're all fucking dead when I get my fucking hands on you!"

Lukas ignored my outburst though. "Skeet? Grab some of the heated towels. And a cool damp cloth."

Skeeter took off to do as he was told, probably more than happy to escape me for five minutes. Hunter fetched me a glass of water, holding it for me to sip as I recovered from the contraction. "You're doing good, Hot Shot."

"I've changed my mind, I want the hospital and all the drugs," I insisted, but Jade cringed.

"You don't have time for that. You literally have a head coming out."

"Well put it back in and let's go!" I cried. "I can't fucking do this!"

Lukas took my hand, letting me squeeze it again. "Yes, you can. You want to lean on me? Put all your weight on me and bear down when Jade tells you to. You've got this, babe."

"No, I don't! It fucking hurts and I haven't even started pushing yet!" I exclaimed, glaring at the guys who stood back from me. "And all these useless cunts don't give a shit!"

"They do, you asked them to leave you alone," he said gently. "Now, hold onto me."

I did as he said, gripping onto him and hoping it would be over soon. I definitely wasn't doing this again.

I had no idea what Jade was doing behind me, but I stopped giving a shit. If she was going to be the person to take charge and get these fucking babies out of me, she could do what ever she wanted.

This time when a contraction rolled through me, Jade spoke firmly. "Okay, push."

I bore down, stopping when I felt like I was going to shit myself. "Nope, I'm going to shit myself."

"It doesn't matter. Lots of women shit themselves while giving birth. It's normal," she explained, but horror filled me with that knowledge.

"I'm not going to shit myself in front of everyone!"

"Yeah, you probably are. I shit myself too, but I was laying down. Trust me, no one cares if you do."

Skeeter jogged back in, making me snarl. "Took your fucking time!"

"The towel warmer was off! I tried!" he threw back, stepping towards me and narrowly dodging my fist.

"Get away from me! This is your fault!"

"How the fuck do you know it's my fault? I bet it was

Rivera or Ortega," he growled. "This has their names written all over it."

"Like fuck, you dick head. I bet it's you! You're an over-achieving piece of shit! You've got to be the best at every-thing!" I shouted, trying to lunge at him but another contraction hit me like a fucking train. "Mother fucker!"

Skeeter looked like a deer in the headlights, pain filling his face at knowing he couldn't make it stop hurting.

Jade snatched a towel from him, not putting up with our arguing. "Push, Rory. The head's almost out."

I parted my legs more, pushing and trying to remember to breathe. It was fucking hard.

"That's good, baby. Keep going," Lukas murmured, peering over his shoulder to glare at the guys. "Can one of you get her the damp cloth?"

Skeeter cursed, but Jensen took off to grab it for me, returning seconds later. He approached me slowly, only placing the cloth against my hot skin when he knew I wasn't going to maul him to death. It felt good as he pressed it against my forehead, moving it around my neck to cool me down.

"I'll need medical scissors," Jade instructed, fear spiking in me.

"The fuck for? You're not cutting my vagina open!"

"It's for the umbilical cord, not your pussy," she said calmly, snapping her fingers at the guys. "Are you listening? Medical scissors."

Marco darted from the room, running back in with the scissors when he heard me crying out in pain as I pushed more.

"The head's out!" Jade beamed, celebrating way too early for my liking.

I cursed the guys out as they got closer, but I grabbed onto Skeeter's hand when he was close enough, needing to pull strength from him. He stepped closer, taking some of my weight from Lukas and allowing me to turn slightly so Jade could get a better look.

Jade grabbed a towel in her hand, giving me a grin. "Once the shoulders are out, it's practically over. You're doing so good."

"Then I have to do it again!" I snapped, almost breaking Lukas and Skeeter's hands as I pushed again. I definitely shit on the floor.

"Breathe, baby girl," Skeeter murmured, and he was lucky I didn't hit him.

"On your next contraction, give me one big push," Jade encouraged. "They're almost here."

I gripped the guys' hands, and the moment I was ready to push, I pushed hard.

I felt the relief as the first baby finally squeezed out of me, landing on the towel Jade held in her hands.

"You've got yourself a boy!" she exclaimed, holding him up so I could get a look at him. He was fucking perfect. He let out a broken squawk, warmth filling my chest.

"Why isn't the other one coming out?" I murmured, suddenly realizing I didn't feel the need to push again. My legs were tired, so Skeeter and Lukas helped me lay down on the couch as Jade followed close with the baby. She clamped and cut the umbilical cord, but I forgot all about everything else as she cut down the center of my shirt, completely exposing my chest before placing the little boy on my skin, covering him with a towel.

"Skin on skin is important. Keep him warm. The other one is still coming. They can take another twenty minutes to come out," she said, making me groan.

"I'm fucking tired."

"They can be quicker. If you're getting tired, stay laying down. Hopefully this one's easier," she said with a small smile. It wasn't though. It took forever for baby number two to grace us with their presence, and I hated that I had to hand over our little boy once I needed to push again. Marco took him, holding him against his bare chest and keeping him warm while the others kept encouraging me to push.

Finally, it was over.

"It's a girl!"

Skeeter

I STARED at Rory in awe as she slept. She'd been in labor all day, and after the doctor finally answered his fucking phone and came to check on her and the babies, she was out like a light. Both babies were fed and sleeping in the bassinet beside the bed, and I couldn't take my damn eyes off them.

Now that they were cleaned up and a few hours old, there was no denying it. They were totally mine.

An arm slipped around my waist, and I turned to find Marco leaning into me. "How's she doing?" he murmured, making me smile.

"Still sleeping."

"You know they look like you, right? They have your nose and lips," he chuckled, kissing my shoulder. "She's going to murder you."

"Nah, they're cute as fuck. She can't be mad at me," I grinned, glancing over at Lukas who was sitting in the chair in the corner, his eyes never leaving Rory. He'd been amazing with her, not letting his emotions get in the way and making sure she was okay. The rest of us were fucking hopeless.

"Did she mention names?" I asked no one in particular, causing Lukas to look up at me.

"No. She's been pretty quiet about the names she really likes. We never agreed on any."

"We'll have to discuss it when she wakes up," I nodded, walking over to the bassinet to get a better look. They had black hair, just like their mother, but their faces were totally mine. I put my finger closer to them, my heart tightening with happiness as one of them wrapped their tiny hands around it in their sleep.

"C'mon, we need to leave so they can all rest," Marco whispered, earning the stink eye from both Lukas and I. We weren't going anywhere.

Rory stirred, seeming to panic when her eyes opened. "Where are they?"

"They're right here, baby girl," I promised, drawing her attention to me. "You can rest some more."

She carefully climbed out of bed, ignoring Lukas' request to get back in as she stood beside me. "I'm going to fucking kill you," she warned, but there was no heat behind it.

"Yeah, I figured. Can it wait a while? I want to watch them for a bit first," I grinned, her eyes softening.

"Did you guys have names picked?"

"We were just wondering if you did," I shrugged, placing an arm around her shoulders and kissing the top of her head. She smelled like my body wash. She'd been given the all clear medically, and the first thing she did was have a shower before passing out.

She sighed. "I had one picked, but it's stupid."

"I doubt that. Tell me," I encouraged, wanting to hear what she'd come up with.

"I want to call the girl Beckett."

"Beckett Donovan, I assume?" I smiled, her eyes going wide.

"Uh, how will we figure out the last name? We..."

"She's going to be one tough girl like her mother. I think she should be a Donovan," I chuckled, her eyes filling with tears.

"You mean that? She can have my last name?"

"Of course. Her name would be too long if we threw all our names in," I joked, but I could see how much it had meant to her. "Beckett Aurora Donovan sound's perfect."

"I have a name I want to throw in," Marco grinned. "Hunter, Jense, and I came up with it."

"Spit it out then," I grunted, making Rory chuckle. "We don't have all night."

"Ryder. We really like that name," he nodded, making Rory glance back at the babies.

"Beckett and Ryder Donovan," she hummed in thought, but we could tell by the way her eyes lit up that she loved them.

No matter what, I'd protect those kids with my fucking life. They'd never want for anything, and nothing would hurt them. Between me and their eight other daddies? They'd be the happiest kids in the world.

CHAPTER FOURTEEN

THREE MONTHS LATER

Rory

*B*eckett and Ryder had screamed all fucking day. I'd hardly had any sleep since they'd been born, but I wouldn't change it for the world. Luckily, they had nine daddies who were more than happy to stay awake all night and take shifts so each of us got at least a little sleep.

All our nerves were shot to shit. Between dealing with Lloyd getting in trouble at school, Mikey becoming clingy as fuck, Angel teething, and the twins being awake all the time, we were a fucking mess.

We'd just gotten the twins to sleep, and Sarah had taken the other kids out to the park with Tyler to have a playdate with Poppy. The house was quiet, which was absolute bliss.

Skeeter was practically asleep on his feet, leaning against the kitchen counter as I sat in one of the chairs sipping coffee. I heard the toaster pop, two seconds before a gunshot scared the fucking shit out of me.

I glared over at Skeeter to find a sheepish look on his face and a fucking hole shot through the toaster that was now laying dead on the floor. "Uh, sorry?"

Crying started upstairs from the loud noise, and I gave Skeeter a shove as I stood and walked past him. "I know the toast is scary and dangerous, but couldn't you have tried to negotiate with it before its execution?"

"It was an accident! My nerves are fucked and I'm tired, sue me!" he called after me, and he was lucky I'd already left the room, or I would have punched him. He couldn't complain about being tired, he'd gotten more sleep than me lately.

I wandered into the nursery, reaching into the bassinet to lift Beckett into my arm, managing to grab Ryder with my other arm and carrying them both downstairs.

Marco took Ryder from me the moment I walked into the living room, a tired smile on his face. "Want me to kill Skeet?"

"Yes, please," I grumbled, trying to comfort Beckett as she continued to scream. Skeeter cringed as he joined us, holding his hands out for Beckett.

"I've got her. You go and rest."

I wanted to argue with him, but what was the point? Besides, Beckett always settled quicker with Skeeter.

I handed her over, watching them as Skeeter murmured quiet words to her, causing her loud screams to turn into small cries. Before long, she was silent. Without his sister crying, Ryder settled too, making me breathe out a sigh of relief.

"You know these are the only kids I'm ever birthing, right? We're never doing this again."

Marco grunted. "Angel made babies seem easy. She was so quiet."

"I bet she becomes a little terror when she's older," I muttered, thinking about all the trouble Lloyd had been getting in. Fights in the playground, taking a knife to school, and back talking in class. We had no idea why he was acting out so much, but we put it down to his trauma catching up with him from when he'd been kidnapped. He was getting therapy, but I refused to medicate him. He'd learn to control his emotions eventually.

"Hey, Lex and Charlie are on the way over," Hunter said as he wandered into the room, tucking me under his arm and kissing me.

"Without Hendricks and Rage?" I scoffed. "I don't believe you."

"I never said that," he chuckled. "They're coming too."

"It scares me that they're getting along," Skeeter grumbled, making me grin. I wouldn't say Rage and Archer had become best friends, but they seemed to be spending a lot of time together lately. Archer was one proud uncle, and he spent time with his nephew, Zane, every chance he got. I was surprised he had the energy to make so much time for him because Lexi had given birth two weeks earlier and their little girl, Tempest, had a good set of lungs on her.

Both Charlie and Lexi were insane. They were counting down the days until they could try for their second baby. Fuck that.

The guys managed to put Beckett and Ryder back down for a nap not long before the girls arrived, but I knew it wouldn't last. Not with Tempest screaming the house down from the moment they walked through the door.

I glanced at Lexi as she tried to get Tempest to feed, but the kid was too focused on the task at hand of making sure my entire household was awake. At least Zane was content to just nap. He looked tiny in Rage's arms.

"Where are all your kids?" Charlie asked as she sat beside me on the couch.

"The twins are napping, if Tempest doesn't wake them up,

and the others are having a playdate with Poppy," I smiled, glad they were making friends. Lloyd was probably beating some kid up on the slide, but that was Tyler and Sarah's problem.

It was like the second we signed the adoption papers, Lloyd flipped a switch and became a different kid. He was respectful to us, but to others? Not so much.

He didn't like being left at home when we went out to do crew business, and I'd caught him following us to the shed before. The little fucker stole my damn Ferarri.

He'd made a few friends at school that seemed to be trouble, but their parents were shit scared of me, so they kept an eye on Lloyd whenever he was at their houses after school.

Surprisingly, I'd been invited to multiple playdates by some of the parents, probably so they could gossip about me the moment I left. People loved seeing me up close, it was like a fucking exhibit for them. I'd only threatened one mother, but that was because she made a joke about wanting to fuck Skeeter. She didn't make another joke after that.

"While we're here, I've heard that there's been another crew sniffing around," I said dryly, making everyone's heads swivel towards me.

Skeeter scowled. "You didn't think to bring this up earlier? When did you hear that?"

"When I visited Kat last week. She said some of the girls have mentioned another crew that she hadn't heard about before," I shrugged. "Hell's Demons or some shit."

Archer snorted. "No way in fucking hell. I slayed their entire crew years ago when that fucker tried to take Lexi from me. Justin Lopez is as dead as a dodo, and no one would try to repair that crew."

"Well, someone's using their name. Kat doesn't make shit up, and she wouldn't tell me if she wasn't sure. Maybe it's just gossip," I sighed. "I don't like the risk of someone trying to take over everything we've built, so if it's true, we need to do something about it."

"Not possible. There was no one left," Archer said, shaking his head. "Wet Dreams was a fucking blood bath. The Demons didn't get out alive."

"That doesn't mean someone hasn't stepped up to reclaim their legacy. Maybe one of their kids has grown and wants to take back what they think is theirs? Either way, it's only talk through the prison system, so I don't think we should worry, but we should definitely be aware."

Lexi groaned, Tempest finally feeding silently and giving my brain a rest from the screaming. "Some of them had older kids. The Demons didn't play by the rules, and that was their downfall. Maybe an angry wife or something has decided to take charge? It's not unusual for women to get involved these days. Rory set a new trend," she said, giving me a grin.

A lot of crews had opened up to women, but I didn't think any of it had a single thing to do with me. Sure, I'd been one of the first women to become accepted into a crew, but it wasn't unheard of that they ruled in other areas. There were all women crews that had started coming out of nowhere, too.

"You might be right. What if the wives have all come together to get revenge or something? Do we worry, or do we let them take Hendricks and call it a day?" I smirked, making Lexi scowl.

"You're not using my husband like that."

"Why not? It sounds like it's his fault. Should have gunned down all their connections too if you wanted to wipe them from existence," I shrugged.

Archer glowered at me, crossing his arms. "I wasn't going to murder a bunch of women and their children. The Demons were dealt with because of Justin's stupidity. It's his fucking fault. We all lived peacefully until he wanted Lexi."

Hunter rolled his eyes and pulled his phone from his pocket. "They were bad news. I think Hendricks did the right thing in getting rid of them. I'm going to call Axel and see if he wants to join this meeting. He doesn't like them either."

"Has everyone except me dealt with these guys before?" I demanded as he left the room, making Rage snort.

"You didn't start causing trouble until after the Demons were killed. Trust me, the moment I heard about you, I was straight on to trying to get rid of you," he explained, making me smile sweetly.

"Aw, thank you for that wonderful story. It's a shame it never got its ending. I'd go back to jail for killing you any day."

"You're full of shit, Donovan. You won't leave all those damn kids behind. We can test it if you like? I say we do an old western shoot-out on main street," he grinned. "I'll let you pick your own coffin first."

"You guys suck," Charlie groaned. "Can't you just be nice?"

"No," we both replied, making her roll her eyes.

"I'm waiting for the day you actually succeed. Then I'll have to kill whoever lives."

"I'll be waiting for you. I'll be the one standing above your dead husband."

She grumbled about us being assholes as Hunter wandered back in.

"Axel's on his way. He heard something about the Demons being back too."

"We should have called this meeting ages ago," Slash grumbled, but Skeeter shrugged.

"We should do a lot of things. Doesn't mean we will. I don't like all these crews in my house, to be honest. This is becoming a common occurrence."

"You have the biggest home out of all of us. We won't all fit into mine," Archer scoffed, and Rage grinned.

"Mine either. I guess we'd better make ourselves at home."

"Haven't you rebuilt at the docks yet, Hendricks? I heard that's going to be spacey," Skeeter stated bluntly. After Lexi, Jade and I had burned down Archer's boathouse, they'd been living in one of the Reaper's safe houses. It wasn't really safe now, everyone knew they lived there, but he'd always wanted to rebuild at the docks. It was where his business was for starters, but it had always been his home.

Archer gave him a dirty look. "I'm building a small crew house. It's for the Reapers to use like how you guys have the shed, and the Devils have the warehouse. We don't go near your establishments, so stay away from mine."

"Touchy," I grinned, glancing up as the rest of my guys joined us. Lukas wasn't bothered by the pending argument in the room, giving me a kiss and sitting on the couch.

"It's tense in here. If anyone wants to start shooting, do it outside."

"Wow, got a new boss?" Rage chuckled, giving him a dark smile. "You want to play with the big boys, Lukas? It's about time. You've always been a little bitch."

"How'd you cope with Charlie's birth, Rage?" Lukas asked dryly. "I heard you fainted."

I sniggered. "Yeah, Angry Man. I heard that too."

"I didn't fucking faint. I just got a little light headed," he gritted out, trying not to yell and wake Zane. It was hilarious to see him having to keep control of his temper. He always had the damn baby in his arms, so he couldn't throw punches for the sake of it anymore. Rage was a really good father, and that was one thing I couldn't talk badly about. His kids would either be the cool kids at school, or the kids that were treated like the plague because they had a scary dad.

We chatted amongst ourselves until Axel showed up, and he filled us in on what he'd heard.

Archer scrunched his face up, now sitting beside Lexi, proving a point that Axel couldn't have her. It was ridiculous between them. Axel respected their marriage, and he wasn't going to try and steal someone who didn't want him. Lexi loved Axel as a friend, but that was it. Sadly, their friendship was now tarnished due to the pissing contest Archer and Axel kept having.

"You believe they're back? Have they tried to reach out to you? Razor and Lopez were pretty close," Archer stated, making me roll my eyes. Of course they were friends. Razor was a piece of fucking shit, so it sounded like him and Lopez were a match made in heaven.

"I haven't heard from them personally, I would have told you if I had," Axel grunted with annoyance. "I might not like you, but I'm not stupid. If a crew like that tries to take over, I'll be standing beside you to push them back out."

"I might throw you in front of me as a shield," Archer growled, scowling as Lexi slapped his arm. I wasn't going to put up with one of their arguments when we had more important shit to discuss.

"So, back to the Demons. Have you just heard gossip, or have you seen something?" I asked, turning the conversation back to business. "We can't have them hanging around, thinking they can take over. We all have our own businesses to run, and we've all learned to play nice together. We don't want to end up with war on the doorstep again. There's too many damn kids involved now."

Axel sighed, running a hand through his hair. "Just talk so far. You know how most of my crew live outside of town?" I nodded, waiting for him to continue. "Two were approached by someone three days ago, asking about our connections and if we'd be interested in partnering up with a new dealer on the block. My guys told them to fuck off and thought that would be the end of it."

"You just fucking said you hadn't heard from them!" Archer barked, but Axel snorted.

"Yeah, and I'm not lying. My guys thought it was some try-hard gangster trying to make a quick buck, so they shooed them away and didn't tell me shit. Until this morning when one of my fucking pill dealers showed up dead."

"You think it's the Demons?" Archer asked, his voice strained. "I don't want to deal with those fuckers again. They were cunts to get rid of last time."

Axel glanced at me, his voice low. "Have you seen the Demon's symbol? Or their calling card?"

I groaned. "Why would I have seen those? I wasn't part of this shit until they were gone, remember?"

He looked at Slash, and I knew it was going to be bad when his face scrunched up with frustration. "My dealer was left without his damn head. He had a bloodied cross carved into his chest."

"Sure it wasn't Angry Man over here? Sounds like something he does in his spare time," I grinned, but Rage scowled.

"The Demons have always been unhinged. They like to play mind games and don't have a pattern, other than that calling card. I haven't seen it since before the massacre, so unless someone's impersonating them, we might possibly have ourselves a rival crew problem."

"Nope, it still sounds like you. Where were you between the hours of…" I started, but Skeeter interrupted me.

"Donovan, not now." *Oh, no one was in a good mood now.*

"Sorry. I just find it hard to believe that there's worse people than Rage and the Shadow Kings out there," I shrugged, earning a disgusted look from Rage.

"I never once said they were worse than me."

"You sound scared of them."

"I'm not fucking scared of them!" he growled, passing Zane over to Charlie. "They're a major pain in the ass, that's all. They're messy little fuckers, too. They never clean up after themselves."

"Aren't they the crew who Archer said was small and useless?" I frowned. "I feel like I remember having a conversation about this."

Archer nodded. "I've said that, yes. They were a small crew, stupid as shit too because they never planned anything, they just rolled with whatever mayhem was created. I don't think they were that difficult to deal with, they were just annoying. But, if someone's coming after us to avenge the fallen members? We might have a problem. If this is their first message to us, I'd hate to see what else happens if we aren't careful."

"What if they're actually dangerous? Should we run this past our crews and form a plan?" I sighed. "I'm too tired for this shit."

Everyone mumbled their agreement, and I couldn't help but wonder who the fuck was really behind the attack on the dealer. Hopefully they'd fuck off and we'd never know.

THE WORST THING happened to me the next week. It was worse than the Demons causing trouble.

"No, no, no! Not again!" I begged the universe as I stared at my doctor in horror. She was finding this shit fucking hilarious. She'd become a good friend of mine since I'd found out about being pregnant with the twins, and she had no issue being blunt.

"Yes, again. I told you how easily it was to get knocked up while your body was still healing. I did try and convince you to get the implant in your arm, remember?" she chuckled, making me scowl.

"I thought you were just testing my blood for iron deficiency and shit. Why'd you go and ruin it with a pregnancy test?" I demanded, probably loud enough for the people in the front office to hear.

"I gave you a list of all the things I was testing for. You signed to state you read it," she deadpanned. "You're five weeks, by the way."

"I can't do that shit again. Fuck, I'm not coping with the twins! They don't sleep, they've sucked my tits dry, and the only time they actually decide to nap, is when I need to take them somewhere," I groaned. "It has to be a mistake."

"I promise you, it's not a mistake. Maybe you should have been more careful? Just because you needed to wait eight weeks to have sex so you could heal, that didn't mean your body wouldn't latch onto any sperm you decided to shove up it. You must have waited until eight weeks to the day. It's only been thirteen weeks since you had the twins." If her boss heard her speaking to me like that, they'd fire her. Not that I'd let that happen.

She'd spent multiple times at our place for dinner, and she'd been helping Jade with more medical practice on the side.

"I'm aware, Pam," I snapped, dread pooling in my stomach. The guys were going to freak when I told them. "Fuck, what if it's twins again?"

"Go home and tell those hunks of yours the good news. I bet they'll be excited," she suggested, making me snort.

"They agreed we wouldn't have any more. I swear to God, if this one's Skeeter's too, I'm going to bury him in the backyard."

She raised an eyebrow, leaning back in her chair. "You know he's the father of the twins?"

"They look just like him. Little devil spawns pretending to be angels," I grunted. "All the guys say he's the father."

"And what do they think about that? Does it bother them?"

"How'd this turn into a shrink appointment?" I scowled. "But they don't care. They're raising them, so they're all their fathers. We don't want to see proof, but it's hard to ignore what's right in front of us. They're definitely Skeet's. Beckett's such a daddy's girl, too. He's the only one who can get her to calm down usually."

"They'll settle eventually. It's hard getting twins into a routine sometimes because they keep each other awake. Maybe separate them at bed time?" she offered. "It can stop them waking the other up by crying."

"We tried that, it was worse. They got separation anxiety or something. We don't like splitting them up to sleep, but we have them in separate bassinets now. They kept bumping each other at night, then screaming the house down."

She looked thoughtful for a second before smiling. "Have you tried wrapping them up so their arms aren't flailing around? Pretty sure I suggested that a while ago."

I shrugged. We'd thought about it, but I felt like it was going to be too tight and hurt them. They were tiny, so I was worried I'd do it wrong. "I was worried it would hurt them."

"Girl, you need to go to some parenting classes. You'd learn the right way to do things without worrying yourself into the damn ground," she scolded, amusing me slightly. We'd argued about parenting classes multiple times. I'd tried once, but one of the dads had hit on me. Lukas tried to start a fight with him over it, so we stopped going for everyone's sake.

"Have you seen me? I freak people out when I walk into a room. Especially one that has innocent babies in it," I grumbled. "I'll watch some youtube videos and see if I can learn something."

"Good. For the record though? You're doing a good job with them, Rory. You should be proud of yourself. They're very healthy little babies," she smiled, patting my arm before giving me the paperwork about my results. The guys were going to lose their shit.

I drove home, my thoughts taking over. How would we cope with six kids? Four of them under two? I needed to get the twins onto bottles before this one was born, my tits wouldn't cope with three of them.

I parked the car in the garage, heading inside and finding Caden laying around on the couch, Ryder asleep on his chest. "Where's Beckett?"

He glanced up at me, his smile still managing to melt my panties after all these years. I'd never become immune to it. "Lukas has her. She had a diaper explosion and needed a bath."

I sat on the edge of the couch by his feet, hesitating before holding the piece of paper out to him. "We have a problem."

He frowned, taking it cautiously. "What kind of problem?"

"My blood results came back for my check-up. I'm five weeks pregnant," I sighed, exhaustion taking over at the thought. "We should have been more careful."

His eyes widened as he read over the results. "No shit?"

"No shit. What if there's more than one again, Holloway? I can't do that shit again."

He gave me a soft smile, carefully sitting up beside me, not wanting to wake Ryder. "You did it before and you didn't think you could. I doubt it's twins again, but it's not the end of the world if it is."

"How can you say that? When did you last do a headcount

of the kids in this house? We already have five," I cringed, but he didn't seem fazed.

"Yeah, and then we'll have six or seven. These two will be settled by then, Mikey will be close to going to kindergarten, and Angel will be two. We've got this, baby," he promised, giving me a quick kiss.

"What's going on in here?" Lukas grinned, placing Beckett in my lap and giving me a kiss. "I missed you."

"I was gone for an hour," I snorted, but he rolled his eyes.

"Yeah, a long hour."

"Hey, bro. Guess what," Caden smirked, handing him the piece of paper. "Guess who's pregnant again."

Lukas' eyes darted to me, his entire face lighting up. "You are?"

"Can you let me process this before getting happy about it?" I mumbled, but I couldn't help but smile at the look on his face. He looked ready to burst.

"Can I tell the guys when they get home? Please?" he grinned. "I can't wait to see the looks on their faces!" He was such a dick sometimes.

Caden

RORY WAS PRETTY calm for the rest of the day. She played in the pool with Lloyd after he got home from school, continuing to teach him how to swim. I think he benefited from one on one time with her, so I called Mom to help me and Lukas with the other kids so they weren't interrupted. He might have been lashing out at school, but at home, he seemed to relax. Hopefully he'd become comfortable at school over time, and I think having friends was helping.

By the time Mom left and the guys started arriving home for dinner, Lukas was bursting at the fucking seams to tell them the news. I'd hoped he would be gentle about it considering Rory's concern of another baby, but there was no such luck.

"So, which one of you knocked up our girl again?" he asked with a smirk as we all sat around the dinner table. Skeeter dropped his knife onto the plate, Jensen choked on the food he was chewing, and everyone else just flicked their eyes between Lukas and Rory, waiting for one of them to laugh and say it was a joke.

"You're pregnant?" Hunter asked slowly, a small smile on his face. "How far?"

"You're having another baby?" Lloyd asked, a big grin lighting up his face. He'd been an awesome big brother to the others, so I wasn't surprised to see him so excited.

Rory nodded, leaning back in her chair and patting her flat stomach. "Yep. Five weeks. I found out today at my doctor's appointment."

"Did they say how many's in there?" Slash grunted, making Marco throw a fry at him.

"They can't tell that early, dumbass."

"I was just asking," he mumbled, his lips twitching with amusement. "One hundred bucks says it's Skeet's."

Complaints went around the table, but Rory scowled. "If it is, you'd better help him pick a coffin. I'll start digging the hole the moment we finish eating."

Skeeter chuckled, patting Jensen on the back as he kept coughing. "Nah, my money's on Rivera."

They threw guesses around the table, and Lloyd piped up saying it was Tyler's because he'd seen them naked wrestling. It eased the tension on Rory's face, and she cracked up laughing. It was good to see her happy.

I couldn't lie, six kids was going to be hard, but it was manageable.

Rory had complained about her stomach losing it's toned

surface, and her hips having stretch marks. She was a fucking goddess, and her body had been a temple for our kids. She might have freaked out about being a mom, but she was so fucking good at it.

She hardly touched alcohol, she'd gone off the drugs completely, and she'd managed to get rid of the cigarettes, too. Most of us had given up the bad habits too, making it easier for her, but Skeeter was struggling to quit smoking.

That was fine, he'd get there eventually.

Being fathers had changed us all, and I couldn't wait to watch our next little one grow.

CHAPTER FIFTEEN

FOUR YEARS LATER

Rory

"*A*re you sure this is the place?" I frowned as I glanced over at Diesel, his jaw tight.

"Yep. It's apparently where he keeps him."

We'd been chasing leads on the Hell's Demons for years, but nothing ever popped up that was useful to helping us find them. They were like a fucking ghost.

The latest information we discovered was that they'd taken over the skin trade, which was something we'd been trying to bring down ever since we got involved with the Shadow King's mission that brought us our three eldest children.

Apparently, the Demons liked to keep a particular child around, never trading or selling him. I wasn't sure if it was true, but all leads had brought us here, to this run down house that seemed empty.

I glanced down the road at Skeeter and Caden who were moving in from the other side, and Slash led Tyler and Harley around the back, making sure we had all entrances blocked. Hunter was working at Devil's Dungeon and Marco was watching the kids with Lukas and Jensen. Lloyd was fourteen, so he was a helpful set of hands too. Luckily for us.

Mikey had just turned seven, Angel was five, the twins were four, and our other two daughters Riley and Marla were three and one. That was a lot of kids to juggle, especially when we all worked so fucking hard at our jobs on top of it.

Knowing this kid we were looking for was a favorite of the Demons, made my stomach twist with disgust. People like that only kept kids around to enjoy them, if you knew what I meant.

We crept towards the house, relief filling me when no one shot at us on arrival. Maybe we'd gotten it wrong after all.

We went right through the whole house, my heart sinking when I realized the kid wasn't there. We'd saved a lot of kids over the years, and Rage had brought down part of the skin trade market up north with his MC club. He'd been trying to stay home more, but it was hard when so many kids went through the trade each week. We couldn't save them all, but we'd fucking try.

Charlie had ended up moving closer to the MC so Rage could continue his mission, their two kids being protected well by the club and the insane security system Rage had installed. Zane was four now, and their little girl Phoenix had just turned two. We didn't get to see them much anymore, and Rage had pulled away from us a lot.

Archer had been devastated when they'd left, and he didn't get a lot of time to visit them. Tempest was about to turn four, and Luna was three, so he was kept quite busy at home with Lexi, or helping run Wet Dreams so Lexi could stay home with the kids.

Harley had closed the bar for the night to come with us, not wanting Alex to have to work. Jade still didn't cope being alone, so one of the guys was usually with her and Landon, making her feel safe.

We were about to leave the abandoned house when my eyes landed on the rug on the floor, the corner lifted slightly. I pulled it back, finding a trap door underneath. I didn't waste time as I yanked it open to reveal a small room.

"Dammit, Killer. Be careful," Slash growled in my ear, stepping in front of me to make sure it was safe first. He couldn't talk, he'd gotten shot in the leg last time we were out shooting at the bad guys. I hated not knowing who they were, but they were skilled with guns, that much we'd discovered.

The little boy was curled up on the ground, facing us with a blank look on his face. He flinched when Slash moved towards him, so I pulled him back and approached on my own.

"Hey, little man. What's your name?" He didn't answer, his eyes dropping back to the ground and acting like I wasn't there.

I reached out slowly, carefully lifting him into my arms and hugging him to my chest, his body limp. His shirt was dirty, and his pants were wet, so I assumed he'd pissed himself. When we got him into the light though, Diesel spoke softly.

"We need to get him to the hospital."

"I'll call..."

"He needs the hospital, babe. He's bleeding," he said, cutting me off, his voice cracking.

I glanced down at the kids back, anger burning inside me to find the wetness on his pants was mixed with blood. They'd been sexually assaulting him. They must have only recently left him, too.

"Call BG, tell him to meet us there," I forced out, carrying the kid towards the car and cradling him on my lap. Skeeter jogged towards me, climbing into the driver's seat and taking off, glancing at the kid every so often.

"Is he still conscious?" he asked, the boy flinching slightly in my arms. Not much, but I noticed.

"Yeah, he's awake," I murmured, stroking the kid's hair and trying not to fucking cry. This was the worst case we'd found. Most kids were a little battered and bruised, but this kid had definitely suffered sexual trauma. He was skinny, so they hadn't been feeding him much either. "It's okay, baby, we've got you," I whispered, wishing he knew he was safe.

He didn't move the entire drive to the hospital, and BG took a step back when he realized what had happened to him. "Shit, is he even alive?"

"He's awake, but he hasn't moved. We found him curled up on the floor. He hasn't spoken or tried to fight us. I want him in a private room, I'll pay whatever it costs," I growled, carrying the kid inside with BG and Skeeter right behind me.

It didn't take long, and they rushed him into a room, shutting us out for privacy. He wasn't my kid, but he didn't have a mother there to hold his hand. He would have been fucking terrified, and I hated that I couldn't take that away from him.

"I'm running out of places to put all these kids you keep finding," BG grunted, scrolling through his phone as he sat in a chair beside me. "Some of the last bunch ended up back with family, which was good. A lot of them we haven't been able to track down information for."

"This one can stay with us until we find his family," I said without a second thought as Skeeter sat beside me and dropped an arm around my shoulders in silent support. He was a complete softie with the kids, and there had been a few he'd been sad to part with when their families had been found.

BG snorted. "You have seven kids. Do you really want to take this one on too?"

"Is the foster system going to pay for the medical bills and psych appointments he's going to need? He's going to need a lot of therapy over the years. He probably doesn't know how to talk, or do anything that normal kids get to do. I have money burning holes in my pocket, and a big ass house with plenty of free bedrooms. He looks similar in age to our kids, so hopefully he'll settle in easily too."

"Do you want to discuss this with the guys?" he asked slowly, making Skeeter growl.

"She said she'd take him in, didn't she? There's nothing we need to discuss."

"Alright. Saves me finding somewhere to put him," he grunted. "You know the drill. You'll have a stack of forms to fill out."

"Yep. As long as he comes home with me, I don't give a shit," I replied bluntly, ending the conversation.

Marco

"ANOTHER ONE?" I asked with a chuckle as Slash explained to me what had happened. He nodded, a grim look on his face.

"The kid's been seriously abused. Skeet just called and let me know they're filling in the paperwork to get him into our care. Sounds like he'll be spending some time in the hospital first though."

"Beaten?"

"Raped and starving," he scowled, fury flickering through my veins. I'd never understand why anyone would hurt a child, especially like that. It was fucking disgusting.

Lloyd walked through the front door, making my eyes narrow. "Why aren't you at school?"

"It was either I left, or beat the shit out of Tony," he shrugged, leaning against the wall.

"What did he do?" Slash grumbled, already not liking the kid from when he spilled soda in his mustang the last time Slash had picked him and Lloyd up from school.

"He fucked Gia."

"The brunette you've been talking to?" I smirked, his face thunderous as he glared at me.

"Yeah, my girlfriend." *Shit.*

"Sorry, dude. I say we go back and throw hands. How long until he's eighteen? I wanna smack him too," I said flatly, earning a small smile.

"Thanks, Dad. I guess he just showed me my girlfriend's a whore."

"Sounds like it," Slash agreed, and I gave him a shove.

"Don't encourage him to call them that."

"What? If it acts like a whore, speaks like a whore, or walks like a whore, it's a whore," he answered, clipping Lloyd behind the ears gently. "But we don't call them that within ear shot." He was such an asshole.

Lloyd scowled, rubbing his ear. "I've heard you call them worse."

"Doubt it. I stopped calling women names when your mother set me straight. The only time it's acceptable to call the woman you love a whore, is if they like it in the bedroom. Make sure you ask her if she's into it though, or you'll get your ass beat."

"And make sure when you're choking her, that you remember to let go," I deadpanned. "How'd this become a sex lesson?"

"I'm not stupid, I know what girls like," Lloyd said smugly. I stepped closer to him, the look dropping from his face.

"You'd better be using condoms, you little shit. We have

enough kids here, we don't need grandkids too. You shouldn't even be having sex at your age."

"I bet you had sex all the time at my age. Back door, no babies. Right, Dad?" he asked Slash over my shoulder, the big fucker chuckling with amusement.

"Yep. Just so you know, the pull out method doesn't work."

Lloyd's face tensed, his eyes going wide. "It doesn't?" I was going to kill him, I swore to God.

"You've been using that method?" I demanded, giving him a dirty look. "You can still get herpes, you know?"

"No offense, but I don't need you two telling me that kind of shit. Nine of you share one woman, and I doubt you use condoms," he threw back, and Slash laughed loudly, making me glare at him. Lloyd soaked up information like a sponge, and the last thing we needed was him knocking someone up.

"Would you cut it out and take this seriously?"

"I could, but this is just too fucking funny," he grinned, turning to Lloyd. "Oh, by the way. You're getting a new brother."

"Mom's pregnant again?! You guys need to get off her!" he growled. "She's scary when she's pregnant!"

"She's not pregnant. We have a kid coming to live with us. He's three or four, and he's been through a lot. Don't be an asshole to him, alright? He's got a lot of trauma."

"Like me?"

"Sort of. He's been very abused, so be nice to him and if he wants to play, you play with him. Make him feel safe," I said firmly, knowing he'd been a bit of a bully to some of the other kids.

He nodded, seeming to realize the importance of it. "I'll be nice. Is he staying long?"

I chuckled, giving Slash the side eye. "Knowing Rory, he won't be leaving."

Rory

IT TOOK a week for the hospital to release the poor kid. He'd perked up a little, showing more emotion than he had when we'd found him. And by that, I meant he was feral. He tried to attack me in the fucking car on the way home, desperate to get out and run away from me. I couldn't blame him, he probably thought he was sold to some bigger and badder assholes to hurt him.

Once I got him home, he hid in the living room for most of the day, growling at people but still not speaking. I was starting to think he'd never learned.

"Baby, leave him alone," I warned Beckett as she toddled towards the living room, her light green eyes full of curiosity.

"But Mooooom."

"Let him get used to the house, then we can see if he wants to play," I said gently, knowing it wouldn't happen. She let out a huff, making me snort. She was so much like me, and she had way too much sass for a four-year-old.

I put together some snacks for the kids, and it wasn't until I was finished that I realized Beckett had vanished. I groaned, knowing exactly where she was.

I poked my head around the doorway to the living room, finding her sitting on the floor in front of the little boy, his face wary as she shuffled closer.

"I'm Beckett. I'm four." She was so cute when she wanted to be.

The boy watched her silently, but Beckett didn't mind. "I have a bike. You can ride it if you want. We have a pool, and grass, and lots of stuff."

She talked randomly to him, and just when I thought she

was going to give up on trying to force his friendship, he spoke. "I'm Maddox. I'm four."

I quietly darted up the hallway, startling Skeeter with my abrupt entrance to the bedroom. "Jesus, baby girl. Where's the fire?"

"He's talking to Beckett!" I whisper-yelled. "She's been talking to him for ages, but he didn't say anything back. He just said his name and his age."

He stood from the bed, dropping the Xbox controller onto the mattress. "He did?"

"Yeah. Guess what his name is, Skeeter Maddox?" I grinned. "It's Maddox!"

"It is?" he asked with surprise, following me down to the living room where the kids were still talking. Ryder had joined them, but Maddox stayed close to Beckett, not seeming sure of her twin.

"Do you like TV? I like the cartoons," Beckett said as she handed him a stuffed teddy bear. "This is my favorite teddy. You can have him to sleep with if you want?"

Skeeter nudged me, a small smile on his face. "She doesn't even let Ryder touch that teddy."

"I know. She'll probably want it back later," I chuckled, turning and heading into the kitchen, grabbing the small platter of fruit and crackers for the kids. I took it into the living room, and Maddox instantly darted to the opposite side of the room, a snarl on his face. It was good to see the fight in him, it meant he hadn't given up.

"Hey, guys. I brought you something to eat," I said gently, placing the plate on the coffee table and backing up a few steps. Ryder snatched some apple and shoved it into his mouth like the savage he was, but Beckett gave Maddox a smile.

"Mom makes good snacks."

He didn't want to get closer to me, so I walked back

towards the door, making sure he knew it wasn't a trap. He eyed the food, and I swore I heard his stomach rumble.

Beckett gave me a grin. "Thanks, Mom! I love berries!"

"I know you do, baby. Make sure your friend gets some, okay?" I hoped Ryder didn't fucking eat it all. That kid could eat an adult meal if I let him. Luckily, he burned a lot of energy throughout the day.

"His name's Maddox. He's four like me!" she beamed. "Can we watch TV?"

"Is he? That's awesome. Can you show him where the toilets are if he needs to go?"

She nodded, turning her attention away from me to focus on Maddox who still had his back pressed against the wall. "You like berries?"

After a moment, he took a step closer to her, and another until he was beside her at the table, staring at the food with uncertainty. She grabbed a strawberry, holding it out to him. "This one's my favorite berry. Mom puts them on pancakes sometimes for me."

He hesitated before taking it from her, shoving it into his mouth and chewing furiously, snatching more off the plate as if someone would take them away from him. Beckett giggled, putting her hands on her hips. "Don't eat all of them!"

He stopped chewing, glancing at me with worry. I chuckled, trying to keep my voice quiet so he wouldn't startle. "You can eat them all. I can get more if you like them."

He didn't growl at me, so that was a start.

We left them alone to play, and by the end of the day, he was curled up asleep on the couch with Beckett, the two of them snuggled up under a blanket while Ryder slept on the other couch, all of them worn out.

IT TOOK a few days for Maddox to get used to such a busy household. The guys tried to leave him alone until he was more comfortable, but Beckett always made sure he had her by her side. They were basically glued together when she wasn't at kindergarten, and my heart warmed at knowing they'd formed such a quick friendship. Beckett didn't make friends well. She was usually mean to most of the kids, but she'd taken a shine to Maddox.

He'd been sleeping in her room, curled up at the bottom of the bed with his own blanket, but I'd found them curled up together that morning, telling me he trusted her.

He'd started to play with Ryder and Riley too, which was good. Slowly, he opened up more until one morning I felt a little hand tug on my sweats, finding Maddox beside me.

"Can I have water?" he asked carefully, relief crossing his face when I smiled.

"Of course you can. Are you hungry?"

He nodded, so I put a bottle of water on the table and pulled the chair out. "Sit here, I'll make you some pancakes."

He was quiet while I got to work, but he eventually crawled up onto the chair and got comfortable. "Do you want strawberries on them with syrup?"

"Please," he mumbled, not sure about all the nice stuff he was getting. I got it, it was hard to adjust, but I was happy he seemed to be trusting me now, too.

I made a big stack of them, proud of my efforts. Lukas and Jensen had been helping me make things lately, and I was getting good at it. I put two pancakes on each plate, placing one in front of Maddox before calling the others, their feet running through the house and into the kitchen. Beckett sat beside Maddox, not wasting time as she shoved a strawberry into her mouth, while Ryder and Riley sat at the other end of the table, making sure there was room for Angel, Mikey and Lloyd.

Angel sat down, picking at her food like she always did, but Lloyd and Mikey shoveled theirs in as if they didn't eat two servings of fried chicken the night before. Once Beckett started eating, Maddox started picking at his food too, his eyes lighting up as it hit his taste buds.

"Never had pancakes before?" I asked with amusement as I joined them at the table with a plate for myself. He shook his head, taking a big bite and dripping syrup all over himself.

"Rory? You home?"

Maddox froze, the new voice scaring the shit out of him, making me sigh.

"Yeah, Uncle. Come in."

Axel walked in, looking panicked which set me on edge. I got to my feet and approached him, halting when I noticed he had a baby's car seat in his hand. "What is that?"

He looked ready to pass out. "She was dropped off on my doorstep this morning by the fucking cops. Remember that girl I was seeing ages ago? The one with the eyebrow piercing?"

"Vaguely."

"She was found in her apartment, dead from an overdose. I didn't know she'd been on that shit again. She was clean. Fuck!" he snapped, and Maddox fled from the room.

"Can you calm down and talk quietly? We have a new kid and he's terrified of everything," I warned. "What does this girl have to do with…"

"She had a fucking baby. My baby, apparently. She's been in foster care, but after the cops searched the house and found the kid's birth certificate, they tracked me down. I can't take care of a baby, Rory."

"Can I take her out of the car seat?" I asked, wanting to get a better look at her. He nodded, placing it on the ground and unclipping her, his hands shaking slightly as he lifted the little girl and handed her to me. She was adorable.

I placed her against my chest, rocking her gently as she fussed. "How old is she?"

"She's almost one. I don't..."

"We'll help you. If I can do it, anyone can," I chuckled, the little girl giggling at me. "Is that funny?" She continued to giggle, and I glanced back at Axel. "What's her name?"

"Harlow Leary. She even used my last name on the birth certificate," he choked out, sitting in one of the kitchen chairs to watch me. "I don't know when to feed her, or..."

"The cops can help you get her medical records, and I can help you figure out a routine for her. It might take her a little while to adjust to the changes in her life, but she'll be fine," I smiled. "Has she eaten at all since you got her?"

"I don't know what to feed her!" he groaned. "Like, can she have toast?"

"She needs something nutritious. Marla has plenty of baby puree. I'll get her some and see how she does with it," I suggested, relief filling his eyes.

"Thank you."

I spent the day helping Axel with a few things, but he was still freaking out by the time he needed to go home. Marco gave him a grin, holding Harlow and gently patting her back. "Want me to come and crash tonight? I'm getting really good with babies, I'll help. You look ready to throw up."

"You'd stay? All night?" he asked hopefully. "That would be awesome."

"I'll grab a few things. Here," he smiled, offering him the baby and rolling his eyes when Axel hesitated. "She doesn't bite."

Maddox hid behind me, but he was trying to get a look at Harlow.

"You want to see her?" I asked, waiting for him to nod

before I took her from Axel and squatted beside him, holding Harlow on my thigh. "She's only little, so be gentle."

He stepped closer, reaching out to touch her hand, jerking back when she tried to grab him.

"She won't hurt you. She wants to be friends with you," I grinned. "Make faces at her, she'll laugh."

He didn't look convinced, but he eventually stuck his tongue out at her, making her giggle loudly and clap her hands. Maddox found it hilarious. They continued their game until Marco was ready to go, then Axel strapped her into the car seat and they headed off for the night, Marco giving me a kiss on his way past.

I shut the door and glanced down at Maddox who was yawning. "You want to watch a movie?"

He nodded, following me into the living room and climbing onto the couch, sitting beside me and getting comfortable. An hour into watching cartoons, he laid down and rested his head on my leg, making me hesitate before running my fingers through his hair. He was tense at first, but then he relaxed and focused on the TV again. He fell asleep pretty quickly after that.

"Want me to take him up to bed?" Jensen murmured as he poked his head in. Most of the guys were at the shed for fight night, so it had been peaceful.

"I've got him. I don't want him to freak out," I said softly, gently lifting him into my arms and carrying him up to Beckett's room. She was already asleep, so I carefully tucked Maddox in beside her, backing out of the room and leaving the door open in case he woke up and panicked.

I watched TV with Lloyd and Jensen until midnight when the guys got home, and I couldn't help but notice that Lukas had a split lip. I raised an eyebrow, and Skeeter grinned.

"You should have seen this fucker. He kicked the crap out of some dude in the cage. I didn't know he had it in him."

"Luke was cage fighting?" I snorted, but Lukas looked so damn proud of himself.

"Yep, and I fucking won."

"I didn't know you could fight," Lloyd interrupted, eyeing him with disbelief.

Jensen chuckled, grabbing Lukas' hand and tugging him down between us. "Luke used to fight dirty in high school. He beat Caden up once."

Caden rolled his eyes, but he was smiling. I'd heard that story many times, and it never got old.

Lloyd asked a million questions until we convinced him to go to bed, and I quickly checked on the others on my way to bed myself. Riley was sleeping soundly, being the easiest kid we'd ever had. She was definitely a mommy's girl though, preferring to spend time with me over the guys, whereas Beckett and Ryder liked being with the guys more. Probably because they got to ride dirt bikes and play outside. Marla was pretty happy with anyone, and Angel still loved Marco like he was a gift from God himself. They had the best relationship.

I glanced into Mikey's room, finding him asleep with his arm hanging off the side of the bed and his light still on. I turned it off and crept further down the hallway, peeking in at Lloyd to see him snoring on his back with the blankets kicked off. It freaked me out that he was already a teenager.

I checked on Beckett and Maddox, finding him spooning her, and I knew we'd have to get him used to his own room sooner rather than later. For now, they were kids, and if she made him feel safe? It was worth it.

I left the hallway light on, walking into the bedroom to find the guys already waiting for me, and I quickly stripped down and put on one of their shirts, diving into my spot in the middle and groaning as I sank into the plush blankets. "Today was a long day."

"Every day's a long day," Skeeter snorted, snuggling up to me to kiss my neck. They each gave me a good night kiss, mumbling they loved me, and as I got comfortable with Skeeter behind me and Lukas in front of me, I realized just how lucky I was.

I went from being an angry, bitter teenager that had no one on her side, to having nine guys who'd kill for me, and eight kids who I loved more than anything.

The best part? For once, I wouldn't change a fucking thing.

EPILOGUE

BECKETT

Fourteen Years Old

*S*tudents parted as I stalked through the crowd. I might have been a freshman, but that didn't mean shit. My parents reigned over this town, and no one stood in my way. Sure, some girls liked to try and throw their bullshit at me, but it was out of jealousy or disgust because I had nine dads. I thought it was pretty fucking awesome.

My brothers Maddox and Ryder always had girls chasing them, but they regularly turned them down to spend time with me. We were family, and no amount of pussy or dick would get in the way of that. I might have had some kind of twin bond with Ryder, but I'd always been closer to Maddox. It had been like that since Mom saved him from the Hell's Demon crew's skin trade. It took him a few years to adjust to having a family who cared, but he'd been my best friend since that day. We'd only been four.

"Where's the fire, Becky?" Jett Emerson grinned as he jogged up to me, making me growl. He was Ryder's best friend, and he'd been living with us as a foster kid for the past couple of years. His parents were pieces of shit, abandoning him the moment they thought he could fend for himself.

Of course, my family took him in, because that's what we did. If you needed somewhere to call home, whether it was for one night or forever, my parent's would open their doors to our family home, making sure no kids had to sleep on the streets.

I wasn't Jett's biggest fan. He was too charming for his own good, and the past year had been full of him chasing girls around. He never left me alone, the fucker swore he'd get a kiss from me one day. I'd cut his balls off if he tried again. He'd gotten a warning punch to the nose the first and last time he'd attempted.

"Fuck off. I've got shit to do."

"Hot girl shit, I bet. You look so mad," he continued to grin, keeping up with me as I headed towards the football field.

I spotted my target, the red headed bimbo leaning into Maddox and giggling at something he said. She thought she could try and push me out of the way and step up as queen, taking her place beside Maddox as if she had a right to be there. She didn't.

So far she'd started rumors about me, making me out to be a slut to try and get the other students to talk shit about me. I also knew she was behind me getting detention the day before, spinning a sob story to the teachers that I'd tried to corner her in the bathrooms and taken her money.

Why the fuck would I need her money? My family was rich as fuck. She wanted me to get in trouble? I'd make sure it was for a good fucking reason.

"Hey, come bucket!" I snapped as I strode towards her, amusement filling Maddox's eyes as I approached. Tory, the red headed cunt, turned and gave me a scathing look.

"Excuse me?"

"Move," I warned Maddox, and he stepped back two seconds before my fist slammed into her nose, sending her tumbling backwards onto her ass.

"You bitch!" she screamed as she scrambled to her feet, coming at me like she had a chance. Having parents who ran street crews meant I was raised knowing how to fight. They wanted to make sure I could defend myself if I needed to. Tory had no hope.

I dodged her fist, slamming my elbow into her chest and swinging my fist hard at her face again, blood pouring down her chin from her busted nose.

"Beckett Donovan!" *Mother fuckers.* It was like the teachers hovered whenever I was around.

I went to throw another punch, but arms wrapped around my middle to pull me back, a chuckle sounding beside my ear.

"C'mon, she got the point. Don't get yourself in more trouble than necessary," Maddox murmured, keeping a firm grip on me as he tugged me back, away from the crying girl who wanted to play innocent victim. She'd done it to herself.

"I just came in my pants," Jett announced as Ryder jogged over to see what was happening, his face scrunching up with disgust.

"You'd better not be talking about my sister, you dick."

"Of course I am. No one gets me off quite like..." Ryder punched him in the cheek, glaring at him.

"Shut your mouth, asshole."

"Why? She's hot," he grinned, rubbing his cheek as he winked at me. "You love me. Right, Becky?"

Maddox scowled, holding my bicep with one hand, while taking a menacing step towards Jett. "If I start smacking the shit out of you, I won't stop," he warned as the teacher reached us, worry in her eyes as she tried to assess the situation. It wasn't the first time we'd been in fights on school grounds, so the teachers knew it could escalate to a complete family fight.

"All of you, go to the principal's office. This will not be tolerated!"

"Even me?!" Jett exclaimed. "I didn't do anything!"

"I highly doubt that, Mr. Emerson. Now, get moving!" she barked, pointing towards the office angrily. The principal wouldn't do much. He was too scared of my mother's wrath to permanently expel me.

"You're going to be suspended," Maddox laughed as he dropped an arm around my shoulders, leading me away from Tory before I could attack her stupid face again.

"Good. Then I can go to work with Skeet," I snorted, preferring to spend a few days watching my father torture people than doing a science project.

As predicted, I was suspended, while the others all got detention.

I waited patiently in the office for someone to arrive to take me home, and I glanced up when the door slammed open and my father, Slash, stalked towards me. "The fuck, Beckett?"

The office lady frowned at his language, but they should have been used to it by now. Mom came down here and cursed us out all the time.

"She deserved it," I shrugged, getting to my feet.

"Did it have to be today though? We're busy as fuck and don't have time for this. Get in the car, we'll talk about this later," he snapped, not talking to anyone else before storming back outside, waiting for me to follow.

We climbed into his Mustang, and the moment he put his foot on the gas and headed towards the shed, I knew they'd been doing something important. "I'm sorry. What did I interrupt?"

"Those Demon cunts left a dead kid in front of the shed today. Skeet's losing his shit. We've got the cops there at the moment, and once they leave, we're going to hunt the fucker down and rip him apart," he snarled, slamming his palm against the steering wheel.

"Do you know who they were? The Demon dude?" I asked quietly, my heart hurting. So many kids had been going missing lately, but it was rare we came across one we couldn't save. My family would feel this hit badly.

"Yeah. We don't think he's one of the Demon's, but he definitely works for them. They've been sneaky, finding people to do their dirty work so we can't catch them. It's like they're a fucking myth, and it's driving us insane. We can't stop a damn ghost crew," he bit out, calming slightly when I gave his large bicep a squeeze.

"You'll get them, Dad. Every day, you get closer to destroying them. Who found the kid?"

"Skeet and Caden."

"Are they alright?"

He sighed, shaking his head. "No. They're out for blood."

"Then make sure they get it," I nodded, staring out the window and letting Dad think in peace for the rest of the drive.

I got some dirty looks from a few people as I walked into the shed, my mother frowning when I walked over to her. "You need to be more discreet with your revenge plans, Honey. We don't need the school calling us every day when we have other shit to handle."

"I know, I just snapped a little," I grumbled, crossing my arms and looking over at Skeeter to find fury on his face. I thought he was mad at me for a second, but he walked over and hugged me tightly, kissing the top of my head.

"You shouldn't be here, but I'm glad you are. I can't imagine what these parents go through when they lose a child so horrifically," he murmured, relaxing as I hugged him back tightly. My dads were all ruthless and brutal, but they were still human. They always felt the pain when they had to deal with hurt kids, so I knew he'd be taking this hard.

"You won't lose us. We're like little terminators, thanks to all that self-defense you threw at us," I smiled.

"You're not invincible, Beckett. Just because your mother thinks she is, doesn't mean it's true. She didn't pass down an immortality ability," he warned. "Which kid did you beat up this time?"

"Tory."

"Ugh, I hate her dad," he grumbled, making me grin. Tory's dad had always made it obvious he didn't like my family. He acted like some rich privileged asshole in a suit, but he made minimum wage and cheated on his wife a lot. Last time he'd tried to start shit with my family, Skeeter had punched his lights out, spending the night in a damn jail cell to cool down. Mom had been pissed about the whole thing, so she'd slashed Tory's dad's car tires and threatened him with the knife, landing her ass in a cell too. It was hilarious.

Skeeter stepped back, motioning for my big brother, Lloyd, to join us. "Yeah?"

"You don't need to be here. Take your sister home and make sure she doesn't make anyone else bleed today," Skeeter asked dryly, making Lloyd scowl.

"Can't she walk? It would take less than half an hour."

"You like wearing that Psycho's jacket? Then remember I've asked you as your boss, not your dad," he grunted. "Do as you're told. I don't want to have to call Mikey and pull him out of classes to come and get her."

Lloyd looked ready to argue, but he knew better and pulled his keys from his pocket. "Fine, but we're getting burgers on the way home. I'm starving."

"I don't care, just take her home," Skeeter scowled, kissing the top of my head before turning and heading back to the others who looked deep in discussion.

They'd plot the guy's murder, track him down once it got dark, and torture him for information until they had enough and killed him. It was cool to watch them work sometimes.

I glanced at Lloyd with a grin as we approached his Dodge Viper. He liked to illegally street race, so his car was a fucking machine under the hood. He was a regular at the racetrack, too. "Can I drive?"

"No. Get in," he muttered, unlocking it and climbing into the driver's seat. He'd been teaching me to drive since I was ten, but he always made me drive one of the other cars. No one touched his baby.

"When can I race at the track? You said once I'd learned…"

"You need more practice. You can't drift properly, and it's a huge part of racing. You need to have good reflexes and be focused, two things you suck at," he chuckled, starting the engine and making me smirk. "But, once you learn to control all of that, then I'll see what I can do. It's dangerous, Beckett. It's not a game."

"I know. Remember when you crashed Mom's Ferrari?" I laughed. "She was so mad."

"Yeah, so can you see why you need to wait? I was cocky and overconfident before I had a right to be. That crash taught me that I had more to learn. Put your damn seat belt on."

I knew without a doubt that I'd be just like Lloyd when I got older. I'd watched a few of his races, and it was amazing. The racetrack had been built years ago, thanks to my mom, so a lot of kids hung around there to watch the older kids race. It was a lot safer there than on the streets, so the cops usually turned a blind eye to it.

Lloyd was a legend there, and everyone respected us because of him.

One day, I'd take over that title, and nothing was going to get in my way.

Fucking nothing.

THE END... or is it?

FROM THE ASHES SERIES

You didn't think I'd stop at the end of Rory's story, did you? Get ready, because the next generation is coming!

King of Carnage, book 1
BLURB

This town knows who runs the streets.
With the cops on the payroll and my family literally getting away with murder, it's obvious.
My parents built a goddamn empire.

I run the local college and the racetrack with my siblings.
No one crosses us, they wouldn't dare.
Everyone knows I don't hesitate when it comes to my blade.

Problem is, things are about to crumble at my feet.
What do you do when your best friend is the one to cross you?
Especially when it's your adopted brother?

In this life of fast cars and power, family means everything to me.

He ripped my heart out with his fist, and I'll destroy him just as much as he destroyed me.

Maddox is about to learn just how dangerous I really am.

I can't let him weaken me, I already have Jett knocking my walls down a little at a time.

My dads would kill me if they knew what was about to happen under their roof.

I know it seems wrong but if I can't have Maddox, no one can.

I'll kill any other girl who tries.

My name's Beckett Donovan, and I take after my mother. I never really did play by the rules.

Pre-Order:
getbook.at/KingofCarnage1

**This is a dark romance book and is MFM. This is Beckett, Maddox, and Jett's story.

Pretty Little Psycho, book 2

Pre-Order:
getbook.at/PrettyLittlePsycho2

**Blurb coming soon. This is Riley Donovan's story and is an F/F romance.

Princess of Pain, book 3

Pre-Order:

getbook.at/PrincessofPain3

**Blurb coming soon. This is Ryder Donovan's story and is an M/F romance with self harm/mental health issues. There are also pain kinks and rape play.

**There will possibly be more instalments in the series in the future. For now though, these are the only three I'm promising.

ALSO BY R.E. BOND

Watch Me Burn series (Completed)

WARNING

This series MUST be read in order despite the characters changing. It follows one storyline. These are dark romance books with violence and multiple trigger warnings depending on the book.

Book 1: Pretty Lies

Book 2: Twisted Fate

Book 3: Beautiful Deceit

Book 4: Ignite Me

Book 5: Perfectly Jaded

Book 6: Don't Fear the Reaper

Book 7: Wrath of Rage

Book 8: Sinners Reign (Final)

From the Ashes

(Watch Me Burn next generation)

Book 1, King of Carnage (Coming 10th June 2022)

Book 2, Pretty Little Psycho (Coming 2022)

Book 3, Princess of Pain (Coming 2022)

Reaped series (Completed)

Co-written with C.A. Rene

WARNING

This reverse harem series is full of violence, gore scenes, and a lot of dark spice, with MM included.

Book 0.5: The Reaper Incarnate

Book 1: Hunting the Reaper

Book 2: Claiming the Reaper

Standalone

Co-written with C.A. Rene

*This book is a psychological thriller.

To the Grave (Coming 7th December 2022)

ACKNOWLEDGMENTS

What a fucking ride! To everyone who's still here at the very end, THANK YOU! I know this was a long series, and I appreciate you all for sticking by me while I navigated the start of my author journey.

When Pretty Lies first released on the 10th of August 2020, I never expected it to grow to what it is today. I cherish every single one of you for loving these characters and books as much as I do.

Massive shout out to everyone who's helped beta read, ARC review, or promote these books over the past year and a half. I wouldn't be where I am today without each and every one of you.

Writing is HARD, and I was blindsided by the amount of work that goes on in the back ground to get a book published. It's consisted of a lot of learning and paperwork, as well as hundreds of hours of social media time. Connecting with my readers is my favourite part of this job, and you guys have helped keep me going on those days where I got overwhelmed and wanted to quit.

You are my book fam, and I think the world of you all. Thank you for everything, and I can't wait to see what else I write and get to share with you.

I hope you loved Rory's final. She needed more than a quick epilogue, but I didn't expect to get a full book out of it. I've been so excited to write the next generation, and I've been smashing out words for King of Carnage like crazy. I hope you'll love Beckett, Maddox, and Jett's story.

Love you bunches,

Rachael Xx

STALK ME!

Stalk the crap out of me you little freaks, I love it!

Facebook:

https://www.facebook.com/indieauthorrebond/

Facebook Readers Group:

https://www.facebook.com/groups/prettypsychos

Instagram:

https://www.instagram.com/author.re.bond/

Goodreads:

https://www.goodreads.com/rebond

Newsletter/website:

https://www.rebondbooks.com/

Tik Tok:

https://vm.tiktok.com/ZSJRKKhr4/

Amazon:

https://www.amazon.com/R-E-Bond/e/
B08DV2C21Y/ref=dp_byline_cont_pop_ebooks_1

BookBub:

https://www.bookbub.com/profile/r-e-bond?list=about

ABOUT THE AUTHOR

R.E. Bond is a dark romance author from Tasmania, Australia. She is obsessed with reverse harem books, especially if they have m/m! She collects paperbacks as a hobby, has read or written every day since she started high school, and constantly needs music in her daily life. She loves camping and rodeos in the summer, and not getting out of bed in the winter. Coffee and books are life, and curse words are just sentence enhancers.